THEN YOU FOUND ME

A CAPITOL ROMANCE

PIPER ASHBY

Connect with Piper Ashby

Instagram: authorpiperashby

Facebook: authorpiperashby

Website: piperashby.com

ISBN 979-8-9879737-0-7
ISBN 979-8-9879737-1-4 (ebook)

For the Hubs

QUINN

I took a deep breath, enjoying the moment. Dreams were coming true. Hard work was paying off. Memories were ready to be made. My future was finally starting, allowing me to leave my past in the past where it belonged.

Walking into the Capitol building overwhelmed me every single time. Since my first time coming to the Capitol during a fourth grade field trip, I never lost my wonder of its majesty. While other students were excited to be out of school for the day, I couldn't stop looking at the beauty of the architecture and the artwork crafted into the walls. It was weird for a 10-year-old, but there was something about that building that felt warm, safe, and secure. As an adult, that feeling continued.

Important things happened in that grand old building. Some were wonderful. Some monumental. And, some things were bad. But, despite the current political climate, the home of our state government deserved to be revered. And I revered it.

My favorite place at the Capitol was the rotunda. I could

spend hours studying the four enormous mosaics that circled the ceiling of the dome, seeing something new in them each time I visited. Three of the mosaics represented the different branches of government, but the fourth was my favorite. A beautiful woman dressed in green to represent hope. She guarded an orb, which some say symbolized the ballot box. Named Liberty, she watched over all those who entered the cavernous space. Liberty stood for justice.

Wisconsin added warmth to its Capitol building by choosing rich red and green marble for the walls, and stunning gold accents throughout the building. It was a welcoming place, the people's place, and it was unbelievable to me that I was going to work there.

After my traditional touristy gawking was complete, I found my new office on the first floor. It wasn't a large office, but it was all mine. Well, at least for the next eighteen months. A light green color warmed the walls. A sturdy oak desk, two matching bookshelves against one wall, and a round oak table in the corner flanked by two leather library chairs filled the room. I tried to contain my excitement, but I was unsuccessful. After closing the door, I did a private happy dance around my office.

I was astonished to be given this position, considering the caliber of candidates I was up against. The governor chose me to spearhead his Art for the People project, or "that silly art project," as the human resource manager liked to call it. They gave me an 18-month contract to develop, curate, display, and conclude the project as I saw fit, with practically no guidance or oversight.

Last year, I finished up my art history doctorate. Aside from student teaching, this would be my first real-world project. They chose me, even though there were more experienced curators up for the position. I wasn't about to let the opportunity to have unlimited creative freedom pass me by.

Governor Swift commissioned the Art Project to recognize local artists and bring art to the local schools. I remembered that my high school struggled with funding to keep our art programs running, so I was positive this project would make a difference in our communities.

I spent most of my first day settling in and working on the agenda for my committee meeting. Noticing the time, I realized I was about to be late for that meeting.

Why does this always happen? Why couldn't I be better with my schedule? I couldn't be late for my first meeting with my new team. What kind of example would that be? I had to get some control over my natural tardiness. Grabbing my laptop, my notes, and a building map, I ran out of my office to find the meeting room.

My heels, which I rarely wore due to my inherent clumsiness, clicked on the marble flooring as I ran up the stairs. Cursing my roommate's name for forcing me to wear the simple black heels to make a good impression on my first day, I slipped and slid down the hallway, rounding the corner. Without paying attention, I ran face first into a rock-solid man. My heel wiggled beneath my foot and my ankle gave way as I fell backward. The next few moments felt like they were happening in slow motion. I saw my notebook and map flying out of my arms, but I refused to release my laptop, so I couldn't stop myself from falling backward. Squeezing my eyes shut, I prepared myself for the forthcoming impact with the marble floor. I waited for the pain.

But the pain never came. Instead, I found myself suspended in air. It felt like I was floating.

Held in powerful arms wrapped around my waist, inches from the cool, unyielding ground, I opened one clenched eye, for fear that opening both would cause me to drop to the floor like the coyote realizing he overshot the cliff.

My breath caught. I'd like to say it was due to my narrow

escape from impending pain and humiliation, but truthfully, it was due to the man. There, in front of me, was the most breathtaking face I'd ever encountered. He was gazing down at me with concerned, deep blue eyes. We stared at each other a little longer than was necessary, then he lifted me up and steadied me on my feet. When he seemed confident I wouldn't tip over, his arms dropped from around me and I instantly missed the warmth of his body next to mine.

"I'm so sorry," I whispered, looking down at his feet, "I'm always running late because I'm terrible at keeping track of time and I wasn't paying attention. I really am so sorry. Are you okay? Did I hurt you? I'm such a klutz. Wow, I really am sorry." I knew I was rambling, but I couldn't seem to stop myself. Unnerved, I attempted to straighten my skirt and reposition my laptop in my arms.

Realizing my rudeness by apologizing to his feet instead of his face, I looked up and saw humor and concern in his eyes.

Even wearing heels, which added three inches to my five-foot frame, I had to stretch my neck to stare up at this handsome man who towered a foot above me. I wobbled a little and his powerful hands were immediately back on me, holding my upper arms, steadying me, and sending sparks of electricity up and down my arms from his touch.

As I came to my senses, I noticed his hold on me lifted the sleeve of my shirt up my arm enough to put part of my scar on display. I pushed myself away and tugged the sleeve back down.

Surely, I looked like a lunatic. I glanced around to find my map and notebook. But before I could get there, the victim of my clumsiness grabbed them and held them out to me. I took them without making eye contact, not sure how to end this awkward encounter.

I stared at the map, as if it would show me the way out. I

felt his finger lift my chin to look at him. This time, the electricity ran straight down to my toes solely from his touch.

"Are you okay?" he asked with a tone of sincere concern. His voice was a full baritone that sent tingles through me. His eyes scanned up and down my body to make sure I was unharmed.

Not knowing how to handle the rush of heat through my body that was completely foreign to me, I let my shyness win. "I...I...I'm late."

I glanced up at him, his eyebrows scrunched as he looked at me, as if he were trying to figure out a riddle, then I stepped around him to get to my meeting. Wobbling on a twisted ankle, I tried my hardest not to look injured. I forced myself not to look back, even though everything inside me wanted to.

I reached the room scheduled for my meeting and looked at my watch. Running five minutes late, I mentally reprimanded myself about making a bad first impression.

Since I was already late, I took another moment to collect my thoughts and emotions, trying to clear the attractive stranger's face out of my head.

Three people were already there. Calmly, I walked to the head of the table to start with introductions. My first day wasn't going as I expected.

2

DEVON

*W*ell, that was interesting. It is not every day a little ball of energy and nerves runs into me. It was surprising, but I can't say that it wasn't enjoyable. I watched her run off to wherever she was going. Her hair, which was up in a knot on the top of her head, was just a little messy. I wasn't sure if it was that way to begin with or if it ended up that way after the fall, but either way, I had a powerful urge to pull the pins out and watch it fall down her back.

I couldn't stop myself from admiring how nice she looked from behind in the professional black pencil skirt she was wearing.

Even though she wasn't standing in front of me anymore, I could still smell her. A faint scent of mint and strawberries lingered on my shirt.

Staring a little too long after she went out of sight, I turned and continued down the familiar halls of the Capitol. My mind wandered back to the tiny little brunette as I head down the east wing and turn into the governor's office. I couldn't figure out why I was so distracted by her. Being rather tall, I was typically attracted to taller, more model-like women, like my ex, Heather. But her gray eyes stayed on my mind; the color of the overcast skies above Lake Michigan in December. They were striking.

"How is it going, Janet?" I casually asked the secretary, leaning my elbows on the counter in front of her desk.

"Hey Devon. Things are going well," she said. "You look a little flustered today."

Guessing it was still showing on my face, I said, "This woman ran right into me in the hallway on my way here."

Shaking her head, she said, "Those tourists. They can be so inconsiderate when they're visiting the Capitol. Never looking to see where they're going. They act like they own the place." She made a *tsking* noise with her tongue as she chastised a woman she didn't know. "You can go right back; your dad is waiting for you."

The Governor's office was traditional, with its rich oak trim and oversized mahogany desk. I smiled as my gaze went over to my college baseball bat hanging on the wall. I gave it to my dad when he was running for governor. It was the bat I hit the winning run with during my college championship game. I told him it would bring him good luck, like it did for me, and when he won, he put it on display in his office to remind himself of his family's support.

Family has always been his priority. As far back as I can remember, the public always considered him an extremely important man. People would come up to us on the street just to shake his hand. But my sister and I never felt neglected. Even when he was growing Swift Corp, the company I now run, he made it a priority to show up at all of my baseball games and all of my sister's theatre performances. It wasn't until I was in my early teens that I even realized my dad wasn't like other dads, or even that we were rich, since he made a point of making sure we live as normal a life as possible.

He was staring down at some papers lying on his desk. He looked up and smiled at me when he saw me at the door. I hugged him before taking one of the chairs in front of his desk.

"You looked pretty deep in thought, Dad. What's going on?"

"Yeah. I'm trying to find the funding for the Arts in the Schools' program I've been planning to go along with the Art for the People project, but I'm hitting roadblocks all over the place. Nobody seems to want to support this simply because it's the right thing to do. They all want something in return"

"Is that what you called me here for? You know Swift Corp is willing and able to make a sizable donation to the school project, just like we did for the Art for the People project."

"No, I'm confident the people will fund this program because their kids are important to them. I'll work around the politics of it all. And, no, that is not exactly what I asked you here for, but we'll get to that later."

Even though I was curious, I knew it was best to let him take his own time to tell me. "How is Mom doing?"

"Oh, you know your mother. She's running herself ragged trying to work on all the charities and committees she's on. Her illness won't keep her down. She's happy, if not a little bothered that you haven't made it out to the house in over a week. If you go much longer, you know she is going to show up at your office and get all dramatic about never seeing her long-lost son," he said.

I laughed, but only because I knew he was speaking the truth. Like my dad, there wasn't anything more important to Suzanna Swift than her family. She was a force and kept our family connected despite all the craziness we each have going on. My dad runs the entire state of Wisconsin, I run the family business, and Tate was promoted to manager of the bookstore that she would one day like to own. We each have our own lives, but it's Mom that holds us all together.

So, yes, she would absolutely show up at my office and put on quite a show if I didn't make time to see her soon.

Even if I didn't have the time to see her, I knew I would make the time, anyway. They diagnosed her with leukemia last month and were going to start chemotherapy next week. Her strength has gotten our family through some tough times. She would try to use that strength to make her illness easier on us, and I needed to convince her she couldn't do that this time. This was the time her family would be strong for her, not the other way around.

"Don't worry, Dad. I was planning on taking Mom out for lunch this week, anyway. I'll call her tomorrow and set it up. She doesn't need to come storming the castle," I said. My dad laughed at the mental image.

"Do me a favor and take Tate with you. Your mom hasn't seen your sister in a while, either. She would be relieved to see you both together."

Tate has been distant for almost a year now after a bad break-up, but she is slowly coming back around to her optimistic self. Hanging out with my little sister would be a relief to me as well. She wasn't one to dump her problems on her family, but when I saw her in person I was usually able to get her to open up to me a little.

"Sure will."

I enjoyed my dad's company, but I was ready to find out why he asked me to come in.

"The last time you called me to your office, you broke the news about Mom's leukemia. How about you tell me why I'm here so I can stop coming up with all the worst-case scenarios?"

Recently, my dad has been wrapped up in a new community art project, so I was hopeful that I was there for that instead of hearing more bad news about my mom. Dad was a business major in college because that's what his parents expected of him, but he minored in Art History because that was what moved him. Growing up, we were surrounded by all the arts; paintings, sculptures, photography, music, theatre, and dance. Our parents believed education made us smarter, but art made us human, and it was easy for us to believe them.

When he took office, he vowed to follow through on a campaign promise he made to bring the arts back into the schools and our communities. He started fundraising for his Art for the People project his first week in office. Many people across the state contributed, which supported his conviction that the communities wanted to support the arts. He got a few companies, mine included, to donate to the project, found someone that believed in and understood his vision to lead the project and now it was becoming a reality. I couldn't be happier for him.

The second part of his plan was what he considered his legacy project. Something he could leave behind when he was out of the office. It was also where he was struggling the most. He wanted to increase school funding for the arts. He wanted his year-long project to only be the kickoff to bringing arts back into the schools. But, from the sounds of it, he wasn't having the best of luck with the senators or the assemblymen to get their backing.

"Devon, I asked you here because I need a favor."

He shifted in his seat as if he were uncomfortable with what he was about to ask. My dad didn't like to put a burden on anyone, so asking for favors was hard for him.

"I have asked for support from the largest donors to join the Art for the People committee. I know the business is all-consuming, but this would only be an hour or two a week, maybe a little more when the project launches."

My money was easy to give. My time was so much harder to part with. "I don't know, Dad. You know from personal experience how much time Swift Corp takes. An hour a week is not something I have to give right now. Maybe you could get Tate to go on behalf of the company."

He knew I was full of it. Swift Corp was like a family and ran just fine when I had to be away for things.

His smirk made me feel like I was going to lose this battle.

"Devon, I would say that I was asking you as the donor on behalf of Swift Corp, but you and I both know the donation didn't come from Swift Corp. So, I'm asking you, as the personal donor, to be on the committee."

Well, I guess he found me out. My mind scrambled for a way to explain this and still get out of joining the committee.

"I didn't want to take any money away from the company for this because I want to give out decent Christmas bonuses this year. That's the only reason I used my own money for the donation. I don't want it out there that it was a personal donation. You know that. Heck, you would have done the same thing when you were running the place. Plus, it looks better for the company if the community thinks Swift Corp was the one that made the donation."

"I know, Devon, and the public can continue to believe the company made the largest single donation to the project, and the best way for people to continue to believe that is to see you on the committee as a representative of the company and its donation. Plus, I know you share the same passion for art that your mom and I do. It would make your mom so happy to see you do this."

He swung for the fences and hit it out of the park. My dad just won the game. Well played.

"Fine." I gave in, knowing I wouldn't fight him on this one. "When is the first meeting?"

The sparkle in his eyes concerned me. "It actually started about 10 minutes ago on the second floor. I've hired a woman named Quinn Hill to run the project. Ask Janet for the room number." And, with that, he put on his reading glasses, gave me a smile, and picked up some papers to read.

After checking in with Janet, she already had the room number written on a piece of paper for me, the traitor. I went upstairs to find the meeting.

The door was open, so I walked in. Standing there, at the end of the table, was the beautiful woman who tried to knock me out earlier in the day.

"Excuse me, can I help you?" she asked with bewilderment in her voice.

Surprised by seeing her again, all I could say was, "Uhhh…my dad sent me."

3

QUINN

*C*onfused, I stared at the man, the brick wall I ran into earlier today. Wow, he looked amazing, standing there in his black slacks and crisp white dress shirt with the top button undone and his sleeves rolled up. There was something so sexy about a man with his sleeves rolled up. But I didn't understand what he was doing at my meeting.

"I'm sorry. Did you say that your dad sent you? Who is your dad?"

Giving me a quizzical look, he fumbled his words, "Oh, uh, yeah. Well, I'm Devon and my dad sent me to represent one of the donors for this project. I'm just here to help."

My pulse was racing at the thought of working with this man that I couldn't think clearly around. But I refuse to ruin this opportunity given to me, so I needed to get myself under control. His vague answer confused me, but I thought the awkwardness of the whole situation was probably the cause.

"Oh, okay. Well, please have a seat. We were just finishing up our introductions, so let me do a quick recap for you." He sat down. "I'm Quinn Hill. The governor asked me to head up this project." I gestured to the older gentleman to my right. "This is Mr. Millard Yates, the curator here at the Capitol building. He will help me with placing the exhibit each month. He will also get us all the permissions we will need to use any of the pieces held here at the Capitol."

With a nod of recognition, Mr. Yates greeted Devon, "Good afternoon Mr…"

"Devon," Devon interrupted as he looked around the room. "You can all feel free to call me Devon."

"Yes, of course. Good afternoon, Devon," Mr. Yates repeated. He had a funny look on his face as he said it.

That was odd, but I kept going and introduced the handsome 30ish gentleman sitting to my left. "This is Preston Henry, representing Henry Paper." I watched as Devon looked at Preston.

"Hello Preston," he said coldly, as if he were meeting the man who ran over his childhood cat.

"Devon." Preston responded with a nod of his head and a look of annoyance in his eyes.

Okay. Was I the only person in this room that didn't know anyone? I gave my last introduction, waving my hand toward the stunning woman sitting next to Preston. "This is Ms. Heather Winston. She is representing The Palette Studio. They have kindly offered to provide a few pieces for the exhibits." And, again, I saw recognition in both their eyes.

"It's been too long, Devon," she purred. She seriously purred at him. My stomach clenched at the sound of her voice. She was far too familiar with him. I don't know why, but I didn't like it.

Fantastic. I can't even imagine how horrible it was going to be trying to lead a group of people that all knew each other but didn't know me. I just wanted to go home and curl up in bed.

I already struggled with social situations, and this was

supposed to be different because it was my job. But since they all knew each other, I couldn't help but feel like I was the weird kid that wasn't part of the cool kids' inner circle.

Not wanting to prolong the awkwardness of me not knowing anyone, I chose not to have Devon tell me about the company he was representing. Based on deduction, I could probably figure out that he was representing Swift Corp. Since everyone else already knew him, I decided I would have to confirm his background later.

It was time to take control again and move things along, so I dove into the project details. Our first display month was going to be January, which meant we only had about three months to come up with the theme and curate the artwork.

"Since you all had little advanced notice of the project, I suggest that we go with my idea for the first month, since I had more time to think about it. What I want to do is start off the project with Wisconsin's most famous artist, Arthur Leary."

Devon and Heather both began speaking at the same time, but Devon gestured for her to go first.

"I personally own one of Leary's earlier pieces, A Winter's Walk, that I would be willing to loan for the project." Heather turned to Devon, "I think we found that piece together in Milwaukee, didn't we?"

Devon ignored her question.

"I think the university has a Leary hanging in their library. I would have happy to reach out to them and see if they would be willing to loan it to us."

I wasn't sure what the tension was between Devon and Heather, but I was thrilled that we already had a couple possibilities for the first exhibit.

We spent the rest of the hour tossing around ideas for what to use in our first exhibit, and by the time we called the meeting to an end, I was filled with hopeful excitement.

Once the nerves from the beginning went away, I quickly realized this group truly wanted the best for this project. For the first time since I accepted this position, I was relaxing into the idea that this year could be a lot of fun.

Mr. Yates left first, but Heather stuck around, striking up a conversation with Devon that I couldn't quite hear. She was leaning into him and running a finger down his chest. My belief was that the meeting leader should be the last to leave a meeting, kind of like the captain going down with the ship, but there was something about seeing her flirt with Devon that made me want to run out of the room like it was on fire.

I closed my laptop and reached for my notebook so I could leave when Preston walked over to me. He put his hand on my arm. My first thought was that his hand was in the same place where Devon's hand was earlier, but his touch didn't cause any electricity to shoot through me like Devon's touch did.

In a smooth voice I assume he used with all women, he commanded me, "Come out with me. Let me buy you a drink."

I gave him a look that said there was no chance I was going to say yes, but then stopped myself because I needed to work well with these people for this project to be successful. So, I needed to find a more tactful way of saying no.

"I appreciate your offer, Preston, but this is my first day on the job, and I'm pretty sure that I'm going to spend most of my evening working on the things we discussed here," I said, hoping that was the politest way to turn him down without hurting our working relationship. I quickly found I was wrong.

"Come on. This is a year-long project. Taking one night off to go out for a drink won't hurt anything in the long run."

I stood there trying to come up with the best reason to

decline, but I wasn't sure how to say no again without causing issues between us.

Seeing my hesitation, he added, "You can give me more details about your vision for Art for the People. Henry Paper is contributing a lot of money to this project, so I should at least get to hear more about your ideas."

My pulse raced. Was he really going to use his contribution against me to force me to go out with him? I didn't want to lose any money towards this project, so I was about to give in when Devon appeared at my side.

"Seriously, Preston, are you so hard up for a date that you have to threaten Ms. Hill with pulling your dad's money to get her to go out with you? That is pretty low, even for you."

"You know it's my money too, Devon. And you know that wasn't what I was doing. I don't have to threaten a woman to go out with me." He growled, "I have a sincere interest in this project going well since my company's name is going to be associated with it, so I was just trying to get a better feel for our new leader."

"I know what you were trying to get a feel for, Preston, and I doubt she would appreciate how you would go about getting that feel," Devon huffed.

I knew I needed to put a stop to the show of testosterone they had going on. "Thank you both for your concern. Preston, I appreciate the offer, and I want to make this project worthy of you putting your company's name on it, so that is why I'm going to stay here and work a little longer tonight." After a moment, he nodded with acceptance.

And, to put an end to the conversation, I added, "I thank you both for the time you spent coming to this meeting and for your commitment to this project. I will see you both at our next weekly meeting." With that, I broke my personal rule of the meeting leader being the last to leave and walked out the door.

I spent another hour in my office, so I wouldn't be a liar for telling Preston I was going to work late. Then, I packed up my things and went back to my apartment.

I changed out of my work clothes and pulled on a pair of black running leggings and zipped up a red sweatshirt over my white t-shirt. I thought maybe being dressed for a run would make me want to go. But I knew it wasn't likely.

I was replaying my day over and over in my head. I needed my roommate, Olivia, to hurry home so I could dump my first day on her and let her sort it out.

Olivia and I met when we were assigned as roommates our freshman year at the University of Wisconsin, Madison. I couldn't afford a single room and I didn't have friends in high school I could request as roommates, so I had to take a random assignment.

When I walked into our dorm room, she freaked out with excitement and told me how much fun we were going to have together. Her energy was infectious. She was the exact opposite of me: outgoing, talkative, extroverted, and confident. But she didn't seem to mind that I wasn't any of those things. She gave me no choice but to love her. She wouldn't allow anything less.

Shortly after, we became friends with Jillian and Sydney, who roomed together across the hall from us. By the end of our freshman year, the four of us were inseparable. We picked up one more, Jace, our sophomore year and our group of friends was complete. We've been a tight-knit group for years. We weren't just friends. We were the family each of us needed.

I sat on the couch waiting for the door to open.

I was so frustrated with how my first day went. And, while I should have been thinking about the project, I spent my time thinking about the way I felt when Devon had his hands on me.

I wasn't the kind of girl who got all mushy over a boy. Watching my parents when I was younger was enough to make me realize I never wanted to be tied to a man. I only dated one guy in all my 28 years and that was only because Olivia and our other friends from college wouldn't get off my back about never dating.

Olivia was a serial monogamist. She would go from one long-term relationship to another, rarely taking time off in-between. By the middle of our sophomore year of college, she had had enough of me not dating and convinced her boyfriend, James, to set me up with one of his friends. That was how I met Troy.

Troy was at UW Madison on an athletic scholarship. When I asked him what he majored in, he said football. I should have put an end to things right then and there, but Olivia insisted I give him a chance, so I did.

We went out a couple of times with Olivia and James. Being with other people made it easier to endure our polar opposite personalities. I let him kiss me goodbye a few times, but I felt nothing. I told Olivia, and she said I just needed to keep spending time with him and the feelings would grow. After a few weeks, he wanted to go out, just the two of us.

He picked me up from my dorm, and we went to the movies. He started with his arm around my shoulder, which wasn't so bad. Olivia was always smiling when James had his arm around her shoulder, so I assumed it was supposed to be a good thing. About halfway through the movie, he moved his hand to my leg. As the movie went on, his hand went further and further up my leg under the hem of my skirt and he leaned over to kiss my neck. I felt like this was what was supposed to happen on a date, so I let him continue.

When the movie was over, he walked me back to my dorm room. Olivia was spending the night at James' dorm, so when I opened my door and Troy noticed my room was empty, he invited himself in. I sat on my desk chair and he sat on my bed. He reached his long arm over to take my hand and pull me onto the bed with him.

Part of me, well, most of me, didn't want to be there with him, but the other part of me thought I should just do it and get it over with so I wouldn't have to be a virgin anymore. It wasn't a label I was holding onto for any specific reason. He was kissing me and grabbing at me, and it didn't feel good like I thought sex was supposed to feel. He lifted my skirt and slid his hand up my thigh. His hands were so rough from playing football that it hurt when his hands scraped across my skin. When he started working on his zipper I just closed my eyes. It was over in less than a minute. Troy zipped up his pants, told me he would call me later, and walked out the door. That was the last time I heard from him.

Laying there on my bed with my skirt still bunched up around my waist feeling confused and misled solidified my decision to stay away from relationships. Maybe I wasn't built for relationships. I told Olivia what had happened. She didn't bother me about men from that day on. She also used Troy as her excuse to end things with James.

I heard the door to our apartment open and watched Olivia walk through. She ran the front desk of our neighborhood police station and was done with work for the day. She wore her black polo shirt with Madison PD embroidered on it and the police department's emblem sewn above the city. Her backpack was slung over one shoulder and she was carrying Chinese food. Just the smell of it made my stomach grumble.

"My hero!" I shouted as I relieved her of the food. "I'm starving."

"I thought we could skip cooking and get right to you telling me about your first day over dinner."

Livy was exactly who I needed to talk to, so I was thrilled that she was finally home.

We each took a takeout container of food and got comfortable on the couch. I told her about how amazing it was to have an office in the Capitol. And I told her about the people I met and how the first meeting went, and how the whole team seemed to know each other. I admitted how uncomfortable their familiarity made me, because I knew she wouldn't judge me for being petty.

"That Preston guy sounds hot. Why didn't you go out for a drink with him?"

"I'm not really sure," I said as I reached for another egg roll. "He is very good looking. I think it was the way he said it. It was more like a command to go out for a drink with him rather than a question. I'm probably projecting too much onto the situation. You know I'm weird around men."

"I know you are, and I still love you. But there's more to the story you're not telling me," she stated matter-of-factly. "What is it?"

It's been years since I've been able to hide anything from her. History had taught me that she would badger me until I gave in and told her, I saved myself the trouble.

"Yes, there is something else that happened today, but it is so minor I didn't think it was even worth mentioning."

She finished chewing her Kung Pao chicken and perked up her eyebrows. "It can't be that minor if it's written all over your face that something else happened. Spill it."

"Okay, so I was running late for the meeting…"

She rolled her eyes at me. My tardiness is well known in my circle of friends. "I was only running late because I had on those stupid shoes that you made me wear, and I wasn't exactly paying attention when I went around a corner and ran right into this man. I fell and almost landed straight on my ass, but he caught me and helped me up and then I went on to the meeting. But it turned out he was part of my meeting. End of story."

"What's the rest of the story that you are still not telling me?"

My shoulders slumped because I was embarrassed to tell her the rest. Even though she was my best friend, talking about men was still an uncomfortable topic for me.

"It's nothing, really. It's just when Devon was holding me after he caught me, I kind of felt something. I don't know what it was. I'm sure it was just appreciation for him helping me up, but it was a weird tingly feeling in my arms."

"Devon?" she questioned.

"Yes, he's the one I ran into who is also part of the project committee," I explained.

"Devon Swift?"

"I don't know. He showed up late and was all buddy-buddy with the people in the room, so I didn't ask him what his name was or what company he was representing. I assumed the people at Swift Corp sent him to represent their company. Why?"

"Do you not recognize the name?" She looked at me and saw from the confused look on my face that I clearly didn't have a clue what she was talking about. "Was he super tall with wavy blondish brown hair and blue eyes you could swim in for days?"

It surprised me she described him so spot-on. "Yes, that sounds like him. Do you know him?"

"Seriously, Quinn? Do you not know who Devon Swift is? The governor's son, Devon Swift? The CEO of Swift Corp, Devon Swift?"

My heart stopped for a moment. I wanted to punch her for saying his name over and over. No, he couldn't be the governor's son. That couldn't be possible.

Olivia pulled out her phone and looked up a picture of

Devon Swift, who turned out to be the same Devon from my meeting today; my Devon.

Apparently, I turned a paler shade than I normally was because Olivia asked me if I was going to be okay.

"No! No, I will not be okay! Livy, I felt electricity with my boss's son. Electricity! That is not okay! How did I not know the governor had a son?" I panicked.

But I knew the answer to my own question. I stopped reading newspapers and magazines when I was 15. I also didn't listen to the news or read it online, so I was completely out of touch on anything going on in the world of the popular people. That was exactly how I didn't know about Devon Swift.

She laughed at me. "I think it's great you had a moment with Devon Swift. I met him once at the precinct and he was gorgeous, but down to earth, which I didn't expect. Even though I was just the receptionist, he took the time to ask my name and chatted with me for a bit while he waited for the captain to come out. You could do worse, Quinn."

"First, stop calling yourself just the receptionist. You know you're so much more than that. And, second, I'm not DOING anything. It was nothing and I'm going to make sure it stays that way. I won't jeopardize this position by flirting with the boss's son!"

4

DEVON

*W*alking into the Capitol building the next day, I thought about finding out which office was Quinn's so I could stop by to see how she was doing. Preston was an ass after the meeting. I didn't like him making her feel uncomfortable yesterday. But she dealt with the situation well. She held her own.

Preston and I had too much history for me to watch him screw around with another woman's feelings the way he did with Tate's feelings last year. I stood by and watched him change my sister from the sweet, confident woman she once was into an untrusting and skeptical one.

Thinking about Preston made my blood pressure rise, and I wanted to hit something. The idea of working with him for the next year was unbearable. It took my sister months to get over how he treated her, and I wouldn't let him do that to Quinn.

I couldn't put my finger on why, but there was something about Quinn that brought out my protective side. Maybe it had something to do with how soft and fragile she felt in my hands yesterday when I helped her up. But, after seeing her in the meeting and how she handled herself, it was obvious she had things under control and didn't need my help.

Once she got past the sticky introduction part of the meeting, things got better. She changed into a confident, self-assured woman when she started talking about the project. There was light in her eyes as she passionately discussed her hopes and dreams for bringing art to as many people as possible. She showed her extensive knowledge and appreciation of a variety of art forms without coming across as snobby about it.

It was exciting to watch her during our meeting. She captivated me as she walked us through her plans and invited each of us personally into the project. But, as soon as the meeting ended, the passionate woman disappeared. She morphed back into the shy woman I encountered in the hallway. It happened as instantly as the flip of a switch. I wanted to know what was behind both sides of Quinn I saw yesterday.

Deciding not to check in on Quinn, I put my focus back on my purpose for visiting, which was to see my dad and check on his progress on the school art funding. It might not have been my real purpose for coming back to the Capitol, but I didn't feel like I wanted to face what my real reason likely was.

Huge oak doors lined the hallway leading to various offices. Walking past one door that was cracked open, I heard a woman's laughter carry into the hallway. It was a reserved laughter, followed by a voice that automatically filled me with rage.

It was Preston. As I slowed to listen, I recognized the woman's voice. It belonged to Quinn. I apparently found her office without even trying. What was Preston doing here talking to Quinn?

I knew I would come across like a caveman if I were to

burst into the office and start pounding on his face like I wanted so badly to do, so I stood outside the door to listen.

"You didn't," I heard Quinn say in a light tone.

"I did! And the professor never caught on that it was me in the back of the room making the noise. The rest of the students in the class treated me like I was a hero from that day forward," Preston bragged. I cringed.

With the same tentative laughter I heard in her voice earlier, she teased, "Well, I guess that means I'm going to have to keep a much better eye on you during our meetings going forward."

"How about I promise never to do that during our meetings, and you agree to let me take you out for a drink tonight?"

I could hear a momentary pause. I hoped that she was trying for find a polite way to turn him down again. I considered stepping in to save her from having to come up with yet another reason to say no when I heard her hesitantly respond, "Sure, why not?"

Sure, why not? Had I heard her right? What was she thinking? I could see it in her eyes last night that she didn't want to have anything to do with Preston, so why was she agreeing to see him tonight?

"Fantastic!"

I heard him giving her the time and place for them to meet. It sounded like she was writing it down. Then I heard him say goodbye. I hurried down the hall and around the corner so he wouldn't see me when he left.

I wasn't sure why I was so bothered by Quinn agreeing to meet Preston for drinks. I barely knew her. Just the run in we had in the hallway and then an hour in a meeting together. It had to be Preston. Being near him had to be why I was all worked up. I couldn't see any woman being with Preston since no woman deserved the heartache he caused.

I walked back down the hall towards the east wing to see my dad, but something stopped me as I passed Quinn's door. I couldn't let it go, so I turned around and walked back to her door, which Preston closed when he left.

I was about to knock when the door opened. Quinn was standing in front of me, looking beautiful in a floral dress with her hair up in a messy knot on the top of her head. That put an end to my wondering from yesterday. Apparently, her knot was messy before the fall.

Her striking gray eyes looked up at me. She seemed even smaller than she did yesterday, then I noticed she was wearing flats instead of heels.

"Devon? What are you doing here?"

Still not wanting her to know my father was the governor, I lied and said, "I think I forgot my phone here yesterday. I was just stopping by to see if it was in the room we met in."

"Oh, can I go up and help you look for it?" she instantly offered to help.

"No, it's okay. I'll run up to the second floor. I don't want to bother you. I'm sure I'll find it," I said. Lying again.

"It's honestly no bother," she offered again. "I lose my phone all the time. Let me help you look for it."

Her genuine kindness shook me.

And, as if I had offended the gods of truth with my lies, my phone began buzzing in my pocket.

Quinn face twisted as she realized I had just lied to her. Her eyes drifted down to her shoes. I hurt her and my gut wrenched at the thought.

"Well, look at that, I guess I didn't lose my phone after all. I just forgot where I put it?" Knowing my newest lie was the stupidest thing I could have come up with, I just prayed that she would lift those beautiful gray eyes back up to mine and find the humor in the situation. But that didn't happen.

She looked up at me, but there wasn't an ounce of humor there. I couldn't make out what she was feeling. It didn't look like anger. It kind of looked like sadness.

"Mr. Swift," she said with an almost inaudible sigh, "why do you feel the need to lie to me? Are you trying to make fun of me?"

Okay, I was busted. It was silly for me to think that I could have kept my identity hidden from her. I wasn't even sure why I wanted to. I guess I wanted to get to know her as a regular guy. When women find out who I am, they get weird. They want to be around me because of my father, or they want to be around me because of my money, but I don't think they ever want to be around me because of me.

I didn't want her to get weird before I even had a chance to see what kind of person she truly was. There was something about her that made me feel she was different from most of the women I knew.

"Please, Quinn, accept my apology. I should have been straightforward with you yesterday."

She bit her bottom lip as I apologized. I couldn't tell if she was considering giving me another chance.

"I don't know why I didn't want you to know I was the governor's son. I guess I didn't want it to distract from the project."

"But they all knew who you were. You were only hiding it from me. You were only lying to me. That doesn't seem like it was to prevent distractions from the project. So, why did you lie to me about who you were?" And she was right. I did only keep it from her. I could see how that could come across as hurtful and I felt shame over hurting her.

"I guess it was because you were pretty flustered after our run-in that morning in the hallway, and then I clearly surprised you when I showed up for the meeting. I guess I didn't want to add anything more to your stress level when it was your first time meeting with the committee." At least I was telling the truth about that much, so I didn't feel bad leaving out the part about wanting to get to know her more before she found out who I was.

She stood there, wringing her hands discretely. I waited patiently to see if this was something she could let slide. I got the impression she wasn't a woman who took being lied to lightly, and I could admire that about her. After a few tense moments, it sounded like she was letting me off the hook.

"Well, I guess I should thank you then, for your consideration of my feelings yesterday. I think you're right. I probably would have freaked out if I had known my boss's son was on the committee during the first meeting. At least now I can say I've had one meeting without the embarrassment of knowing it was the governor's son I nearly trampled." She laughed stiffly.

Even though she said the words, there was a look in her eyes that said any possibility of trust was gone. She was definitely not a woman that easily forgave someone for lying. I royally screwed this one up and I had an overwhelming urge to correct it.

Changing the subject, she asked me, "What did you really come here for, Mr. Swift?"

Mr. Swift. I would give anything to go back to being Devon to her. And her question was going to be a tough one to answer, because fuck if I knew why I was there. Something drew me to her for reasons I couldn't explain. Maybe that was why I was there. I couldn't tell her that, but I knew deep down in my gut that I didn't want to lie to her ever again. I couldn't ever remember getting a look of hurtful distrust from anyone before and it caused an ache inside me unlike anything I've ever experienced. It wasn't something I wanted to feel again. But what was I going to tell her?

Being uncertain around a woman was also a strange

feeling for me. It was a feeling I hadn't felt since I was a gangly teenager asking Tiffany Anderson out to the prom. But, even then, I had the whole rich kid thing going for me, so it wasn't unbearable. I don't think being the rich kid was going to help me out this time. Honestly, I thought it might actually be to my detriment with her.

Trying to find something to explain my presence at her door, I blurted out, "I came to share an embarrassing story about myself to put you at ease about your fall yesterday. That way we would be even in the meetings. Want to hear it?"

My question brought embarrassment into her eyes, which made me feel terrible for even bringing it up. But she nodded, so I continued.

"My junior year in high school, I was walking down the hall with this girl from my calculus class and doing a terrible job trying to flirt with her. I wasn't smooth back then at all. In case you hadn't noticed by my awkwardness right now, I have improved very little over the years." I heard a little laugh come from her. "Well, I was being overly animated in my gestures as I spoke to her with one huge swing of my arms. I connected with the principal as he walked out of a classroom. I knocked out one of his front teeth." To save a little face, I added, "In my defense, I was going through a major growth spurt at the time and my arms didn't want to cooperate with the rest of my body. All the students there to see it happen spread the word and the whole student body called me Fight Club for the rest of the year."

I watched a change come over her, as if telling her embarrassing stories of my past made me more likable. She was even smiling, still looking down at the ground, but smiling nonetheless. I would never have considered that making myself sound like a dumbass would appeal to a woman. It was becoming clear to me Quinn wasn't like the women I usually hung around.

She lifted her chin to look up a little, and I got a better look at the smile gracing her full, feminine lips.

"Did you get the girl?" she asked.

"Nope. She wouldn't give me the time of day from that moment on, which was a blessing anyway. She was your typical mean girl, so I was better off not getting involved with her."

Still not quite meeting my gaze, she confessed with a chagrined tone, "It was pretty embarrassing yesterday. I hate it when I'm clumsy."

"I'm sorry for running into you."

My apology brought her eyes up to meet mine directly. "Oh, goodness, no. It wasn't your fault. You have nothing to be sorry for. I just need to pay better attention when I'm going places and not always be late, so I won't have to run."

"I know it wasn't my fault, but I was at least 50 percent of the collision, so I can still be sorry."

That brought a smile to her face.

"Now that we both know embarrassing stories about each other, how about we start over?" I asked. I reached out my hand to her as I stood up more formally and spoke to her in a proper British accent, "I'm Devon Swift. It is a pleasure to meet you."

She reached out to me, and I took her hand in mine. Her pale skin was buttery soft, and her petite hand was swallowed by my large one. Her smile was radiant as she continued on with our conversation, using the same proper British tone, "Thank you, Mr. Swift. The pleasure is all mine."

Being bold, I offered, "Ms. Hill, may I take you to lunch to make amends for my foolishness? I would most certainly like to rectify the errors I have made."

She dropped the accent and the smile. "I'm so sorry, Mr.

Swift. I actually have plans to meet my friend Jace for lunch today."

So, we were still at Mr. Swift and not back to Devon yet. I would need to fix my fuck-up and get back on track. One reason is because Mr. Swift is my father. And the other reason is I would like to see more of the woman from the committee meeting yesterday, and I don't think I would get to see her if she wouldn't drop the formality my lies caused.

Then the rest of her words caught up to me. Jace. Was he her boyfriend? Of course, a woman as kind, beautiful, smart, and cultured as Quinn would have a boyfriend. Then my protectiveness came out again, and I wondered if he was the reason she has those moments of fearfulness. Was he the one that brought those moments out?

"Maybe another day?" I asked.

"Of course. I really should be going, though. I'm running late for my meeting with Millard about the location for the Leary exhibit." She closed the door to her office and walked away from me with a slight nod in my direction.

After she walked out of sight, I turned and made my way over to the east wing to see my dad.

Janet grinned at me as I walked up to her counter.

"Twice in one week, Devon. What an honor."

"Yes, well, I just can't stay away from you, Janet."

"Devon, I have known you since you and your sister were in diapers. Do not think that your teasing has any effect on me. Go on in. Your dad doesn't have anyone in there right now."

She handed me a watermelon Jolly Rancher, my favorite, and gave me a slight head nod and a smile as I walked by. Janet was the best.

Dad was sitting behind his desk on a phone call. He waved his hand, letting me know I should come in and sit down, so I did. He finished his call and let out a heavy sigh as he hung up the phone.

"Devon, I'm surprised to see you today. Is everything all right?"

"Yeah, everything is fine, Dad. I just thought I would check in to see how things are going with making movement towards the school arts funding." Despite my distractions today, it was important to me that this funding was put in place for the kids.

"Not great." He leaned back in his chair looking defeated.

"What's up?"

"There are two senators that will only support the funding if we find a way to put certain tax cuts into the budget. Two other senators will only support it if there are certain tax increases budgeted. On the assembly side, one assemblyman told me he would only support it if I could find some financial support for the roadwork project needed in his district."

"Sorry, dad. Fucking politics."

"I know. It is all fucking politics, but that's not the part that's killing my funding. I think I can actually make all of those things happen. My problem is what Senator Spenser wants in exchange for his support of my project. He wants to be Senate President, but there was no way I can persuade enough people to vote for him. He just isn't a likable man, in the senate or out of it. I know everyone is hoping that he won't be reelected next year, but that won't help me with my funding issue."

He ran through a bunch of options for trying to get Senator Spenser on board, but each one was a bit worse than the one before it. I jokingly offered that have him taken out, but he declined.

Sighing in frustration, he changed the topic. "How did the committee meeting go last night?"

"It was good. Ms. Hill's passion for this project is impressive. You picked a good one." I saw a smirk on my dad's face that I ignored. "I wish you would have given me a heads-up that Preston and Heather were going to be on the committee too, though."

"I should have told you. I'm sorry, son. Mr. Henry found out about the project and insisted that Preston get involved for the publicity. I almost said no because their donation was so small, and Preston is such a dick, but Henry Paper is one of the largest union employers in the area and I need to keep up good working relationships with them."

His frustration showed on his face. "As for Heather, I actually didn't know about her joining the committee until after the meeting. When I spoke with Greta, the owner of The Palette Studio, she said she was planning on representing the studio herself. I guess she sent Heather last minute. Are you going to be able to work with them?"

He knew as well as I did Preston was going to be a nightmare. But with Preston's history of being extremely lazy, I hoped he would stop coming to the meetings altogether.

As for Heather, she was going to be a bigger challenge. She and I dated, but our relationship ended last year. In her head, our dating was going to lead to us walking down the aisle together, but I couldn't commit myself to someone that was so self-absorbed. She spent a small fortune on her clothes and makeup. She never gave a thought to anyone or anything unless it directly benefited her.

Even with all the signs I gave her showing her I was unhappy in the relationship, she was livid when I ended things with her after two years of dating. I was a little worried she had become mentally unbalanced. Since our break-up, she still seemed to believe we were going to find our way back to each other, giving her the happily ever after she felt she got cheated out of.

Heather worked the system to make things happen in her favor. It wouldn't surprise me if she had found out I was going to be on the project from Greta and then asked her boss to let her go in her place. She's tried so hard to cross my path since we split. Once, she paid my driver to find out what restaurant I was taking a date to and then just happened to show up and run into me. She made my date feel so uncomfortable that we ended the night early and didn't go out again.

"I'll be fine. I've been dealing with Preston and Heather for years. A few meetings a month won't be an issue."

"Good. I'm glad to hear it." He leaned back in his desk chair to stretch out. "Now, tell me more about Ms. Hill. Her resume was impressive and some of her ideas for the project were outstanding, even better than what I was thinking. But she was awfully quiet during our meetings. My only worry was she wouldn't be able to lead being as shy as she was."

It didn't surprise me Dad picked up the same personality traits I saw.

"She was pretty quiet in the beginning, but as soon as she started talking about the art, wow, she was a totally different person. Confident and commanding. Like I said, I think you made a good choice in picking her."

Knowing how protective my dad was over people, I hesitated, telling him the next part. "Preston asked her out for drinks last night. He insinuated he would pull his funding if she didn't go out with him. She could say no last night, but he was in her office when I got here and I overheard him asking her out again. They're meeting for drinks tonight." I watched my dad's face pale, knowing his mind went directly to Tate and what she went through.

"Damn it," he swore as he sat back up in his chair. "Tate was strong and you can see what Preston did to her. During our background check on her, I found Ms. Hill has some issues from the past that she is probably still dealing with. My guess is that's why she was so quiet. I can't imagine what Preston could do to someone with struggles in their past."

I knew Dad wouldn't break anyone's confidence by telling me what those issues were that Quinn was struggling with. But knowing they existed made me burn with anger.

"Do you want me to take him off the committee?" Dad offered. "I can find some way to smooth things over with his dad. Maybe I can get a street named after him or something."

"No, don't put yourself in that kind of position. You don't want to be indebted to the Henrys. I'll make sure I'm at all the meetings and Preston will get bored with things and stop coming eventually."

With that all cleared up, we spent the next hour getting caught up on other things going on at home and in the Capitol. My stomach growled, so I knew it was time to excuse myself and find some lunch.

I left the east wing and walked by the entrance to the north corridor, where Quinn's office was. I glanced down the corridor just as Quinn opened her door for a man standing outside it. She came out of her office and jumped up into an enormous hug. The man, dressed in corduroy pants, a denim shirt, and a plaid scarf around his neck, looked like a history professor. I watched as he set her down, then bent down and kissed her forehead. It was such a familiar, intimate gesture, it made my stomach tighten. He must be Jace. Damn, he was a lucky man.

5

QUINN

*I*t occurred to me I probably shouldn't be as boisterous at work as I just was, but it was so good to see Jace. He had some unexplainable calming effect about him that all four women in our little group of friends took advantage of often.

"I'm so glad to see you!" I practically shouted as I squeezed him one more time before letting him out of my death-grip hug. "Sorry if my hug hurt a little."

"No worries." He smirked at me. "Liv can't keep anything secret. She called Sydney and I last night to give us the rundown of your day yesterday. Jillian was working, so she's still in the dark for now. But, after talking to her, I knew I would be in for a squeezing." He lifted his arms, and I saw the white bags in his hands. It was then I noticed the delicious smell of Italian food surrounding him.

"Come in, come in! I'm hungry." I backed through the door and helped him with the bags. We sat at my office table and spread out the food.

"Lasagna. Jace, have I ever told you how much I love you?" I cooed as I bit into the steaming pasta.

"You have once or twice."

We ate together, and I confirmed what Olivia had told him last night. It didn't bother me that she called him. Our closeness was one of the most comforting things about our friendships. We all cared about each other. There was no judgment or criticism. We only had support for one another.

I moved on to my third breadstick and told him about my interaction with Preston and then with Devon. Both were so weird.

"I mean, it feels odd to me that Preston would stop by like he did. I don't know him well enough for a surprise visit to feel normal. And then Devon. I don't even know where to start with him. He purposefully hid his identity from me yesterday, which he tried to fix with a weak explanation, but then he flat out lied to my face about looking for his phone. I hate it when people lie to me. Why does he have to be that guy? It's just not cool with me."

There was recognition on Jace's face when I said I hated to be lied to. He was one of the few people who knew about my parents, so he understood how much it truly hurt me when someone broke my trust.

"The hardest part was that my impression of Devon after last night's meeting was a positive one. His input during the meeting was so thoughtful. I felt like he was going to be someone that wanted to bring this project to life for the right reasons. I mean, it's pretty clear to me Preston was only there for the publicity and Heather was only there for Devon, but I thought Devon was there with good intentions. Now I just don't know what to think." I dipped another breadstick into the warm marinara sauce and took a big bite as I sat back in my chair with a thump of frustration.

"Oh, babe, there is so much there, I don't even know what to start with. First, do you think you should go out with this Preston guy tonight? I know Liv said he sounds totally hot," he said in a mocking, somewhat hurt voice, "but if you know already just from the first meeting that he is only in it for the publicity, then he doesn't sound like the kind of guy you should be going out with."

He cared so much about all of us. Jace was a good man.

"You have my total agreement on everything you just said. I'm going out with him tonight because he has asked me out two days in a row and I don't take him as the kind of guy who's going to give up. I have to have a good working relationship with him. So, my plan is to go out with him tonight, only talk about art, and bore the tears out of him. Then, hopefully, he'll stop asking me out and focus on the project."

Jace's face lit up with laughter at my ability to come up with a plan like this. I think I saw a hint of pride as he looked at me.

"Fantastic plan, Quinn, just fantastic. But, just in case, how about I get Liv and Jillian to go with me to the bar you're meeting him at and we just hang out at a different table in case you need anything?"

Relief washed over me. I was terrible at dating, even if it was a guy I was actually interested in, so going out with someone with questionable motives wasn't something I was looking forward to. It meant so much to me to have my friends look out for me.

"Do you mind?" Which I knew was a dumb question.

"Of course not. I know Sydney is working late on a segment at the studio tonight, otherwise all four of us would be there for you." He pushed his takeout container away from himself and groaned with satisfaction. "Now, the next issue to discuss. This Devon guy. Why do you think he came to see you today?"

"I truly don't know, but I wish I did. I just have so many questions about him, like why did he show up late for our meeting? Why didn't he want me to know he was the governor's son? And why did he show up at my door today with the stupidest lie and excuse? Why would he tell me that lame story about his principal? Why would he find someone like Heather attractive?" My last question surprised me when it came out. It shouldn't matter to me who he's interested in dating.

"It sounds like you've been putting some thought into him. I won't push you about it, but you might want to spend some time figuring out why all of those questions are bothering you so much."

"Fine," I snipped at him. "I'll put some thought into it."

He gave me a warm, comforting smile and I took a deep breath, letting it all go.

"So, let's move on to you now. Why haven't you started forming a campaign committee yet? You aren't changing your mind, are you?"

Jace was a fantastic human being. He ran a non-profit that provided meals to the underprivileged children in Madison and spent most of his free time serving at the local homeless shelter. He even gave blood every other month. Seriously, he put the rest of us to shame, but he still loved us, anyway.

When he told us a few months ago that he was considering running for senator in the election that was just over a year away, we all just about lost it. He would be the best representative of our state because he had the biggest heart. But each time I was over at his condo, I saw his campaign ideas notebook on the entry table. I worried he might change his mind and not run.

"Don't worry, Quinn, I'm going to turn it in. I have all the signatures I need and all the paperwork is complete. I just want to wait until we get closer to next year's June 1st candidacy declaration submission deadline."

Confused, I asked, "Why would you want to wait? Don't you want to get out there right now and start campaigning?"

"I hired a campaign manager. Charlotte. She wants to do a little more research on my competition before I announce. You know I'm going to be running against Senator Jeffrey Spenser, right?"

I nodded at him as I dug through the takeout bag looking for the cannoli I was positive Jace would have brought for me. I smiled when I found it under all the napkins.

"You do realize Sydney hates you for being able to eat all that you do and still stay so tiny, right?" He laughed.

"I accept her hatred, because I know she still loves me." I said, as I took a big bite of espresso cannoli.

"Anyway, as I was saying, Charlotte and I did some looking into him and we confirmed my first impressions of him. He won't be an easy man to run against. He's known for backroom deals, unethical voting, and mistreating his staff. My concern is once he knows I'm running against him, he is going to make things difficult for me. We just don't want to give him extra time to prepare. So, that is why I'm waiting a little longer before I announce anything. I talked it over with Liv when she called last night and she agrees with me, so I feel like I'm making the right choice."

I couldn't stop myself from smiling. Of course, he talked it over with Olivia. And, of course, Olivia agreed with him.

Jace had been in love with Olivia for years. I was pretty sure it went all the way back to the day he saved her from some drunk guys at a barbecue we were at our freshman year of college. And, while it was easier to read it on Jace, I felt it deep down that Olivia also felt the same way about him for the last decade.

I understand that they're afraid to act on it for fear of changing the dynamics of our group, but the rest of us see it and are completely okay with it. Watching them go through boyfriends and girlfriends over the years has been torture. At the moment, Jace wasn't with anyone, and he was extremely verbal about his dislike for Olivia's current boyfriend, Trenton. But in Jace's defense, we all had a strong dislike for Trenton. I thought it was possible that even Olivia had a strong dislike for Trenton, but her strange need to always be in a relationship was stopping her from moving on.

"So, you talked to Livy about this?" I gave him an unrepentant grin.

Knowing where I was going with this conversation, because I was the only one in our group willing to have it with him, he quickly said, "No, Quinn, we're not doing this."

"Come on, Jace. You know you have feelings for her. You guys talk nightly and go to each other with all of your problems before you bring them to me, Jillian, or Sydney. Would you please just tell her how you feel?"

He ran his hand through his hair in frustration. "She's with Trenton right now. She is always with someone. And I don't want to do anything that ruins any of our friendships. What if we dated and things didn't work out? Which side would you pick? You're her roommate, so you would have to pick her side. And Sydney was my roommate for a while, so she would have to pick my side. That would leave Jillian. She's so passive. Having to pick between us would break her. So, she wouldn't pick any side and would just go off to marry Matthew and we would all never see one another again. One selfish decision on my part would totally tear apart the best group of friends I've ever had. I won't do that to any of us. I value our friendships too much to let that happen."

"Wow." I giggled. "Dramatic much?"

"Oh, I hate you sometimes, Quinn." He took a deep breath, let it out slowly, then sat back in his chair.

"Jace, that was just a bit over the top, don't you think? For being such a positive person, you went all doom and gloom."

His posture showed just how disappointed he was over the thoughts he had about a potential relationship with Olivia.

"Maybe, just maybe, you wouldn't crash and burn. Maybe you'd tell her how you feel about her, she would finally ditch Trenton the Terrible, you guys would turn your friendship time into sexy time, you'd get married, with me as the maid of honor, Sydney as the best man, and Jillian as the flower girl, and you would both live happily ever after on the same street with me and Sydney sharing the house next to you, because we had to move in together, and Jillian and Matthew living in the house across the street." I was a little lightheaded because I rambled the whole thing out with one breath.

He burst into laughter at the sunshine and roses story I just made for him. Even though he wouldn't do anything about the Olivia situation today, he at least made a move forward by admitting out loud that he thought about what a relationship with her would look like. If only he could get his vision to look a little more like a rom-com and a little less like a post-apocalyptic tale of woe.

We spent the next hour chatting about everything and nothing at all, and I felt more at ease about what was going on in my world by the time he left.

"Now, we're going to be at the bar a little before 7:00 tonight," Jace spoke with his big brother voice, "and we'll leave you guys alone unless you need us. You have a tendency to give people the benefit of the doubt, which is an endearing quality, but sometimes you need to shut that off. If anything doesn't feel right to you, you walk away. If he doesn't find you as boring as you are going to attempt to be and he wants more, just give me the look and I'll be right over at your table. Got it?"

"Yes, I've got it." With hopefulness, I added, "But I don't think I'm going to have to call in the calvary to save me from this date. I have been successfully repelling guys my whole life. I'm confident in my abilities to bore him senseless tonight."

I gave him a big, enveloping hug and sent him on his way.

I didn't trust men. I couldn't even remember a time where I did trust men. Jace was different. I started looking at him as a big brother from the first time I met him, so I never really thought of him as a man. He was the protector in our group. The non-judgmental guy's point of view we all sought out frequently. He was the only man I trusted.

Getting ready for drinks with Preston caused panic to grow inside me. Aside from going out with Troy in college, I hadn't gone out on a date before. And, if tonight went anything like it went with Troy, I would prefer to stay home in my pajamas reading a good book.

I didn't want to dress up, since my entire goal for tonight was to turn him off, so I put on an oversized cream-colored cable-knit sweater and a pair of my favorite jeans. I looked at myself in the mirror and decided my long hair was better pulled up into the messy knot again.

I wasn't the girl who put a lot of effort into her looks. Which was probably why I never wore my hair down. My mousey ash-colored hair always felt so boring, especially when I stood next to Olivia with her thick, rich black hair, so it was just easier to toss it up than try to do anything with it.

Any color of eye shadow just made my gray eyes look freaky, so I didn't do much with makeup other than a little mascara and some lip balm. I wasn't looking to attract attention, so I kept my look simple.

The piano bar I met Preston at was dimly lit by votive candles at each table. When I arrived, I didn't see Preston there yet, but I saw my friends huddled together at a table near the back. I wished I could just grab a drink and join them, but I knew I had to get this over with. I ordered a glass of red wine from the bar and took it over to a table near the door. That was when my friends started texting me.

Olivia: Your guy is late.

> Me: He is not my guy and he is only 2 minutes late.

Olivia: If I were going on a date with you I wouldn't be late.

> Me: Would you be late if you were going on a date with Jace?

Olivia: Shut up!

Jillian: Holy crap – did you see the gorgeous guy that just walked in?

I turned to the door and saw Preston sauntering over to my table. I waved my hand towards him.

Jillian: Damn! That's Preston?

With that, I put my phone back in my purse and smiled at Preston. He leaned down, gave me a quick kiss on the cheek, and told me he was going to get a drink from the bar. I watched him flirt with the blonde bartender. Her cheeks turned a bright shade of crimson at something he said to her. He took his drink, and she watched him until he reached my table.

"You look beautiful tonight, Quinn." He looked at me with warmth in his eyes.

"Thank you, you don't look so bad yourself." And I meant it. He was stunning. I would guess he was about 6 feet tall, with wavy dark brown hair. He looked confident in his navy-blue dress pants paired with a lighter blue button-down shirt. He went without a tie, but wore a suit coat that matched his pants, and finished off the ensemble with brown leather shoes that probably cost more than a couple months of my rent. I definitely felt a little underdressed next to him.

If someone had asked me before our date how things would go, I would have said it would be over in thirty minutes or less and he would never come around again. Boy, was I wrong. We sat there for over two hours talking and laughing like we were old friends. It turned out we had a lot in common.

We discovered similar tastes in books and music. He was truly interested in art, not just for the recognition of being part of the project, but because he had an appreciation for it. While my favorite form of art was painting, which I enjoyed doing a little of on my own time, his favorite form was the symphony orchestra. It was interesting hearing his different thoughts on art.

When it was just the two of us, he seemed like a different man. He seemed completely focused on me and didn't come across as pushy or cocky as he did at the meeting. Although I didn't feel that spark people talk about feeling, I felt like he might actually be someone I could enjoy spending time with.

Preston treated me respectfully when it came to the end of the evening. He asked if he could drive me home. I explained my apartment was within walking distance, so he asked if he could walk with me. Since I hadn't enjoyed a man's company this much since, well, forever, I agreed.

Being the beginning of September, there was a slight chill in the air. He saw me shiver, so he took his scarf off and wrapped it around my neck. He held his arm out to me and we walked arm in arm to my apartment. I didn't feel right asking him up, since we were practically strangers, but it didn't seem like he was going to push the issue, so I was off the hook.

We said our goodbyes and then he leaned down, put one hand on my hip and the other in the middle of my back, pulling me to him, and pressed his lips to mine. Immediately, it was a deep, demanding kiss, but not a passionate one. It didn't fill me with desire, or even butterflies and flutters. But, with my limited history of kissing to compare it to, it was a decent kiss. With that, he told me he would see me at our next meeting on Monday and watched me as I made it safely into my building.

6

DEVON

I wanted to see Quinn before the meeting to let her know about a plan I had come up with for the Art Project. Unfortunately, she wasn't in her office when I stopped in to see her. Resigned to waiting for her in the meeting room, I walked in and saw that Heather was the only one to arrive for the meeting so far.

I could feel her gaze following me as I walked over to a seat at the table. She looked at me like she was a tiger that hadn't eaten in months and just saw a rabbit. She sauntered over to me and sat on the table facing me.

"Hi Devon," she purred.

"Hey Heather," I said coldly as I pushed my chair back to put some distance between us.

My skin burned when she reached out to run a finger down the side of my face.

"I've missed you, Devon."

I looked at her, and she was flawless on the outside. Her red dress clung to her body in all the right places. Her long legs had a glow that shouldn't be achievable in Wisconsin. I remembered those long legs wrapped around me and that memory should have caused some kind of yearning in me, but all it did was make my stomach churn.

"I'm sorry to hear that. But you know that won't change things, Heather. We aren't good for each other."

A moment of anger flashed in her eyes, but then she turned the sweetness back on. "Devon, you just need a little more time to realize how good we are together. A little more time to sow your oats or whatever it is you're doing right now. We make sense. We complement each other. Together, you and I make the strongest power couple in the city. You need to finish this little temper tantrum you're having, and we will get back to being the couple we're supposed to be."

I needed to make things as clear as possible for her, despite knowing it wouldn't make a difference. "Listen, I'm not sowing anything, and I have no desire to be a power couple. Your need for us to be on top of Madison high society was one reason we broke up in the first place. I don't want the same things you do and I don't trust you. Understand this, Heather, we will not be getting back together. It's not going to happen. Ever."

She slid off the table onto my lap, putting her arms around my neck. Leaning into me, she whispered near my ear, "You will come back to me." She slid one arm down my chest and onto my pants. "You know you miss this." With that, she started rubbing up and down, with mischief in her eyes.

I let out a momentary groan, a normal human reaction to someone rubbing against your dick. But quickly gained my wits and reached up, putting a hand on each of her shoulders to push her off my lap. It was at that moment I heard the door to the room open. I glanced over and saw Quinn standing in the doorframe with a blush on her cheeks. Dammit, how much of Heather's show did she see?

Quickly, I stood up, forgetting Heather was sitting on my lap. She fell back onto the table.

"I'm sorry," Quinn said quietly. "Would you like me to come back? We still have ten minutes until the meeting, so I can, um, leave you the room to, ummm, finish what you guys are doing."

"No," I said.

At the same time, Heather said, "Yes, that would be lovely."

"We were finished with our conversation, Quinn," I said.

Giving Heather a look, making it clear to her not to contradict me, I added, "I'm glad you got here early. I wanted to talk to you about something I set up."

She took a breath and seemed to relax. I watched Heather glare at Quinn as she walked to the table and took a seat. Thankfully, Quinn wasn't looking up as she walked, so she didn't notice Heather's disrespectful attitude.

Heather sat in the chair next to mine and leaned towards me. Intensely frustrated with the whole situation, I turned in my chair and directed my attention to Quinn. Before I could say anything to her, I saw Quinn look up as she heard someone else entering the room. I watched her face change from a look of sadness to one of maybe hopefulness, excitement, happiness? Her smile grew and the glow in her eyes was what I would love to see when she looked at me when I walked into a room. I turned to see who was getting her attention.

Preston Henry.

Seriously, how could that be? He made her uncomfortable each of the last two times I saw them together. What could have changed between then and now?

Preston had his naturally cocky grin on his face as I watched him strut into the room and over to Quinn. He lifted her left hand to his face and kissed the back of it.

Quinn's cheeks flushed. What was going on here? And why did I feel so protective of her for this to bother me so much?

She was beautiful, and sweet, and listening to her speak so passionately about art moved something in me. And she fit perfectly in my arms when I held her. I've only interacted with her three times, so why was she affecting me so strongly? Or was this all because it was Preston, who had just walked around the table and taken the seat right next to Quinn, who was the one making her face light up?

Millard was the last to show, then Quinn brought our attentions to the meeting. "Okay, thank you for joining me again. I hope you all had a wonderful week last week."

"I had a great week," Preston interjected, and Quinn blushed again.

"That's good to hear, Mr. Henry," Quinn said as she turned to the group. "I reached out to the University, and they said they would be more than happy to let us use their Leary for January's exhibit. They just asked to be given credit for loaning it to us, which I think is the least we can do for them. Did anyone else find any leads on other Leary pieces?"

Heather gave a slight lift of her hand and said, "I think The Palette Studio is going to be able to loan out two pieces and I have an inquiry out to another art gallery that might get us one more."

"That is great. But we're going to need more than just these few. I knew it would be hard starting with a show dedicated only to one artist. It's so much harder to get enough pieces from just one person," Quinn said with a concerned tone in her voice.

This was my chance. I had the answer that was going to brighten her day, but I wanted to wait to see if anyone else had something before I hit her with my plan. Nobody was making eye contact with her, which made me think they had found nothing to contribute. I was happy to see Preston didn't put in any work. So, now was my time.

"I have something."

Quinn's face brightened as she looked at me.

"What did you find, Mr. Swift?" she asked.

Why did we have to be so formal still?

"I spoke with Mr. Leary's assistant of 30 years, a Mrs. Ida Elmsworth. She started a B&B on Washington Island in Door County after Mr. Leary passed away a decade ago. I explained to her how the Art for the People project was going to be a showcase of Wisconsin artists and how we want to start the project with a month dedicated to Mr. Leary. She was so excited to hear about the project and started coming up with ways she could help."

I watched the excited expression grow on Quinn's face. She looked at me with adoration and I couldn't imagine anything feeling better than her approval.

I continued, "She said she has about 30 pieces of his that he had given her over the years. Many of which have never been on display before."

Quinn put her delicate hand up to her mouth as she sucked in a breath, waiting to hear the rest.

"She said she would be more than happy to loan us those pieces for our exhibit. She also agreed to an interview about Leary. I thought we could place quotes from her interview around the room so people could learn more about the artist behind the paintings."

Her expression made all the time I spent away from my company last week completely worth it. Just seeing the look of hope in her eyes was validation that it was time well spent.

"Devon, that is just amazing. I can't believe you were able to pull this off." Quinn spoke so softly it sounded like a whisper. "When can we meet her?"

"Yes, Devon. When can we meet her?" Preston asked as he glared at me.

"Well, Preston, I don't think you are going to get to meet her. The paintings have to be shipped here from her Florida home. She told me she keeps her B&B open through Christmas, then closes down and spends the winter down south, which is why she keeps the paintings there. She said she would ship them here, but it would take some time. I set up a time with her the week before Christmas. She thinks she can get them here by then. It will be cutting it close, but she assured me they would be ready to display."

Preston growled. "Of course you did. You just happened to set up the time to meet with her during the one week you know the Henrys always go to our cabin in Montana for a family vacation. Quite convenient for you, don't you think?"

"Sorry, I didn't think to consider your schedule. I didn't do it intentionally, Preston. I just picked a time when she was available."

Of course, I didn't mention that I was, in fact, given a few dates that worked for her, but chose the one I did because I did, in fact, know they always take their family vacation the week before Christmas. But he didn't need to know that.

"I thought we could drive up there together," I said, as I turned my attention back to Quinn. "We'd have to leave pretty early in the morning, but I think we could do it all in a day and still catch the last ferry back from the island."

"Did you even consider I might want to be a part of this, Devon?" Heather interjected.

"Sorry, Heather, but I didn't want to assume how much time you were interested in investing in this project, so I just let Mrs. Elmsworth know that Quinn and I would be the ones coming to visit her." It felt like the best out I could give myself for not wanting to spend a whole day with Heather. "I'm sure you are going to find an opportunity like this for one of the other months, and you and Quinn can tackle that one together."

"I think just two people going to interview her and see the pieces might be best," Millard added. "You don't want to overwhelm her with people asking questions when she is being so kind with her time and her possessions." He gave me a little wink when the others turned back to me.

"Well, that settles it. Unless you have any objections, Quinn."

The ball was in her court. I just hoped she was willing to play.

I watched as she looked around at each person at the table. I had a look of excitement, like a kid waiting to see if the toy he really wanted for Christmas was going to be under the tree. Heather, sitting next to me, scowled and wasn't trying hard to hide it. Millard had a knowing smile on his face.

Then there was Preston. He looked pissed, and I didn't care. From the little I knew about Quinn, I knew she was way too good for him. Honestly, I truly believed any woman was way too good for Preston Henry. But I also knew he wasn't going to just let this one go. He might not be going with us in November, but I knew he wouldn't stop pursuing Quinn. If I had to guess, the obvious declaration of interest I just made was probably going to make him try harder to win her, since he had a history of being overly competitive with me.

As if steeling herself for battle, Quinn quietly said, "I think that would be good, Devon. If we leave early enough and catch the first ferry of the day, we could spend several hours with her discussing Mr. Leary and looking at his works. Also, Heather, even though you won't be going to this meeting, I would love to stop by your studio soon and discuss the Andrew Jorgensen photos for February."

I watched as she glanced over at Preston to see what his reaction would be. I still wanted to know what I missed. Why should she care what he thought about this? I know they went out for drinks last Friday, but I've had drinks with Preston before. He is the most boring, pompous jackass there is. I couldn't imagine anything happening that night that would endear him to her. But Preston hid his colors from Tate for months before he let his true self show.

Just thinking about him made me so angry inside. I hated what he did to her and how he changed her into a victim. I didn't realize how upset I was getting until Quinn's sweet voice interrupted my brooding.

"Did you change your mind, Devon? You look a little upset."

"No. Sorry, Quinn. I was just thinking about something I forgot to do at work. I think Mrs. Elmsworth is going to help us tremendously and the road trip is going to be fun. My apologies for the distraction. You have my full attention again."

We spent the rest of the meeting discussing different ideas for the following months. When the meeting was over, everyone seemed to hang back to talk to someone. Except Millard. He happily took his leave of the group. Heather was seeking me out, Preston was seeking Quinn out, and I wasn't sure who Quinn was looking to see, but I was hoping it was me.

Heather got to me before I could catch Quinn's eye and pulled me over into a corner to speak with some privacy. "Devon, I want to go with you to Washington Island. Maybe we could leave Quinn behind and go just the two of us. I have an Art degree too, and I've been using mine in the real world longer than she has, so I would know best the right questions to ask."

She slid her fingers down my arm and tried to take hold

of my hand as she added in a whisper loud enough to be overheard by the others in the room, "And maybe we could stay a night or two at Mrs. Elmsworth's B&B. It's time we get reacquainted, don't you think?"

Quinn was watching us as she spoke to Preston.

I knew Heather had extensive issues from her past that contributed to her behaving this way, but I needed to be firm with her that she wouldn't get her fairy tale ending from me.

"Heather, we are not getting back together. We have no need to get reacquainted. We are not good for each other. You are not what I'm looking for." She cringed at my last comment. "We will work together on this project because it's in the best interest of both of us, but we can only do it as colleagues. Maybe, someday, we can get back to a place where we are friends, but that is as far as it is ever going to go."

"Why can't you forgive me?" She pouted. "I made a mistake. That doesn't mean we aren't good for each other. It doesn't mean we can't get back to where we were. Or is it that I'm just not wholesome enough for you? I see how you look at Little Miss Perfect Quinn over there. You know you don't have a chance with her. Preston beat you to it."

I was so frustrated that she wasn't getting this. My break-up with her wasn't about her "mistake." Sure, it was the catalyst, the proverbial straw that broke the camel's back, but not why I left her. I left her because she made it clear she was with me for the status and the money. That was it. I wanted to connect with her, but there wasn't any substance to her personality for me to connect to.

I will say, though, walking in on her fucking Preston in my bed was definitely a good enough reason to end things, even if everything else was great in our relationship. I went out of town for a business trip and asked Heather to stay at my house to take care of Wasabi, my cat. My business went quicker than I had expected, and I came home two days early.

When I walked in, I found Wasabi locked in the laundry room. I could hear her meowing. When I opened the door, she bolted out. I saw Heather had put her cat food and litter box in there and naturally assumed she spent most of the time I was gone locked in that little room. I was furious.

I went upstairs and heard Heather moaning. Great. Just great. She was getting herself off while my cat was locked up like a criminal. That was when I heard a man telling her how wet she was.

I opened my bedroom door and saw Heather on all fours while Preston was fucking her from behind. They didn't even realize I had walked into the room for almost a minute. During the brief moment I stood there, I heard Preston saying stupid shit like, "Yeah, baby, tell me I give it to you better than Devon. Tell me I make you come so much harder than him."

So, I thought that would be the perfect time to put my thoughts out there. Clearing my throat, I said, "Well, you're not going to make her come harder than me if that is the equipment you are using to do the job. It's no wonder my sister doesn't want to be with you anymore. Not exactly a big stick you're carrying there, Preston."

They both looked shocked to see me there but took it differently. Heather immediately began apologizing and telling me how this was the first time it's ever happened and what a mistake it was. Preston, on the other hand, was pissed off at my comments and tried to tell me that if I was satisfying her in bed, she wouldn't have come looking for him. Which I knew was a complete lie.

I was a big believer in the two-to-one rule. She had to come at least twice before I would come once. And that was the low end of the rule. Most of the time Heather was so exhausted she couldn't move when we were done. So, I knew he was just talking out of his ass.

Preston grabbed his clothes pretty quickly and left, but Heather stuck around and tried to salvage whatever it was we had. Begging for another chance, which I repeatedly refused.

When she didn't catch on that it wasn't going to work, I pointed out to her that I could never be in a relationship with someone that would lock my cat away for days. Her actions told me everything I needed to know about her as a human being.

She tried to cover and tell me Wasabi must have bumped the door and gotten herself stuck in there, but that didn't explain how her food and litter box were both moved in there, too. I told her to leave and walked away from her without a second thought.

So, her trying to say her mistake was forgivable was laughable.

"Heather, this is over and has been for a year now. This isn't about you fucking Preston," I growled in a whisper, "and this isn't about Quinn. This is about you not being what I want." And I walked away to try to get a minute or two alone with Quinn.

7

QUINN

I tried to give all my attention to what Preston was talking about, something about his company's donation to the project, but I couldn't focus because I was catching words here and there from, what appeared to be, a heated conversation between Devon and Heather.

The way she was touching him when I walked in the room earlier made me think they were a close couple. I shouldn't have felt a pang of sadness over that, especially after having such a good time with Preston last week, but I did.

I couldn't imagine feeling close enough to a man to touch him like that in private, much less out in public like she was doing. But the way they were arguing was sending out a different message.

I brought my focus back to what Preston was saying, "So, I think we should have the major donors listed alphabetically on the marketing material. Henry Paper, The Palette Studio, and Swift Corp."

Was he actually suggesting we put his company first when they donated the least amount to the project? As a general rule, I tried my hardest not to judge anyone, because you never knew where they're coming from, what they've experienced in the past, or what their true motives were, but his suggestion sounded pretty selfish to me.

Not wanting to offend him by telling him that I saw the donor list, I said, "I actually sent the marketing images to the printers already and I put the names on the flyers and posters in a random order. Sorry."

"Well, what order was it in when you sent it?" he asked forcefully enough that I immediately became uncomfortable.

Wow, he wasn't going to let up on this. Swift Corp donated over ten times what Henry Paper donated. I put his company's name last on the marketing material for that specific reason. I couldn't think of a good way to tell him that without him getting angry.

"Preston, stop being a dick," I heard Devon say as he walked up to join our conversation. "This is not about whose company gets top billing. These were donations for a good cause and making it the best that it can be is where our focus should be, not on getting credit."

"I'm just saying, Devon, big donations deserve to be recognized. Don't you agree? If your donation was bigger than mine, that's fine. They should list you before me, but I doubt that's the case, is it, Quinn?"

"Back off, Preston. I'm not going to let you come in here and treat Quinn like you do other women," Devon spoke firmly. I felt he might be more reactive than the situation called for, which made me wonder if there was some history I was missing.

"Fuck off, Swift." Preston raised his voice and stood up a little taller, even though he was still not as tall as Devon. He took an aggressive step towards Devon and I could feel my heart racing.

I didn't want to be in the middle of them fighting. I wasn't prepared to handle a confrontation like this again. My breathing was getting faster. If experience taught me anything, it was that I needed to protect myself when the yelling started. My hand went to the scar on my right arm and held on as if I was trying to stop the bleeding again.

Suddenly, I was brought back to my dad yelling at my mom when I was younger. He would get so mad and I would hide under my bed like my mom told me to. I could feel the cold floor as I laid there with my stuffed panda bear for protection. My dad's voice boomed through the house, and I could hear my mom trying to calm him down. It never worked, though.

I didn't want to feel this way again. I could feel a panic attack coming on.

"Quinn." I felt Devon's hand on my arm, grounding me. "Are you okay? You look so pale."

He moved in front of me, blocking Preston from my line of sight, and lifted my chin to look at him. Looking into his eyes brought a calm over me. He held my gaze as I took a few breaths and could feel myself relaxing. Making direct eye contact with people had been an uncomfortable thing for me for years, but with Devon, who was still practically a stranger to me, it was different. With him, it felt safe.

Devon took control of the situation. "Preston, maybe this is not the time to discuss this. Quinn, how about you and I go get some coffee and we can discuss the logistics of the Door County trip?"

Preston jerked his chin at Devon but didn't continue to argue. I nodded my agreement to Devon and pulled myself together enough to tell Preston that I would see him at next week's meeting. Devon picked up my bag and led me out of the room.

Even though it was the middle of September and only had a slight chill in the air, I still shivered as we walked. Devon put his coat around my shoulders as he led me out of the Capitol and down State Street a few blocks to The Hideout Coffee Shop. We didn't speak as we walked, and I was grateful he didn't force a conversation. I told him my order when he asked, and we took a seat on a couch near the fireplace to chat.

I could feel his eyes on me as I looked down at my coffee.

"Are you okay?"

His voice was filled with the comfort of a warm blanket. I felt guilty for causing him any concern, and I knew I couldn't explain what happened back at the meeting.

"I'm sorry, Devon. People shouting tends to make me uncomfortable." That was at least partially true. "I appreciate you stepping in to help."

"Not a problem. I was just concerned when you went so pale. I'll make sure Preston stays under better control from now on." He paused, as if he was unsure of what he wanted to say next.

"Speaking of Preston, I heard you guys went out for drinks last week. How did it go?"

No, no, no. I definitely didn't want to talk about Preston with Devon. Especially after Preston's aggressive side came out today. That side wasn't there when we met for drinks last week. I had to question my ability to judge someone's character. But Devon was gentlemanly enough to step in and help me today, so I felt like it wouldn't hurt to share a little with him.

Should I tell him it's been him on my mind since our first meeting, rather than Preston? Would that be too forward? I didn't understand men. I had Preston pursuing me, which I assumed was for personal gain, and then there was Devon. Devon, who I haven't been able to stop thinking about since the moment I ran full force into him. Even though I let myself be fooled by Preston, I still believed I was right about Devon.

"I had a good time with him. We actually have a lot in common." I saw his face fall slightly at my confession, as if he wanted me to tell him I had a terrible time.

"But he seemed different today. When we were out last week, he was so kind and considerate. Today he just seemed focused on himself and what he wanted for his company." I stopped for a moment to think before I continued. "Maybe he was just having a bad day today. I have those kinds of days sometimes too and maybe I shouldn't judge him for his bad day."

Devon looked at me like I had grown a second head. "You are an honest to goodness good person, aren't you, Quinn?"

Well, that was an odd question. All I could do was shrug my shoulder and look down at my coffee again. I didn't feel like a good person. I've always felt like there was something wrong with me. Like I had a defect others didn't have. The only time I didn't feel that way was when I was discussing art. The arts made me feel like I had something positive to contribute to society. People listened to my thoughts about all different forms of art and my opinions were respected. I didn't know if that small contribution made me a good person, though.

"You don't have to answer my question if you don't want to. I wasn't trying to make you uncomfortable. It was just an observation." He spoke softly as he put his arm on the back of the couch and turned more towards me.

His nearness sent sparks through my body. His voice was more calming than the lavender tea I drank before bed. But, to counter the calming effect of his voice, his scent was invigorating me. His masculine scent made me want to climb up on his lap and devour him, which was also a new feeling for me. I sipped my coffee and tried to focus on our conversation rather than how amazing he smelled.

"I'm sorry I walked in on you and Heather earlier. Despite what our run-in my first day says about me, I do generally try to get to meetings a little early. But maybe you and your girlfriend could take the making out to a different location next time?" As the words making out came out of my mouth together, I cringed. Apparently, I wanted him to think he was out to coffee with a high school girl. I was so embarrassed.

"You do not have to apologize for anything. And Heather is not my girlfriend. At least not anymore."

I gave him a look, wordlessly encouraging him to continue talking, hoping he would pick up on it. And he did.

"She and I dated for about two years and I ended it about a year ago. We wanted different things."

"May I ask what you were looking for that she wasn't?" I knew I was being forward, but I desperately wanted to know what could have possibly been missing with a woman as seemingly perfect as Heather.

He took a long moment of thought before he answered. "I'm thirty-three years old and am to the point in my life where I'm thinking about settling down. I want a family. I see myself coaching my son or daughter in little league, then coming home and having deep, meaningful conversations with a woman that loves me, but also challenges me. Or maybe go to an art opening together." He laughed and nudged my shoulder with his hand that hung over the back of the couch. That sent my mind racing trying to decide what he meant by that touch.

"I would be happy spending evenings with my wife doing nothing at all as long as we're doing it together. When it comes down to it, I want what my parents have and I don't want to compromise. I have no desire to take over the world. I don't want to spend all my time going to fancy parties, being forced to talk to people that offer little to a conversation other than commentary on the stock market. I've done that already and I'm kind of over it. But Heather envisioned a different future than what I was looking for, so I ended it."

He looked so sad. There was tension in his shoulders. I felt like there might be more to the story he didn't want to say, but I wasn't going to push him for it. I appreciated him being as honest with me as he already was.

"How about you? What is Ms. Quinn Hill looking for in Mr. Right?"

For Mr. Right to love Mrs. Right, instead of beating her up. Was that an acceptable answer? We definitely grew up in different environments. How could I explain that to him without explaining my history? Did he know my history? I was sure it had to come up during the vetting process for my job. Did his dad tell him?

"I don't know that I'm looking for a Mr. Right, so I don't think I have a list of things I want from him. I think I just want to be happy. Maybe, someday, I would like to have a family, but I honestly don't know if marriage and family are in the cards for me, so I don't put a lot of effort into worrying about it." I glance down again, not wanting to see the judgement on his face.

I could feel him watching me, like he was trying to see into my soul for all the answers. I thought it would make me uncomfortable, someone staring at me like that, but it didn't. It felt like he was trying to understand me.

"Who hurt you, Quinn?"

That wasn't what I was expecting.

Looking up into his eyes, I said with a nervous giggle, "Aren't we a little off topic here?"

"I'm going to be honest with you, because I feel that's important to you. I want to know you, Quinn. I get a glimpse of a carefree woman each time you talk in the meeting; when we get deep into the art talk, you turn into a rock star. But after, you shut down and become so timid. Where's that coming from?"

I couldn't say anything to contradict his assessment of me, so I just shifted in my seat and took another sip of my coffee, trying not to cry.

Seeing my discomfort, he said, "I'm not going to push you, though. Let's make some plans for the trip. I would be happy to drive. But I'm fine if you'd like to instead."

We spent the next hour discussing the logistics of getting to Washington Island before Christmas. It was a possibility there could be snow by then. Since driving wasn't my strong suit, we decided to take his Land Rover and he would drive. We also came up with a list of questions so long it might overwhelm Mrs. Elmsworth, so we decided to meet for coffee again after next week's meeting to narrow them down.

Once we finished with business, we spent another hour just chatting with each other. We talked about art, music, and theatre, as well as his love of baseball. He told me about his childhood growing up as a Swift and how it made him and his sister close. Not having siblings of my own, I reveled in his stories of the trouble he and Tate got into. Obviously, he cared for her greatly. He asked about my childhood, but I only gave the vague answers practically pre-programmed in my head.

"Quinn, could I take you out to dinner on Friday night? We could go wherever you want. Or we could hit up the Museum of Contemporary Art. Or both. What do you think?"

"I wish I could, Devon, but I have plans Friday night."

I wasn't sure why I lied. My only plans for Friday involved take-out Chinese food and a good Netflix binge. Maybe it was because Preston also asked me out again after the meeting and I turned him down, so it didn't feel right to say yes to Devon. But maybe it was because Devon scared me. Not in the "he's going to hurt me" kind of way, but more like the "he was someone who could damage my heart someday" kind of way.

Devon didn't hide his interest in me. Olivia says I'm oblivious to men hitting on me and I doubted her each time she mentioned it. But I felt fairly confident Devon was hitting on me. I also felt the same way about Preston, but his was him telling me outright he wanted to date me. Devon let me know in different ways.

He touched me frequently. Simple little touches, like when he grazed his hand against my knee when he was reaching for a napkin or how he brushed a strand of my hair away from my face while I was leaning over my laptop, taking notes. His hand on the small of my back when we walked to the door was almost enough to set my whole body on fire. When the light at the intersection changed to WALK, he took my hand in his and guided me across the street. I felt so safe in his presence.

He asked for my keys when we got back to my office, and he unlocked the door for me. I could have turned into a puddle on the floor after that one melted me. I wondered if he was going to demand a kiss like Preston did, but he did one better.

"I had a wonderful time with you today." Then he took my hand in his, put his other hand on the side of my neck, leaned forward, and placed the gentlest of kisses on my forehead. My forehead. Preston's kiss did nothing for me, but Devon's one little kiss on my forehead was going to leave me with weeks of naughty dreams.

"Have a good evening, Quinn. I'm looking forward to next Monday," he said as he walked away.

I needed to talk to Olivia right away.

Me: Hey—where are you at?

Olivia: Work...why?

Me: I need to talk about Devon!

Olivia: OMG! Tell me EVERYTHING!

Me: Meet me at home—tell no one!

Olivia: Not even the gang?

Me: NO! I'm not ready for this to be a thing.

Olivia: Chinese or Mexican?

Me: Is both an option?

Olivia: No...I can't afford to feed you. You eat like a teenage boy. Pick one.

Me: Mexican—and get me a lot of extra chips and salsa and fried ice cream!

Olivia: Fine...I'll bring a Mexican feast because I love you.

Me: I love you too! See you at home!

Olivia got home with two bags of Mexican deliciousness for us and immediately demanded the details. Since she was the only person who knew everything about my past, I didn't feel like I needed to censor anything from her. That's why she's my best friend.

I explained the argument at the end of the meeting and how I could feel a panic attack coming on. She yelled at me for not calling her, but then she continued eating her chicken chimichanga and listened while I continued on with my story.

I covered the discussion we had about Heather, and she

was excited to hear they weren't a couple. Apparently, Olivia and Heather have crossed paths before and Olivia didn't think highly of her. I even told her how he asked me who hurt me in the past. She was disappointed in me for not giving him any details, but she understood, so she didn't give me a hard time. Then I got to the part where we spent an hour talking about everything else.

"Livy, he is so passionate about the performing arts. He's been to New York for so many Broadway productions, and he sponsors the Mendota Players for their Shakespeare in the Park performances during the summer. It's not just talk with him, it's action. He truly loves the arts as much as I do."

"That's fantastic, Quinny. You deserve someone great like him. But what about Preston? I thought you guys hit it off last week."

"We did, but there wasn't a spark. I definitely felt a spark with Devon." Then reality hit me. "Holy shit, Livy, I felt a spark for the first time in my life."

She squealed.

Thinking about it warmed me for a moment, then the anxiety took over.

"I shouldn't be looking for a spark with either of them. I shouldn't be worrying about men, because that's not in my future. And I definitely shouldn't be looking for a spark with someone on the committee."

This was my first opportunity to show the community what I was capable of doing. Dating someone on the committee would only undermine the end result I'm trying to achieve. Remembering Devon's scent on his coat wrapped around my shoulders squashed all those thoughts.

"Devon is such an amazing man, and I'm damaged goods. Nobody wants to see the governor's son, the CEO of one of the biggest employers in the area, with someone like me. Can you imagine?"

"I can imagine, Quinn. And I wish you could too. You are such a beautiful person, inside and out. And he would be lucky to have you. I wish you would accept how fucking awesome you are."

"What, like how you accept that Jace has been in love with you for years, but you still don't seem to think you're good enough for him? Is that how you want me to accept my awesomeness?"

I could tell she was upset with me for bringing up Jace. Their relationship has been unique for as long as I could remember. He pined for her from the sidelines as she went through her string of relationships. She knew everything about my past, but she wouldn't share with me why she wouldn't let Jace into her romantic world. I had a hunch it had something to do with her mom, but she still wasn't ready to open up about it, even after all these years.

I knew she and Jace would be perfect together. Everyone in our group could see they each have feelings for each other. We've all resigned ourselves to giving them time and hoping they figure things out on their own.

"That's different and you know it." She shook her fork at me for emphasis so hard a piece of chicken flew off and bounced off my cheek. We both rolled around laughing.

Neither of us was going to make the other change our opinions tonight, so we agreed to stop trying and watch some reality TV. I went to bed, resigned to avoid being alone with either Preston or Devon, but my dreams didn't get the memo. I dreamt of Devon all night.

8

DEVON

*D*riving home from the coffee shop, after leaving Quinn at her office door, I couldn't help but question everything I did. Was I too pushy? Was I not pushy enough? I switched the conversation over to safer topics when I could see she was getting worked up by my questions, but I desperately wanted to know what she was hiding.

Talking with her about my love of performing arts was freeing. Many of my friends judge me for being so passionate about it. Deep down, I wished I had the talent to perform, but it wasn't in me. So, I left the theatre to Tate, and I stuck to baseball. All of Quinn's opinions about the different topics were so well thought out. It felt like I was having to pull them out of her. But, once she got going, she relaxed more and shared freely. Seeing the real Quinn come out was a gift.

Every moment I spent with her made me want more. I haven't felt that way towards a woman ever. Growing up as the son of a US Senator, and then the governor's son, made it difficult to find someone who wasn't after me for my money, my potential connections, or the fame I could bring to them. Heather was my longest relationship, but only because I was at that point in my life and I wanted someone that would be forever. I fought for our relationship way longer than I should have, and in the end, it didn't matter.

But with Quinn, I felt like she was actually pushing me away, even though I was pretty sure she was interested. Maybe her disinterest was what I liked about her. Pursuing a woman wasn't something I've had to do before. I spent more time respectfully rejecting offers. Being interested in Quinn and having to pursue her was a novel experience for me, but I think I liked it.

And, while her mind absolutely infatuated me, her body was doing damage to me. Her soft curves were perfection. There would come a day where I would see her with her hair down and I couldn't wait to run my hands through those brown locks. And there would come a day, I was sure of it, when I would kiss her pouty lips and finally taste her. I wanted to do more. My dreams showed me that much, but if I could just kiss her, that would be enough.

I also hoped to get her to open up to me. I noticed an angry-looking scar on her right arm. She tried to keep it covered, but it peeked out of her sleeves when she moved her arm to reach for her coffee. I didn't know how far up it went, but I wanted to know the story about it. If she would open up to me about the cause, I feel like it would be the start to her telling me her story. And I seriously wanted to know her story. There was a desperate need inside me to understand her.

Pulling into my driveway, I saw someone sitting on my front stairs. As I got closer, I saw it was my sister, Tate. I couldn't figure out why she didn't wait inside since she had a key, but sometimes she made little sense to me.

"Hey sis," I said as I leaned in and gave her a big hug. She had lost too much weight in the last year. I looked down to see her jeans were practically falling off her body. She wore an oversized flannel shirt to cover up how thin she has gotten, but it only had the opposite effect. She was drowning in it.

"Why didn't you tell me?"

Okay, so she was diving into something I was unaware of. She sounded pissed. But pissed was a good emotion since I haven't seen her feeling passionate about anything in over a year. I would happily take pissed.

"How about we go inside and you let me know what you are talking about?" I guided her up the stairs and into the house. We went to the kitchen, and I grabbed some waters for us.

"Now, what is it exactly that I didn't tell you?"

She was so angry, she seemed to be on the verge of tears.

"Why didn't you tell me you were working with Preston and Heather?" She spit the words out at me.

Everything made sense. I didn't tell her, but I'm assuming she found out from Mom or Dad. I wasn't sure how I should handle this one.

Tate and Preston started dating about a month after Heather and I did. We did everything together as couples. Hiking, bowling, couples' vacations, charity events, dinners, brunches, movie nights, and every other activity we could do together. The elite of Madison were calling for a double wedding. We were that close.

About a year and a half into the relationship, Tate withdrew from our adventures. She and Preston were living together by that point, so he would make excuses for her, saying she wasn't feeling well, or she had something going on at the bookstore. She wouldn't just drop by for a visit anymore and she wouldn't answer the door when I dropped by her place, even though I was pretty sure she was home. I worried about her, but when I confronted her about it, she just brushed me off and told me she was busier than usual.

She assured me things would slow down for her soon and we would all get back to normal.

The day I walked in on Heather and Preston in my bed, I went over to Tate's apartment. I was so angry that I pounded on the door until she opened it because she was so worried something bad had happened. That's when I saw them.

Tate was wearing sleep shorts and a tee-shirt and she was covered in bruises. As soon as she saw the look on my face, she realized I saw them, so she ran to the other room and grabbed her robe.

"What the fuck are those, Tate? Who fucking hurt you? Was it Preston? Did he do that to you?" When I saw the look of shame on her face, I lost it.

"I'm going to fucking kill him! He is a god damned dead man!"

"No, Devon, don't." She pleaded, "It was my fault."

No. No. No. No. No. Not my baby sister. This wasn't happening to my baby sister. I've heard about women thinking they were the reason their boyfriend or husband beat them, but I never thought it could happen to Tate. My sister was stronger than that. We were raised to know women had value and should never be disrespected, much less beaten. She would never stand for that. Oh my God. How could I not have seen this? How could I have let this happen? I knew something was wrong with her, but I didn't push it. That bastard, Preston, was going to pay for this.

I wrapped her up in my arms and rocked her back and forth, repeating, "This is not your fault," over and over. Tears were flowing between the both of us.

After a while, I told her what I saw when I got to my house and I held her as she cried again. I couldn't feel any sadness over Heather because there was no room left in me after the rage over Preston took hold.

She let everything out. She started with how he had

controlled her, which was the reason she couldn't come out with us anymore. He watched everything she ate and called her fat when she had anything other than a salad. She told me how he monitored every text she got and lost it when she would get a text from a man. How he told her she wasn't a good businesswoman so she shouldn't put together a business plan to be ready to buy the bookstore when the owner was ready to sell. How he would comment about everything she wore; it was either too sexy and she was clearly trying to cheat on him, or it was too plain and she was trying to turn him off by looking so ugly. What she told me made me furious, but she made me promise not to do anything to him, and I took my promises seriously.

I helped her pack up her things so she could come move in with me. When we finished loading the Land Rover, she took her key off her keyring and left it on the counter. We were walking to the SUV when Preston showed up. He bolted out of his car and yelled to her that whatever I said to her was a lie. I helped her into the passenger seat and shut the door. He was still yelling at me and begging her to listen to him when I got into the driver's seat without saying a word and drove away. That was one of the hardest things I had ever done. So much of me wanted to stay there and beat the shit out of him, but I made a promise to Tate.

As the days and weeks went by, we discovered that Heather and Preston had been sleeping together for almost a year. She had been cheating on me for almost half of our relationship. But the knowledge that she was doing it with the fuckwad who was abusing my sister the whole time made it so much worse.

Now I had to explain to Tate why I was working with the two traitors.

"I'm sorry, Tate. I wanted to tell you, but I didn't want to open old wounds. Honestly, I'm surprised Dad told you."

"He didn't. Preston told me." Her face went pale.

"When the hell did he talk to you?" My heart was beating faster.

"He showed up at Between the Covers about an hour ago. I was shelving some books, and he just appeared in the aisle. He told me the gang was back together and informed me he needed me back to round it out. He said we should go for dinner soon and discuss our reconciliation."

My fists clenched.

"He also said he thought you and Heather looked like you were getting back together, too. Tell me he's lying, Devon. Tell me you aren't going to take that crazy bitch back." A single tear made its way down her pale cheek.

"Of course I'm not taking her back. She's psycho. Yes, she's been trying to convince me we should get back together, but I'm not giving it any consideration. She's not picking up on how solid I am with my decision, but she isn't my problem anymore. And Preston should know better than to come to your bookstore to talk to you. I'll have a little conversation with him. You won't have to worry about it happening again."

Anger was raging inside me at the thought of him seeking her out. He shouldn't be anywhere near her. Just because I'm civil to him at the project meetings doesn't mean everything is okay between all of us. He must have sought her out after the meeting. What was he thinking?

"Hey, why don't you stay here? You can stay in the guest room tonight. I have to run out and take care of something, but I'll be back soon and I'll bring dinner. Sound good?"

She nodded, and I left, locking the front door behind me.

It was already almost 6 pm, but I knew my dad would still be in his office. Mom didn't react well to her first chemo treatment for the first couple days, but she gradually got better. So Dad decided that he would work longer hours the days before her treatments so he could be with her when she was sick. Her next treatment was scheduled for Friday, so I was sure I'd find him at the Capitol. I made it there in record time.

Janet was gone, so I stormed into his office unannounced.

"Do you know who visited Tate today?"

Stalking back and forth in front of his desk, I couldn't force myself to sit down. I didn't let him answer before I answered my question for him.

"Preston. Preston fucking Henry thought it would be an acceptable idea to show up at the bookstore and speak to her."

There was an immediate change in my dad's demeanor. He stood up and said, "He did what?"

I was still stalking around in his office, like a caged animal. Because it usually calmed me to hold a bat in my hands while I thought, I took my game winning baseball bat off the stand my dad kept it on and started swinging it gently, so not to break anything in the office. I spent so much of my youth and college days with a bat in my hand; it grounded me.

"Yes, he thought he should go see her, suggest they get back together, and tell her he thought Heather and I were getting back together." I wanted to scream.

"Let me call and cancel my six o'clock meeting and we will go have a chat with Preston."

He picked up the phone, and it appeared as though his call was going to voicemail. Since it was only two minutes to six, whomever he was meeting with was probably already on their way. He said we would wait so he could cancel in person and then we would go.

Trying to keep his composure, my dad said, "He stopped by here after the project meeting this afternoon and said he thought things were going well and thanked me for letting him join the committee. I thought it was a turning point in the right direction for him to do that."

I couldn't keep it in any longer. I'd had enough. Since the Capitol was practically empty at that time of night, I let out a guttural yell and swung the bat so hard that it accidentally connected with a ceramic planter on a stand, which shattered when I struck it. I took a breath in and looked up. The door to dad's office was open and Quinn was standing there, white as a sheet and trembling in fear. Fuck, she must have been who Dad was meeting with at six. She took off out of the Governor's Office Suite.

I followed after her as she ran out through the King Street entrance. I called her name, but she didn't slow down. My much longer legs helped me catch up with her when she reached the top of the stairs leading down to the street. She was terrified. Terrified of me.

I reached out my hand to put it on her arm to calm her, but she turned to run again. I watched as her first foot hit the top step at a weird angle, and then I watched her fall down the concrete stairs. There were so many stairs. The scream she made as she was falling was one I knew I would never forget. She stopped at the landing between the upper and lower stairs. She wasn't moving.

I yelled for help. I screamed for it as I ran to her. There was blood coming out of a wound on her forehead and her left arm had a large gash, too. My dad reached us moments after the fall and was also yelling for help as he dialed 911 on his cell.

Paramedics arrived quickly and after some arguing and a little encouragement from the governor, they let me ride with her to the hospital. I held her hand and pleaded with her to be okay.

Nurses took her from the ambulance and told me I would

have to go to the waiting room while they checked her out and ran some tests.

They took me to a private waiting room and my dad joined me not long after. I was sitting there with my head in my hands, replaying everything. I couldn't forget the look on her face when she saw me yell like I was out of my mind and break the planter. It was like she was looking at a monster. I knew I had a short temper, but I have never hit another human being, even though I wanted Preston to be my first. Violence wasn't in my nature. But her expression showed me she thought I was dangerous. How could this have happened?

I felt my dad's hand on my back as he sat down next to me. I didn't look up when I spoke.

"Did they tell you anything when you got here?" I prayed his answer was yes.

"Nothing much. They said it would be hours before they knew anything solid. They were able to stitch up her arm, but they're more concerned about the head injury. She'll need some scans and then they'll let us know."

"The way she looked at me, Dad. It was like she thought I was going to hurt her. I would never hurt her. Fuck, the way she ran from me. I need her to be okay so I can explain I'm not that guy."

"You don't know who she is, do you?" he asked me in his calm, fatherly voice.

"I know she's who you picked to run your project, and she's fucking amazing. I know there must be something difficult in her past keeping her guarded, but I don't know what it is."

He leaned back in his chair and ran his hands over his face, like he was trying to prepare himself for a long story.

"You were away at Notre Dame when it all happened. You probably didn't hear about it. It made national news, but as a sophomore, I'm guessing you didn't watch the news all that often. I think it was in the wintertime."

Frustrated he was taking so long to get to it, I demanded, "What happened?"

"She saw her father murder her mother. Then, the prosecutor talked her into testifying against him in court. She was only fifteen."

There was nothing. No sounds. No talking. For several minutes, we just sat in silence while I let his words sink in.

"Okay, I'm ready. Tell me the story."

9

QUINN

13 YEARS AGO

"Quinn, can you please tell us your story?" the prosecutor asked.

We practiced my testimony dozens of times. She wanted me to tell my entire story to the jury, and she was going to try not to interrupt me. She said the defense attorney wouldn't interrupt much, if at all, because it would make them look bad for badgering a teenage girl who just lost her mom. I didn't look at my father at all. With a courtroom full of people staring at me with pity, some with distrust because they didn't believe me, I told the judge and the jury my story.

"My father was physically, verbally, and emotionally abusive for as long as I could remember. My mom took the brunt of it. She did her best to protect me. When I was little and he would get out of control, she would tell me to get Pandy, my stuffed panda bear, and hide. I usually hid under my bed because it felt the safest there. Hiding didn't stop me from hearing everything from under there. I heard him calling her the worst names. The kind of names that would get you suspended at school if you were caught saying them. I could also hear him tossing her around the house.

"I was almost never in the house alone with him. I think my mom had her schedule worked out so I wouldn't have to be. But, one day, when I was 12, I got home from school and she wasn't home yet. I was going to go across the street to Aunt Betty's house. She wasn't really my aunt, but she let me call her that because my parents were both only children. My dad came home before I had the chance to leave. He wanted to know why Mom wasn't home yet and why the dishes weren't done. I told him I didn't know, so he smacked me across the face. I started crying, and it made him even madder. He took me by my throat and held me against the wall in the kitchen. He kept yelling at me, saying I was useless and he wished I was never born. He said I was the reason he and my mom would fight, and he said they would be a happy family if I wasn't around.

"As I got older, Mom got me into painting. Her therapist suggested I try it so I had some place to put my feelings. Dad didn't know she saw a therapist. Mom told me that some-times you need to ask for help when things get to be more than you can handle. That it wasn't a sign a weakness, but actually a sign of strength when you could admit you were in over your head. She also got me some headphones to listen to music and gave me these books of art and art museums from all around the world. She was very specific about when I was allowed to take them off. While she was getting beaten up by my dad, I was looking at amazing pieces of artwork and sculptures, or I was trying to paint, and I was listening to classical masterpieces."

I heard some people whispering, so I stopped for a moment to take a drink. Then I continued on as the prosecutor asked me to tell her about the night my dad murdered my mom.

"It was the Friday night before Valentine's Day. I was supposed to go to the Valentine's dance at school and then I was going to spend the night at my best friend Amy's house. We went to the dance, but someone spiked the punch and Amy got pretty sick, so I told her I would just go home. I was really looking forward to spending the night at her house because I slept better over there, but I knew I couldn't stay.

"I didn't want to call my mom and bother her if she had already gone to bed, so I walked home from Amy's house. She only lived a few blocks away.

"When I got into our neighborhood, I could hear yelling from our house when I was still four or five houses away. I saw Aunt Betty sitting on her porch swing. She waved me over, so I went.

"She told me Mom and Dad had been fighting for about an hour and it was louder than normal. She asked me why I wasn't at Amy's house and I explained about her being sick. Aunt Betty said I should spend the night with her, but I was worried about my mom, so I was going to go home. She told me she would wait up until the yelling calmed down and that I should come back to her house if they didn't settle down.

"There was a gigantic crash, and I heard my mom scream as soon as I got to the step, so I ran in. When I opened the door, I saw my mom on the floor next to the bookshelf that was knocked over. My dad was leaning over her with one of Mom's kitchen knives in his hand. He was stabbing her over and over.

"I don't think he heard me come in because he didn't turn to me until I screamed. Then he noticed me. He got up off the floor and came at me with the knife. I held my arm up to protect myself and he cut my arm with the knife. I fell over and he was on top of me, stabbing me in my belly. Aunt Betty came over as soon as she heard me scream. My dad ran when he saw her.

"My mom was lying on the ground covered in blood. The paramedics said she was dead before they even got there, so there was nothing they could do. They took me to the hospital, and the doctors fixed the three stab wounds I had in my belly and they put 42 stitches in my arm. I spent two weeks in the hospital recovering, so I didn't even get to go to my mom's funeral. I used to paint, but it's hard for my arm to hold up a paintbrush for any amount of time, and I don't have the coordination in my hand to paint anymore, anyway. But at least I'm alive. At least he didn't kill me, too."

I started crying. I know I was supposed to stop my testimony there, but I still had more to say.

Through the tears, I made the courtroom my confessional. "I could have saved her. I should have called her from Amy's house. I knew I wasn't supposed to change plans without telling my mom. When I heard the yelling, I should have gone straight into the house. If I didn't stop at Aunt Betty's house, if I wasn't such a chicken, I could have walked in before he killed her. I could have saved her. She would still be alive if I didn't make such stupid decisions."

Then, with so much pain in my heart, I looked over at my father for the first time. He was dressed in a suit, which was strange because I had never seen him in a suit before. He combed his hair to make himself look nice and presentable, which was also weird to see. But the hatred burning in his eyes as he looked at me. That was something I was used to seeing. I didn't understand why he hated me so much, but it didn't matter now. I knew this was going to be my last time to talk to him.

"You didn't have to kill her. You aren't a powerful man because you can control a woman and a little girl. It's just the opposite. You're a pathetic man because you felt you needed to try. If you weren't happy, you could have just left. We would have been fine without you. I hate you so much and I will never forgive you for this. I hope you spend the rest of your life in prison."

I heard the defense attorney repeatedly objecting while I spoke, but I didn't care anymore. They were not going to stop me from speaking my truth. I knew I would never see him again, and I needed him to know what taking her from me meant. I needed him to understand my pain. But I knew there wasn't anything inside his dark soul that would allow him to empathize with the agony I was living with. Telling him was what I needed to do for myself. Letting it all out was healing for me. For one brief moment in time, it stopped being all about him.

I didn't stay for the rest of the trial. I didn't want to watch my dad try to justify what he did. The attorney told me what happened when everything was done. My dad tried to plead temporary insanity. Luckily, the jury didn't buy it because of his history of abuse. They found him guilty of my mom's murder and guilty of his attempted murder of me. The prosecutor said she didn't think he would ever walk out of jail a free man. That's when I became an orphan.

After the trial, I thought I was through the worst of it. But I was wrong.

10

DEVON

My hands trembled as my dad finished telling me the story as he knew it. I knew there was something in her past that affected her, but I never would have guessed it would be something so traumatic. How does a person even carry on after something like that? She has to be so strong.

Then it clicked in my head. When she heard me scream and saw me swing the bat, she must have thought I was going to attack her. I would never hurt her. She needed to be okay, so I could tell her she was safe with me. She wouldn't ever have to worry about me lifting a finger to hurt her. Please, God, let her be okay.

We had been sitting in the waiting room for a little over an hour when a crazed-looking woman with jet black hair flowing behind her and a look of panic in her eyes came into the room. She ignored my dad, which is not normal behavior for people, since he is the governor, and came straight up to me.

"You're Devon, right?" she asked in an urgent tone.

"Yes," I said, then she slapped me hard across the face.

"You bastard," she shouted at me and swung her arm to slap me again. This time, I caught her by the wrist so I could ask the crazy lady what her issue was before I let her go.

"The police told me you were chasing Quinn, and she fell down the steps trying to get away from you. She made you sound like such a good guy. What the fuck is wrong with you?"

Still holding her wrist to stop the spitfire from slapping me again, I asked, "Are you, by chance, Olivia?"

"Yes, I'm fucking Olivia and you're a dead man for hurting Quinn."

I released my grip and her arm stayed cocked. She had every right to slap me again. I deserved it.

"I'm sorry, Olivia. This isn't how I wanted to meet. And I am to blame for her accident, but I promise you that it wasn't intentional."

She put her hands on her hips waiting for an explanation.

"I just got some shitty news from my sister and I went to my dad's office to fill him in. I picked up my old baseball bat that he keeps hanging on his wall so I had something to do with my hands. I yelled and swung it out of aggression. I wasn't going to hit anyone with it, but that's when she walked by. Her face. Fuck, the expression on her face when she looked at me. I can't even put it into words. Then she ran."

I couldn't tell if she believed me.

"I didn't know her history. We haven't gotten that far yet."

Gesturing to my dad next to me I added, "Dad just filled me in."

Olivia was so laser focused on me when she walked in, it was like she didn't even realize my dad was there.

"Oh no. Oh, my goodness. Shit. I'm so sorry Mr. Governor, Sir. I'm so sorry. I don't usually act like this. I'm just so scared for Quinny. I'm so sorry."

My dad was great at handling difficult situations with grace and respect. He walked up to her and wrapped her in a big hug that she clearly needed.

"You don't need to apologize for anything. Quinn is a lucky woman to have a fierce friend like you by her side."

She then proceeded to cry on his shoulder for a solid ten minutes.

Over the next hour, three more of Quinn's friends showed up. Jace, the man I saw at Quinn's door the day after I met her, arrived and went straight to Olivia to comfort her. His look of sincere concern put a knot in my stomach, wondering who he was to her. Their friend Sydney showed up next. The last to show up was Jillian. She walked into the room wearing scrubs, and the other three immediately started asking her questions. Putting two and two together, I figured out Jillian worked at the hospital in some capacity.

Jillian held up her hands and told everyone to sit down. She introduced herself to Dad and me and then explained that she was a pediatrics doctor at the hospital and her colleagues briefed her on Quinn's condition.

According to the doctors working on her, Quinn was being treated for a concussion and the cut on her arm. She also had several bruises forming all over her body from the fall. The wound on her head wasn't as bad as it looked and they were able to stitch it up, but the concussion was concerning. She needed to take it easy for the rest of the week. They were going to keep her there overnight, but she shouldn't be left alone for the first couple of days.

Jillian turned to Olivia. "I know you're supposed to leave tomorrow for your brother's wedding, but is there any way you could leave a day or two later? You could still be there by Friday in time for the rehearsal."

"Let me make some calls. I know Tracy will shit kittens when she finds out I won't be there for her bachelorette party on Wednesday or her spa day on Thursday, but she's going to be family, so she'll have to forgive me, right?"

Jace stepped in. "Liv, you don't have to do that. I can close down the immunization program for a few days and Quinn can stay with me."

For some reason, his plan didn't sit well with me.

"I caused this. Let me help fix it," I interrupted, not knowing for sure where I was going with this. They all turned to look at me. "Olivia, you don't have to miss your brother's wedding, and Jace, you don't have to stop immunizing people, if I heard you correctly. I have a huge guest suite in my home and she can stay with me. I can work from home. I need a chance to make this right. If she agrees, would you please let me do this?"

They walked to the other side of the waiting room to have a lengthy, whispered conversation. When they walked back, they looked concerned. I was positive they were going to reject the idea, but I knew I would fight them if that was the case. I needed to fix this.

Olivia stepped forward as their spokesperson. "If she agrees to it, we will too, on one condition. You need to let Jace, Sydney, and Jillian stop by whenever they want to check on her. And if Quinn isn't okay with this, we're going to support her decision."

"Deal."

The next few hours were a blur of doctors and nurses stopping in frequently to give updates. I was fairly sure if we weren't sitting with the governor in the room with us, we wouldn't have gotten that level of attention.

Quinn's four friends were definitely close. They sat together and talked non-stop. From what I could overhear, they had Quinn's next two months planned out for her. I wondered how Quinn would feel about their mother-hen planning. I was definitely worried about her, but I also acknowledged she was a grown woman and should have some say in her life. Maybe it would be a good thing if she stayed with me. They seem to think of her as a wounded bird.

The nurse came out and told us Quinn was awake, but we could only go in one at a time and only for a few minutes each. Olivia went first. She was in there for about ten minutes before the nurse kicked her out. Jace went in next, and the knot in my stomach came back with a vengeance.

Olivia came over and sat next to me.

"Quinn wanted me to let you know that she's embarrassed by her reaction and she doesn't want to put you out since this was all her fault. Those were Quinn's words, not mine. She insisted I make sure to tell you that she blames herself, not you. I convinced her that everyone understood her reaction and talked her into staying with you. Although I'm certain the only reason she agreed to it was because she didn't want anyone else to have to change their plans or cancel anything on her behalf. She's unselfish like that."

When Jace came out, the nurse said Quinn could only have one more visitor tonight. Sydney and Jillian both wanted to go in, but Olivia stopped them.

"Devon should have a chance to go in and clear everything up with her tonight so it doesn't hang over everyone until tomorrow."

I was starting to like the crazy woman who slapped me when we first met.

I walked into her darkened room and took in the sounds of the monitors attached to her. She looked so tired, but still so beautiful. When she saw me, tears flowed down her cheeks. Quickly walking over to her, I took her good hand in mine and sat on the side of her bed so she didn't have to strain her neck to look up at me.

"I'm so sorry," we both said it at the same time, but as soon as we did, she looked away from me.

Taking the lead, I corrected her. "No, Quinn, you have nothing to apologize for. I shouldn't have lost my temper and behaved the way I did, whether you were around or not. I'm sorry for scaring you."

"But I shouldn't have reacted the way I did. Now all of this is going to mess up so many things. Olivia told me how you offered to take care of me, but I know she's still going to worry while she's supposed to be off having a great time at her brother's wedding. Getting her to go to the wedding is the only reason I agreed to this plan. I thought she might worry less if she believes someone is taking care of me." She looked down at my hand holding hers, refusing to look me in the eye. I was pretty sure she was lying to Olivia about agreeing to stay at my place.

"Well, she doesn't have to worry about anything at all, because I will take care of you."

She continued to look down while she spoke softly, "I don't want you to. You shouldn't have to work from home and take care of someone you barely know just because I'm emotionally dysfunctional. My situation isn't fair to you. If you wouldn't mind picking me up tomorrow, so Jillian sees me leave with you, then drop me off at my apartment, I would really appreciate it. I will be fine on my own. It's just a little bump on the head, and I know I can survive perfectly well with the stitches in my arm."

Yes, she's already survived perfectly well with an injured arm thirteen years ago. She wasn't going to do this alone. I knew any of those people in the hallway would drop everything to be the one to take care of her, but she saw herself as a burden. I would love five minutes alone with her dad to let him know exactly what I thought of his parenting skills.

"Quinn, I'm going to pick you up tomorrow, but I'm not

going to bring you to your apartment. You're coming home with me so I can make this right. You think this is your fault, but I know it's mine. If you don't let me do this for you, I'm never going to be able to forgive myself," I teased, not beneath using a guilt trip to help my cause.

"Please, let me do this for you. If it makes you feel better, I will go out of my way to be the worst host possible, so you won't think I'm putting myself out for you."

She laughed at my self-deprecation and looked up at me with tears still swelling in her stormy grey eyes. God, she was stunning, even all battered and bruised.

The nurse came in and said it was time for me to leave. I discussed the general discharge time for Quinn with her and made plans to be back to pick Quinn up tomorrow after-noon, assuming the doctor cleared her for release. Her friends and I all exchanged numbers so we could keep in contact over the next few days. Then I thought it was best to head home and get the guest room set up for her. Shit, the guest room. I totally forgot about Tate after Quinn's fall. I was at least four hours later than I was planning on being.

All the lights were on at home. Shit, with everything that happened, I forgot to check my phone or to reach out and let Tate know what was going on.

When I walked in, I saw Tate, asleep on the sofa in the living room. The streaks down her cheeks made me think she'd been crying for a while before she fell asleep. I pulled the blanket on the back of the sofa over her so she would be warm enough, but the movement woke her. She sat straight up and hugged me.

"Devon, please tell me you didn't do something stupid. I was so worried about you."

"Tate, I'm so sorry. I should have called you. I went to Dad's office and Quinn, the woman running the project, had an accident and had to be taken to the emergency room. I was so caught up in all the chaos that I forgot to call you. Are you okay?"

"Yes, I was worried when you didn't come home. I thought you might have gone to Preston and done something crazy. I'm just glad you're safe. How is Quinn? Is she going to be well enough to continue on with the project?"

"Quinn is an entire story that I've been meaning to tell you."

I sat down next to her on the sofa and settled in to tell Tate everything. We didn't keep secrets from each other anymore, so I figured it was time to talk.

I started from the beginning, with the run-in we had in the hallway. Then I told her about the way she was in meetings when she talked about the arts. I also gently told her about Quinn and Preston. Tate got pretty worked up when I told her about them, insisting I tell Quinn the truth about him or she would. No woman should have to go through what she did. I promised her I would.

Then I got into the accident earlier tonight and explained that Quinn was going to stay with me for a while in the guest room. For the first time in months, I saw a smile on Tate's face. It was wonderful.

"Why the grin, sis?"

"You like her, don't you?" Her grin got even bigger.

Trying to downplay things, I said, "She has a lot of desirable qualities as a person."

Tate launched herself across the sofa and landed on her knees next to me. She reminded me of an excited puppy waiting for a treat.

"No, that's not what I asked. I asked you if you liked her."

I didn't want to drag down her excitement, so I admitted, "Yes, I do like her. I'm completely fascinated by her and I want to get to know more about her. I'm hoping this whole fall down the stairs fiasco doesn't ruin our chances to do that."

"If she agreed to stay here, I think you have a chance. Now, let's go fix up the guest room, since it sounds like she's going to be spending a lot of time in there and it's the most boring room in the house."

Tate had a project now, and it was amazing to see how excited she got. If this was going to turn things around for her, I would give her a million dollars and let her redo the entire house. Anything to keep that smile on her face.

The next morning, she dragged me from store to store picking out new bedding, a TV and a dresser for it to sit on, a chaise lounge chair, and a ton of girly stuff for the en-suite bathroom. By the time we finished shopping, I was offended by the realization that my guest room was apparently so lacking. Nobody had complained before.

I spent a few hours at the office getting things in order. Swift Corp had great workers and my management team was second to none, so I knew the place would run smoothly in my absence. I took a few things with me I knew I could work on from home and dropped all my stuff off at the house.

Tate spent all afternoon putting things together for me. When it was time to go pick up Quinn, my spare bedroom was completely transformed and Tate was ecstatic. It was so good to see her smiling.

I promised her I would keep her posted on everything that happened and told her she could come visit, but not on the first day. Quinn deserved some time to settle in before being introduced to more of my family.

In my head, I knew I was picking up an injured woman from the hospital, but it felt like I was picking up a beautiful woman for a first date. I had to stop thinking like that. I needed to focus on her getting bedrest, not me getting into her bed.

The charge nurse spent about twenty minutes giving me all the care instructions. I didn't want to mess anything up. I knew when every medication was supposed to be taken, how often to check for fever or infection, how to change the bandage on her forehead, how to deal with the stitches itching, what signs were worrisome and required a call to the doctor, and a general guideline of when she should be able to get back to each activity. She also gave me a stern look when she reminded me Quinn didn't need to deal with anything that would stimulate her, raise her blood pressure, or cause her to get excited. When I had a blank look on my face, she clarified. Sex. Quinn should not be having sex any time soon. Well, that bucket of cold water being dumped on me should make it easier to avoid making any moves. At least, that's what I thought.

With a full semester's course worth of knowledge on concussion recovery crammed into a twenty-minute class, I went to Quinn's room, where I heard her voice. I made sure she got a private room, so I couldn't guess who she was talking to when I heard voices as I neared the room. Then it clicked; I knew that voice.

If I was the one with a concussion, I would have ended up back in the emergency room because my blood pressure was through the roof. But I didn't want to scare Quinn again, so I calmed myself down before I entered her room.

Opening the door slowly, I saw Preston sitting on the side of Quinn's bed holding flowers and a stuffed teddy bear with Get Well Soon written across its tummy. Quinn was sitting upright and was smiling at him. I wanted to throw up. They both turned when they heard me enter the room.

"Preston, what are you doing here?"

"I heard from an acquaintance at the Capitol that Quinn took a fall yesterday because you were chasing after her. It's all that anyone is talking about. I wanted to check in with her and see for myself that she's okay."

I hated him. I hated him with every fiber in my being.

"Well, you can see she's going to be fine, so you can leave now. I'm here to pick her up and bring her home with me because she's being released."

The shocked look on his face was priceless.

"She's going home with you? Why would she do that when you're the one who caused her fall?"

I saw Quinn was growing uncomfortable with the conversation, so I suggested we step outside while she got dressed. He followed me as I led him far enough down the hallway Quinn wouldn't be able to hear our conversation.

As soon as we were out of earshot of the room, I turned to him and growled, "You stay away from Quinn and you stay away from Tate. Neither of them need anything from you."

"Awww," he taunted. "Did little Tate come running to her only brother when the big bad wolf came around her door? And, as for Quinn, she thinks I'm great, so she doesn't want me to stay away. I think I'll have that little pixie in my bed as soon as she's healed from these injuries. Shouldn't be too long, maybe a week."

It took everything in me not to punch him in his smug face. It didn't surprise me he knew how long it took to recover from injuries, since he was usually the one causing them. He got away with so much because his dad was the owner of Henry Paper. But I wouldn't let this continue.

"Quinn is going to know the truth about you soon, then you won't have a snowball's chance in hell."

"Like she's going to believe anything you say. She's afraid of you. So afraid of you, she ran to get away from you. I'm sure you had to do some quick talking to get her to come home with you, but that doesn't change the fact that she's afraid of you."

I worried he was right about her being afraid, but I was going to do everything I could to change her opinion of me.

"She doesn't have to believe me. Tate already has a plan to talk to her. Women believe other women, jackass."

That shut him up. He turned several shades of red as he considered what I said. "You wouldn't let Tate talk to her." He spit as he spoke.

"Oh, you are wrong. Now go away, Preston. And stay away from Tate. After all the pain you caused her, she deserves your distance."

He stomped away, mumbling under his breath about how this wasn't over.

I took a few breaths to get my anger under control and walked back to Quinn. She told me to come in when I knocked on the door, so I opened it.

Olivia brought her some clothes to leave the hospital in and packed her a bag for my house. Dressed in black yoga pants and a well-worn, oversized University of Wisconsin sweatshirt, she looked so tiny and fragile. I wanted to wrap her up and protect her from the world.

She held up her bag and said, "I think we're ready."

I called for the nurse, who insisted on wheeling Quinn out to my car in a wheelchair.

I helped her into the passenger seat, put her bag in the back, and hopped in next to her for the drive.

"So, where to? How about an amusement park?" I smiled at her.

"Oh, this is going to be a fun couple of days, huh?"

"Week. This is going to be a fun week, at least." She gave me a confused look. "The nurse said concussion symptoms are tricky, and it would be best to monitor you for at least a week."

"I can't take a week off of work. I have so much to do. We only have three months to get this first showcase pulled together, not to mention plan out February's exhibit. I can maybe take today and tomorrow off, but that's it."

"Well, my dad, your boss, has ordered me to keep you out of the Capitol for the rest of the week. With pay, so don't let that be a worry while you recover."

She stared out the window as we drove in silence to my house. When we arrived, she tried to get out on her own, so I had to run around to her door to help her out. I could tell I didn't have an amenable patient on my hands. This was going to be an interesting week.

11

QUINN

*D*evon led me into his home which I could only describe as picturesque. It overlooked the shores of Lake Mendota and could fit my apartment in it multiple times over. I was exhausted just from the short drive, so he said he would bring my bag up to my room and let me rest before dinner.

If I would have imagined the perfect guest room, even my imagination wouldn't have made one this nice. The king-size bed in the middle of the room, with fluffy pillows and an equally fluffy white down comforter, looked like a cloud. Getting to sleep in that bed might make getting a concussion and some bruises worth it.

It felt like everything in the room was hand-picked for me, right down to the books on the table next to the chaise. He showed me to the bathroom and all my favorite scents were there. Rosemary mint shampoo and conditioner, strawberry body wash; even a vanilla scented candle next to the sunken jetted tub. I might never leave. But I knew I couldn't overstay my welcome, so I promised myself I wouldn't get too comfortable.

He started unpacking my things for me and putting them into the closet and the dresser. When I told him he didn't need to help, he handed me some pajamas Olivia packed for me and suggested I change and take a nap. I didn't have the energy to argue with him. By the time I finished changing in the bathroom, he had unpacked all my things and had the bed turned down for me.

"Do you want me to wake you for dinner, or do you want to rest until morning?" he asked me as I slid into the most luxurious bed ever.

"I think dinner sounds nice. I'll set an alarm if you tell me what time you would like to eat."

"That's probably not the best idea. The nurse told me to help you avoid loud noises for a few days. I know we don't know each other well yet, and I promise I will be respectful of your privacy as much as humanly possible, but I think it might be best if I come in and wake you up. Are you okay with that?"

He was the sweetest person I've ever met. I freaked out on him, injured myself, then let him take me in to care for me while I recover, and he's worried about my comfort level around him? Something had to be wrong with this man.

"Yes. I'm okay with that, Devon." I saw him sigh in relief.

"Good. Now why don't you sleep for a couple hours and we'll have dinner? I know some of your medicines can upset your stomach, so how about some soup and a salad for dinner tonight to see how eating feels?"

I nodded. This man was going to get me soup and a salad for dinner. I couldn't even comprehend him.

"What's your favorite soup, Quinn?"

"Ummm, tomato?"

"Okay, and garden or Caesar salad?"

Was he seriously putting this much effort into deciding what to get for dinner tonight? He was so considerate.

"Garden would be great."

He brought the covers up over me and wished me sweet dreams. Then he went to the windows and closed the drapes before he left.

I couldn't remember a time where I was a trusting person. There were only a handful of people I would say I truly trusted. But I felt like Devon could someday be on that list. There was so much sincerity in his voice when he spoke to me. It wasn't like when Preston talked to me earlier in the hospital room. He spent half the time talking about himself and the other half telling me what things I should do to recover quicker. It was an uncomfortable conversation. I laughed at his inappropriate jokes, but only because I knew I had to continue working with him on the committee. There was something safe about Devon that made me feel like I didn't need to pretend with him.

I pondered their differences for a little while, but then blissful sleep overcame me.

Unsure how long I slept, I woke to Devon's husky voice drawing me out of my sleep.

"Quinn," he whispered as he gently nudged my shoulder, "it's time to wake up."

I groaned as I tried to sit up. Every part of my body seemed to hurt. Falling down a flight of granite stairs will do that to you.

Devon reached over me, took two of the pillows I wasn't using, and propped them behind me to help stabilize me. He had a concerned look on his face.

"Are you in a lot of pain? Do you need some painkillers?"

"No. I'm okay. I think I'm just a little stiff after sleeping. I think getting up and walking around a little should help fix the problem."

He helped me out of bed and held me while I got my footing. There was a warmth from his body that calmed my anxieties. He must have taken a shower while I was sleeping because he smelled like a cedar body wash mixed with his natural scent, which was intoxicating. I wanted to stay in his arms like this for the rest of the night, but forced cuddling would definitely fall into the Overstaying My Welcome category.

We walked through his elegant dining room on the way to the kitchen. He said he didn't use it often because he preferred the relaxed feeling of the kitchen. The smell of soup was so comforting. There was a pot on the stove with a large salad bowl on the counter next to it, and I was confused.

"Do you have a cook?"

"No.

"Did you order in and put the soup in a pot to warm it back up because I slept too long?"

"No. Why do you ask?"

"Devon, did you make homemade tomato soup for me?"

"Yes, I did."

I was constantly being surprised by this man. Nobody, including my mom because she was a terrible cook, had ever made me homemade soup. And, not just soup, but soup that filled the entire room with an amazing aroma. Maybe it was the medicine, but I felt like my heart was going to explode.

He motioned for me to sit on a stool at the kitchen island. I sat down while he pulled out four bowls, ladled soup into two of them, then put salad in the other two. He brought everything over to the island and offered me something to drink to go with it.

I know I was sitting there with the dumbest look on my face, but I still couldn't get over how this act of kindness affected me. The warm feeling this one simple meal brought over me. A single tear escaped down my cheek.

Devon noticed and hurried to my side. "Are you okay? Are you in pain? What can I do?"

"Sorry. I'm fine."

I hated to admit it to him, but I couldn't let him think something he did was wrong.

"It's just that I've never had someone treat me like this. This is a strange feeling."

He took my face in his hands and turned me to him.

"Quinn, I know we are just getting to know each other, but I know in my heart, right now, you deserve millions of moments like this. You deserve to be cared for and respected and treated like the outstanding woman you are."

I choked back more tears. I thought, maybe hoped, he would lean a little bit closer and kiss me. But he didn't. We kept our connection for what felt like forever. Then, when he started to lean in, he stopped himself, dropped his hands from my face, and backed away. There was only coldness remaining where the heat from his hands were and I chastised myself for hoping for something I knew he didn't want.

I didn't want to push it, but I had to know. "Did I do something wrong?" It came out as a whisper as I looked down, afraid that if I looked at him, I would see his face as he tried to ease the blow I knew was coming. He wasn't interested in me that way.

He stepped back to me and lifted my chin. I tried to keep the tears from falling, but I failed. The last two days took a lot out of me and I struggled to control my emotions.

He used his thumb to wipe a fallen tear from my cheek. His presence affected me so intensely that I struggled to breathe. He leaned in close to me, put his forehead to mine, and spoke like he was in a confessional.

"Quinn, I don't know what it is about you, but I have wanted you from the moment you ran into me in the hallway. The more I get to know you, the more I want you. Every new thing I learn about you is even more fascinating than the last. When I came into your room to wake you up, and I saw you, like an angel resting in your enormous bed, it took all my willpower not to climb in there with you and pull you close to me. But we're not there yet. I hope we get there someday, though. And I wanted nothing more than to kiss you just now, but you're injured, and I won't take advantage of you. I don't want you to look back on this moment and think I was only focused on myself and my own needs. I want you to look back and know I respected you."

His words moved me. Everything felt surreal.

With more courage than I have ever had before, I looked him straight in the eye and asked, "But what if I wanted you to kiss me?"

He stared at my lips for the longest time, which made me nervous, so I bit the side of my bottom lip out of habit. He groaned.

"Are you sure that's not the medicine talking?"

I could hear the hope in his voice, and it gave me confidence.

"Positive."

I felt his hands as they started on each side of my neck, then he slid them up to caress my cheeks as he angled my face to him. He leaned in and stopped when our lips were a mere moment apart. I could feel the heat of his breath. I willed him to bridge the distance and kiss me, and finally, he did.

His lips were soft, but strong. The kiss was gentle, lips touching lips, but then it became more insistent. My lips parted in what felt like a natural reaction even though this wasn't natural to me at all, and he took that as an invitation. His tongue explored and I couldn't get enough of his taste. He groaned into my mouth when I met his tongue with mine and my heart might have stopped beating.

Sliding my hands up his muscular sides, I stood up to get closer to him and my world spun. I swayed in Devon's arms, and he broke the kiss.

"Are you okay?" he asked as he guided me back to the stool. The look of concern on his face killed me. The moment was beautiful and perfect, and I had to ruin it.

"I'm sorry. I got a little lightheaded, that's all."

While most men would have taken that as a compliment to their manliness, Devon's expression changed. He seemed upset with himself, which was devastating to me.

"Please stop looking like that, Devon. You didn't do anything I didn't ask you to do, and I liked it. A lot."

"I did too. A lot."

We both laughed and he leaned in and gave me a quick kiss on the lips.

"The soup is getting cold and I can't have you going hungry. I'm pretty sure your gang, I mean friends, would take me out if I didn't take the best possible care of you."

I laughed at the thought of my friends that way. They were a bit intense sometimes. I could only imagine how they were at the hospital with him.

The soup was outstanding. It turned out his mother insisted on teaching both of her children how to cook so they wouldn't live on frozen pizzas and ramen noodles when they moved out.

After dinner, he suggested we watch a movie. Nothing with any action or loud noises, because he was determined to be a mother hen following every rule the nurse gave him. So, we picked the original Sabrina with Hepburn and Bogart. We sat in silence as we watched together. It was a good thing I'd seen the movie several times in the past because I wasn't focusing on it at all. I sat there enjoying the feel of him next to me on the sofa.

About a half an hour into the movie, he reached over to

hold my hand. I wanted to soak in how wonderful all of this felt, but my pain medicine was working against me. Shortly after, I was fast asleep.

I woke up floating in Devon's arms and I thought it was a dream. It turned out he was actually carrying me up the stairs to bed. When we got there, he set me down gently, then covered me up and lightly kissed my forehead.

"I hate to leave you, but I'm right on the other side of this wall if you need anything. Anything at all," he said. And then he walked out.

My body was tired, but my mind was wide awake from being in his arms. I wished he hadn't left. So much had happened over the last three hours and I didn't know how to process it all. But I knew who would.

> Me: Are you up?

Olivia: Yes...how are you feeling?

> Me: Amazing!

Olivia: Why do you feel amazing when you only got out of the hospital a few hours ago? Holy shit, Quinny, did something happen?

> Me: Yup

Olivia: Tell me EVERYTHING!

> Me: He kissed me!

Olivia: And?

> Me: And...then we watched a movie.

Olivia: How was the kiss?

> Me: I've never experienced anything like it! I felt it down to my toes!

Olivia: Damn… that sounds like a good kiss!

> Me: It was…but now I don't know what to do.

Olivia: Go get another one. That's how this works.

I was twenty-seven years old, and I didn't know "how this worked." How embarrassing was that? Until recently, I thought there was something wrong with me. I assumed, because of all of my issues, I wouldn't have a relationship ever, so I didn't have to worry about learning how to date. Devon might have changed my opinion on the topic. But I didn't want to get ahead of myself.

> Me: What if he rejects me?

Olivia: You should have seen him at the hospital. He practically demanded he be the one to take care of you. I don't think he'll reject you.

> Me: What if he wants to go fast and then I have to tell him I'm practically a virgin? I might die of embarrassment.

Olivia: I doubt he's going to go that fast. And when it does happen, if he's the good guy I think he might be, he will be understanding.

> Me: I'm scared of all of this. His kiss made me feel so many things.

Olivia: Don't worry. It's about time you felt something.

> Me: Thanks Livy!

Olivia: Love you, Quinny.

Me: Love you too.

After an hour of trying unsuccessfully to fall asleep, I gave in and turned on the TV to watch the news. About twenty minutes later, I heard a soft knock on the door. I got up and opened it to find Devon standing there in nothing but blue plaid lounge pants that hung low on his hips. His abs were so yummy I wanted to lick them.

Whoa, where did that come from? I've never wanted to lick someone before.

"I'm sorry, was the TV too loud? Did I wake you?"

His eyes skimmed from my bare feet and up my legs that were on display because I changed into my pajama shorts. They went up to my tank top and lingered at my breasts for a moment before they went up and met my eyes. I could see the muscles in his jaw flex. I mentally added those to the list of body parts I wanted to lick.

"No, I was still awake. I was just going to get some water and saw your light was still on, so I thought I would check on you to see if you needed anything."

"Nope, I'm good. I couldn't sleep. Strange house, unfamiliar environment, lots of medicine."

"Is there anything I can do to help?"

"No. But I appreciate you offering."

Unless he wanted to put a baseball bat under my bed like I had at home, there really wasn't anything he could do. But that request would make me sound like a lunatic.

"I'll be fine. I'm so tired, I'm sure I'll fall asleep soon. Have a good night, Devon."

I sent him on his way, laid down, and did all the tricks my therapist taught me to help me fall asleep and finally succeeded.

The dreams always felt so real. It was like I was watching my mother's murder over and over. I tried to get away when my father saw me, but I was never fast enough. He caught me every time.

"No. No. Please stop. I don't want to die." I woke up shouting. But I wasn't alone.

Devon was holding me tight, even though I was covered in sweat.

"It's okay. You're okay. It was only a dream. I've got you."

I clung to his bare upper body, grateful for its warmth, and nuzzled my face into his shoulder. He held me tighter. We sat that way for a long time while he whispered calming words to me. After my breathing slowed to normal, I pulled myself away from him.

"I have nightmares sometimes." Wow, marvelous job stating the obvious there. I mentally kicked myself. I didn't want to explain my story to him. I didn't have the energy to do that tonight.

"Anyone that's gone through what you've gone through would have nightmares sometimes, too," he said in a reassuring tone.

Someone already told him. I was now *that* Quinn Hill to him. Never to be a normal woman to him again. I hung my head in shame.

"My dad told me at the hospital. He thought it was probably why you reacted the way you did. But that doesn't justify how I behaved."

We sat in silence. I didn't know where to go from here. He took the first step.

"Do you worry about someone hurting you while you sleep?"

Feeling like a scared little child to admit it, I said, "Yes. I sleep with a bat under my bed and that helps a bit."

"Would you sleep better if I was in here with you, so you weren't alone?"

Olivia would stay with me when the nightmares were

bad, and it helped. I never had a second one when she was with me. I was so exhausted that I desperately wanted to take him up on his offer. But this was stepping into foreign territory for me.

"Would you mind?"

"I wouldn't have offered if I minded."

I believed he wasn't the kind of man to say something he didn't mean, so I nodded.

With that, he walked around to the other side of the bed and got under the covers. The bed was so big that we would each have our own sides and wouldn't bump into each other, but he had other thoughts. He moved to the center of the bed and lifted the covers for me to move next to him. I slid over as he laid on his back and pulled me to his side. I put my head on his chest and laid my hand on his abs. They were even tighter than they looked when he was standing in the doorway earlier.

"I'll keep you safe tonight," he said, as he wrapped his arm around my waist and I quickly fell asleep.

It was the best night of sleep I'd had in years.

I woke the next morning with him looking down at me. I drooled a little on his chest and thought I was going to die of embarrassment. When he saw the recognition in my eyes turn to a look of horror, he laughed and sat us up. He dabbed the drool off his chest with the sheet and grinned at me.

"I'm so happy that you feel comfortable enough to drool on me."

I felt my cheeks redden.

"I'll go make us some breakfast," he said as he kissed my cheek before getting out of bed. I watched him walk out of my room and he looked as delicious from the back as he did from the front. My cheeks reddened even more, but not from embarrassment that time.

This was going to be a long week.

12

DEVON

I was cooking pancakes when Quinn came down. She still looked a little embarrassed, but I hoped we could get past that quickly.

Last night was wonderful, minus the nightmare, of course. But holding her in my arms and feeling her relax as she let sleep take over was the best feeling in the world. I know it was unfortunate circumstances that threw us into high gear when it came to getting to know each other better. In a normal dating situation, I would have tried to take things slow and let things happen naturally, but I wasn't going to regret how we skipped about ten steps ahead in the dating process.

The bruises all over her body were looking particularly painful, which was a reminder to me I needed to keep myself in check with her. She was still healing.

The doorbell rang, and I asked Quinn if she could watch the pancakes while I went to answer it. I wasn't expecting anyone today, but it wouldn't surprise me if one of Quinn's friends stopped by to check on her. They all seemed to care about her deeply.

When I opened the door, it wasn't her friends, but rather the flower delivery guy. I signed for the flowers and brought them to Quinn, since her name was on the box.

"Looks like someone sent you flowers." She beamed as I handed them to her. How many men have sent flowers to her in the past? I was going to lose my shit if these came from Preston.

Opening the box, Quinn's expression changed from excitement to horror as she slammed the lid back on the box and pushed them away from her.

"What's wrong?" My concern was growing as I saw tears in her eyes.

I reached over to the box and opened it myself.

"What the fuck!"

Inside the box was, what appeared to be, two dozen dead roses with a card on top that read WHORE.

I ran back out the front door to see if I could catch the delivery man to find out who sent him, but he was gone. The delivery truck had a name on it, but I couldn't remember what it was.

Quinn was still in shock when I got back to the kitchen, so I wrapped her up in my arms. I couldn't hold her tight enough to make this all go away, but I tried. All the heat had gone from her and she was trying to hide her tears. I stepped back, and we took seats at the kitchen island.

"Who would have sent those to me?" she asked between sobs.

My first thought went to the person I assumed sent them before we found out what was in the box: Preston. He was a sore loser, and I was fairly confident he viewed Quinn coming to stay with me as a loss, but I don't know why he would take his frustration out on Quinn. I also didn't understand why he took things out on Tate either, so I didn't think I had a good grasp on what Preston was or wasn't capable of.

If Preston knew about what was going on, I was sure Heather knew, too. For as long as I've known her, she's been a deeply vindictive woman. I guess that said something about my judgement in character. But I wasn't going to waste time analyzing Heather's shortcomings while Quinn was struggling.

Then I came to realize I knew little about Quinn's personal history other than what my dad told me. Maybe someone else in her life sent these.

"This feels like an intimate attack. Do you have any jaded ex boyfriends who might not be happy you're spending your recovery with me?"

She laughed so loudly. "I'm not exactly a hot commodity, Devon." Implying I was crazy for even asking such a silly question.

Wow, did she not see herself as others saw her? She was so intelligent, creative, compassionate, and beautiful. How did she not see how wonderful she was?

"I beg to differ with you on that one. I think you are so much more than you think you are." She looked at me blankly, but I needed to know more, so we knew where to start. "How long has it been since your last serious relationship? Did you end it or did he? Did it end amicably?"

She looked down at her hands, which I've learned is how she avoids things that make her uncomfortable. Was her last relationship so bad she didn't want to talk about it? Were there so many of them she was embarrassed about them?

"It's okay, Quinn. There's no judgement here. I promise you. I just want to help narrow down who could have done this."

She sat for a long time, still staring down at her hands. I felt like she wanted to tell me something but had to build up the courage to do so. She was trying to decide if she could trust me with her truth. I began to worry about what bombshell she was going to drop on me when she hit me with one I didn't see coming.

"Devon, I don't have a last serious relationship. I was kind of a freak because of my parents, so nobody wanted to come near me. There was this one guy in college but that only last about a few weeks and then he was done with me." She blurted it all out so quickly the words kind of blurred together.

No previous relationships? Only one guy for a few weeks? Guys didn't want to be around her? None of it made sense. Then it hit me. I didn't think she was the kind of woman to sleep around, but I certainly didn't think she had almost no experience at all. I was not expecting that. Shit, how forward did I seem to her last night?

I wanted to tell her she wasn't a freak at all. That none of it mattered. That there were clearly men who missed out on an amazing woman by not getting to know her, but I didn't think she was the kind of woman who wanted placating words, even if I believed all of them.

"Please say something," she said when I was taking too much time to respond. My mind was spinning over her revelation.

Standing up, I pulled her into my arms, resting my chin on the top of her head and stroking my hand up and down her back.

"I'm sorry I pushed. I was just trying to figure out who all the possible senders could be. There is nothing wrong with you, Quinn. You're not a freak, and I'm absolutely not running from you because of your past. You are an amazing woman, and I will say it over and over to you until you learn to accept it."

I tipped her face up to mine, leaned down, and placed a soft, but intense, kiss on her perfect lips. I needed her to know how I felt and I didn't think she would listen to words, so I had to show her through actions.

Knowing a box of dead flowers with a mean note in it wouldn't get a lot of attention at the police department, I told Quinn, "I'm going to call Olivia," as I continued to hold her. "I know she's out of town, but maybe she can use her connections at work and direct us to someone at the police department who will take this seriously. If nothing else, it gets it on record, so if anything suspicious happens again, they'll know about this too."

I finished making breakfast, then Quinn let me know she was going to take a nap. All the excitement from the morning was taking its toll on her. While she slept, I spoke with Olivia. She made some calls and told me she was sending Officer Matthew Hadaway, their friend Jillian's boyfriend, over to take our report. She also told me there wasn't a lot they could do on this one, since it wasn't an actual threat. But she did give me the name of a private detective she approved of when I asked for a recommendation.

I called the private detective, Sarah Barlow, and she agreed to come by later in the day to get some information. I would pay whatever I had to pay to keep Quinn safe.

When Officer Hadaway came by, I woke Quinn up so she could talk to him. She was a little embarrassed, but she answered his questions willingly. When he finished with his questions, he wrapped her up in a big embrace and I heard murmurings as he was whispering in her ear.

I knew they were friends, and he was dating one of Quinn's best friends, but I still didn't like the feeling in my gut seeing them together gave me. I wanted to be the one comforting her. I was going to have to put some thought into the new feeling of jealousy the kept popping up when I was around her.

Sarah showed up moments after Officer Hadaway left. As

a child, I watched a lot of *Murder, She Wrote* so when I heard she was a private detective, my mind pictured someone older. When Sarah arrived, she was more *Charlie's Angels* than she was *Murder, She Wrote*. Maybe in her early thirties, she appeared professional in tailored black slacks with a crisp, white button-down and a tailored black coat. Her long, sandy blond hair was pulled back in a simple, low ponytail.

Sarah was meticulous in her questioning without being aggressive or overwhelming Quinn. She said she would start looking into things and keep us posted.

Quinn was upset with me for suggesting it could have been Preston or Heather, but I wasn't going to take any chances. They both needed to know those two could have sent the flowers to Quinn.

After the private detective left, the doorbell rang again. This time it was Jace. Knowing they hadn't dated and weren't a couple made me a little less annoyed by his presence, but I still wanted some time alone with her today. She wouldn't get better if she kept having the stress of all these people around all day long. At least, that's what I told myself to feel better about being so possessive of her time today. I gave him a quick rundown of what happened, so she didn't have to answer questions about the flowers for the third time today. He was worried about her and suggested she come stay with him, but he relaxed when I told him I hired a private detective to look into things and I scheduled a security guard from Swift Corp to stay outside the house tonight.

They spent about two hours together and he stayed for dinner. His visit also gave me a chance to get to know him a little, and he seemed like a good guy. The kind you'd want as a friend. Quinn was in better spirits when he left, so it was a good thing he came by.

Knowing she had to be exhausted by everything that took

place over the last several hours, I suggested she head to bed and try to get a good night of sleep. But she hesitated.

"Is everything okay?" I asked.

She bit the side of her bottom lip again and I almost lost it. I wanted to kiss her again, badly. I wanted to hold her and make every drop of hesitation disappear.

"I was wondering if you could stay with me again?" she asked, then looked down to avoid my answer. "But I'll understand if you don't want to."

Don't want to. Was she fucking crazy? I wanted to with every fiber in my being. But could I behave? That was my question. I had to put her needs before mine, so I knew I could be good, but it was going to be hard. Yes, it was going to be uncomfortably hard.

"Of course I will. Give me twenty minutes to finish things up down here and I'll be right up."

I watched as she made her way up the stairs. When she disappeared around the corner, I went outside to make sure Bobby, the Swift Corp security officer helping me out tonight, was in place and had everything he needed to protect Quinn. Before coming to work for me, Bobby worked as a bodyguard for my dad, so I knew I would sleep better with him outside.

After taking a quick shower and putting on a pair of pajama pants, I pondered putting on a shirt to be more respectful. But feeling Quinn's hand on my chest last night was too good to miss out on, so I selfishly went without.

I knocked and she answered the door dressed in those short pajama shorts and a tight tank top again. She was undeniably not wearing a bra under her top. I took a deep breath and walked over to my side of the bed.

How crazy was it that only two nights ago, I didn't have a side of the bed? Two nights ago, Quinn wasn't a daily part of my life. Two nights ago, I didn't know what it felt like to have her body curled up next to mine. So much had changed so quickly. I would take back all the pain Quinn had gone through in the last forty-eight hours in a heartbeat if I could, but I would mourn the loss of how close we'd become.

I slid between the sheets and moved to the middle, as I did last night, and tossed her side of the covers back. "Come here," I said, trying to control the longing in my voice.

Seeing the bruises on her legs helped keep me in check while she climbed over to me, but as soon as I felt her hand slide across my abs, I instantly got hard.

Granny panties, three strikes when I'm up to bat, creamed corn, old men wearing tank tops and socks with sandals. I was trying to think of every unsettling thing that could help my situation, but she smelled so good I couldn't force my erection to go away. I prayed she didn't notice, so I wouldn't become that creepy guy who got a boner when she was recovering from a concussion.

Tonight, I felt her becoming less reserved. Instead of lying on her side next to me as straight as a rail, which couldn't have been a comfortable position for her last night, she slid her leg across mine. Heaven couldn't have felt better than what it felt like to have her body wrapped around mine.

She also became bolder with her hand. Rather than merely resting her hand on my abs, she was drawing circles with her finger. Lord help me, I wasn't going to survive the night.

"Thank you, Devon."

Since most of the blood in my body flowed south, my brain wasn't processing properly. Was she thanking me for letting her fondle me? Because she could do that any time she wanted. Or was the thank you for letting her wrap her tight little pixie body around mine, because, again, any time she wanted to do that, I was absolutely willing.

"Thank you for what, beautiful?"

"For everything. For opening your home to me, for taking such good care of me, for staying with me when I know I'm acting like a toddler that's afraid of the dark. Thank you for making me feel safe."

"You are welcome, but you have to know, there is nothing about you that makes me think of a toddler. You are all woman, and I might be struggling with that a little."

She sat up, pushing on my stomach in the process, and I groaned.

"Am I making you uncomfortable, Devon? I don't want you to feel that way at all."

"I'm not a teenage boy, Quinn. Yes, my body is obviously reacting to you because everything about you is so reaction worthy. But I'm a grown man and I can behave. I needed you to know I feel something for you, and not just here in bed. But this is exactly where I want to be. Now lay back down and cuddle with me."

She laughed and I could feel the tension leaving her body as she cuddled back up to me.

"Can I kiss you goodnight, Devon?"

Was there any reality where she couldn't? I didn't think so, and if there was, it wouldn't be a reality I wanted to live in.

I tipped her chin up and leaned forward to kiss her. She might not have had a lot of experience with men, but her kisses affected me. Her hand slid up to my chest as she took control of the kiss. Soon, our tongues were dancing together. Then she nipped at my lower lip. Damn, the restraint I had was rapidly fading. I wanted everything from this woman, and not only in bed. And that thought terrified me.

I guided my hand under the back of her tank top and up her back. Her skin was smooth like glass, but warm to my touch.

Her hand slid down my chest and went below the covers.

When she reached the waistband of my pajama pants, I knew I had to stop things. I didn't want to, but it was important to me that we didn't do anything she would regret in the morning. I wrapped my hand around her wrist and brought it back up to my chest.

"Quinn, I want you so much right now, but not like this. I need you to be fully recovered, so when we do this it is nothing less than perfect."

She pouted, and it was adorable.

"Trust me, I'm not stopping this because I don't want you. You need to understand and believe me when I say that." I nodded towards the tent in the sheets and said, "You can see I want you, can't you?"

She looked and gasped when she saw exactly how aroused she made me.

"But the nurse was perfectly clear with her instructions. Sex is the last activity to be put back on the table, so to speak. I would never forgive myself if anything happened to you."

"I understand," she said with a sigh. Then she curled back into me and quickly fell asleep.

The rest of the week went the same. We had breakfast together. She would nap while I worked until lunch. We played board games, watched movies, or relaxed, having great conversations after dinner. She was slowly opening up to me. The more I would share about myself, the more she was willing to share with me.

I told her about my mom and my fear of losing her to leukemia. I told her more than I ever admitted to my dad or Tate.

She didn't share anything she wasn't ready to, though. She told me stories of being a young girl and a bunch of stories about her college years with her group of friends, but she skipped over the years from her mom's murder through her high school years. Those were the stories she wanted to hold on to, and I respected her boundaries.

Each night, we went to bed together. After the third night, she didn't have to ask me again. I joined her in the guest room when it was time to get some sleep and we both found our way to the middle of the bed.

Words couldn't do justice to explain how it felt to spend my days with her, laughing and talking, and my nights with her wrapped in my arms. There weren't any other incidents, like the dead flowers, so she relaxed more each day. And I saw her growing stronger each day, too.

Sunday morning, I went looking for her after breakfast. I found her in the guest room, standing by the bed, folding clothes and packing her suitcase.

"What are you doing?" I asked in a panic.

"I'm packing."

"Well, I see that. I guess my question should have been, why are you doing that?"

She put down the shirt she was folding and turned to face me.

"You have been the best host I could have asked for, but I can't overstay my welcome any longer, Devon. Olivia got back into town last night, so there's no reason for me to stay here anymore." There was sadness in her tone. Maybe she didn't want to leave. I knew I didn't want her to leave.

"Plus, I have to get back to work tomorrow morning. I've already lost a week and I'm stressed about falling behind."

Hearing her come up with a second reason made it sound like she was trying to convince herself that it was a good idea instead of me.

I didn't want her to go. Aside from sharing my dorm room in college with my best friend from high school, I haven't had a roommate. Not that I considered Quinn to be a roommate. But I also never had a girlfriend live with me. Not that I considered Quinn to be my girlfriend, either. I just knew I enjoyed having her in my space with me. Over the previous five days and nights she had become a huge part of my world and now that was changing and I wasn't ready for it.

Maybe her leaving was a good thing. Things between us went from zero to one hundred in only two weeks, which was way too fast for me. Maybe this was a chance for me to get back to my normal life and not be so consumed by her.

"Can I drive you home?"

"I was going to call an Uber so you wouldn't have to."

"No, I want to," I practically shouted at her.

"Okay. Thank you. I should be ready in about five minutes."

Shit, there was nothing I could say to stop this. No reason to suggest she stay came to mind. She was feeling better. She didn't need to be watched all day long. Her roommate was back from her trip so she wouldn't be alone if anything happened. She would be back in the comfort of her own space. So, I resigned myself to being her chauffeur and getting to see her again at tomorrow's weekly project meeting.

We drove in silence, and when we got to her apartment, I grabbed her bag to carry it upstairs. Olivia was there waiting for her. It was time to say goodbye.

"I can't thank you enough for all you've done for me this week, Devon. Please let me know how I can repay you."

Don't leave. That would be a good way to repay me. But I couldn't say that.

Her history was scarring enough for me to know I needed to take this at a pace she would be okay with, and I didn't even know everything that happened to her. I vowed to take things slowly with her, even if it killed me.

With Olivia standing there, I felt like a teenager trying to get a kiss goodnight with her parents watching from the window.

"No repayment necessary." I leaned forward, wrapped my arms around her one last time, and kissed her forehead. "I'll see you at the meeting tomorrow."

Then I left, back to my empty house.

13

QUINN

*I*t took over an hour to get Olivia to stop asking me questions. She asked about everything from the roses to my symptoms to my routine over the last few days, and she spent a lot of time asking about the hug and the kiss on my forehead she saw me get from Devon.

I tried to tell her we're just friends. How spending so much time together this week fast-tracked us getting to know each other and we discovered we have a lot in common. She wasn't buying it.

"Did you have any nightmares while you were there?" She knew about my nightmares since I often woke her up because of them. But she never complained.

"I did, that first night."

"Did he hear you? What did he do?"

"He heard me and he stayed with me while I fell back asleep." Saying that brought me back to his tenderness on our first night together. My screaming must have scared him, but he was so calm and comforting.

"So, how did you only have one while you were there?"

She probed with a grin on her face, like she knew the answer already.

I didn't want to hide anything from her. Our friendship was too strong for me to lie to her, and I knew she wouldn't judge me.

"He slept with me each night." I saw the look on her face and quickly corrected her assumptions. "Only sleeping in the same bed. Nothing else."

I watched as the information rolled around in her head.

"Is that all you wanted to happen?"

I didn't know how to answer that. I struggled trusting people enough to be vulnerable with them. And to trust someone with your body seemed like a level of vulnerability I wasn't ready to try again. But there was something different about Devon. From the moment he caught me in the hallway, he made me feel safe. He made me feel like I could let my guard down and be myself with him.

When we watched movies together, he didn't mind my random movie critic comments throughout the whole movie. He wasn't repelled by my intensely competitive nature when we played games together. And he didn't run away when he made me laugh so much I snorted while we were working on a puzzle together. Each day I spent with him, I let my guard down a bit more and it didn't feel scary at all.

Being so near to him each night was torture. Every night, I could feel his erection against my leg. Not being very experienced, it was a concerningly large erection. But he never pushed me to do anything. His respectful restraint made me want to be bold, but I honestly didn't know how.

"I don't know what I wanted to happen, Livy. This is all so new to me. I feel things I definitely didn't feel with Troy. But you know my past. You know I'm not okay with opening myself up and trusting people."

"You learned to trust me, and Jace, and Jillian, and Sydney. So why can't you let one more in there?"

"I only learned to trust you guys because you were relentless and wouldn't stop until I did." We both laughed because it was true.

"I think I need to keep my focus on the project. Devon will only complicate things. Plus, his dad is my boss, and that's just plain weird."

She rolled her eyes at my excuses, which is exactly what they were. But, for my own sanity, I needed to bring the focus back to work, where I was confident in my abilities, because I wasn't sure what to do about anything else.

She finally relented with the questions and we got back to our normal routine. Sunday nights were pizza nights. Neither of us wanted to cook on the weekends. After debating which pizza place to order from, we sat down for our weekly reality TV binge. Olivia got me hooked on some of the worst reality shows. I couldn't bring myself to admit it to anyone, but I loved watching every episode.

In bed, I felt alone. After only five nights with Devon, I missed his warmth next to me. I missed the comfort of his slow, even breathing. I wondered if he missed me, too.

It took longer than normal to fall asleep and I woke in the middle of the night from another nightmare of my father. Thankfully, I didn't wake Olivia this time. I looked at my phone. It was a little after two in the morning. I also saw an unread text on my phone from Devon sent right before midnight. Why was he awake so late?

> Devon: If you have a nightmare tonight, call me, please.

My heart flipped at the text. He was thinking about me. I wanted to call him, but I didn't want to wake him. After about twenty minutes of an internal debate, I texted him. That way, if he was sleeping, I might not wake him.

> Me: I had a nightmare. It was nice not having them for the last few days.

It only took a moment before I saw the bouncing dots showing he was typing something.

Devon: I'm sorry. How can I help?

> Me: I don't think you can.

Devon: I wish there was something I could do.

> Me: Can I tell you something?

Devon: Absolutely.

> Me: I haven't gone four nights without a nightmare since my mom died.

There was a long pause before he started typing again.

Devon: Can I tell you something?

> Me: Of course.

Devon: I don't ever remember sleeping as well as I did when you were in my arms.

Wow. His words made my heart race.

> Me: I think we did things backwards.

Devon: I think you might be right. Sleeping together before our first date is definitely out of order. But we can fix that.

Me: How?

Devon: Go out with me.

Me: When?

Devon: Now.

Devon: Okay, maybe not now, but soon.

Me: Can I tell you something?

Devon: I'm begging you to.

Me: I miss you.

Devon: I miss you too. Does that mean you'll go out with me?

Me: What about your dad?

Devon: I don't think he should join us. I think that would just be awkward.

I laughed out loud in my room in the middle of the night. It was so loud I worried I might wake Olivia up.

Me: You know what I mean.

Devon: He would be okay with it. Trust me.

Me: How do you know for sure?

Devon: Because I talked to him about you this afternoon.

Me: You did what!

Devon: I needed him to know I'm interested
in you and I knew you would be concerned
about how he would view us dating, so I got
that part out of the way. He's cool. Now, will
you go out with me?

The Art for the People project was my first real job, and I
didn't want to jeopardize it by dating the boss's son. Success
on the project would open so many doors to me in a tight-
knit industry. I didn't want to risk my future career opportunities by giving people something else to gossip about.

Sighing, I prepared myself to text him back with a polite
decline, but I couldn't bring myself to type it out. An unfamiliar sense of warmth and security passed over me as I
remembered our last week together. Was I willing to risk so
much to hold on to that feeling? My nerves were taking over,
but I hadn't wanted something this badly in so long, so I took
a chance. I picked up my phone and typed one word.

Me: Yes.

Devon: My night without you just got better.
Let's go out after our committee meeting
later today.

Me: Wow, moving kinda fast, aren't you?

Devon: I don't want to give you a chance to
change your mind.

Me: Tonight works for me.

Devon: Yes!

Me: Good night, Devon.

Devon: Sweet dreams, Quinn.

I slept the rest of the night through without nightmares.

Because of my accident, I rescheduled my visit to the Palette Studio for that morning, before the committee meeting. Our second month of the Art for the People project was going to celebrate a famous Wisconsinite photographer, Andrew Jorgensen. Most of his work was scenic, but he currently had an exhibit running at the Palette Studio of photos of the women of the Oneida tribe. Heather was close with the artist and she got him to agree to share his pieces with the project.

My head still hurt from the fall, but it was getting much better. I didn't want to risk another tumble by wearing heels, so I dressed casually. Jeans, a navy-blue cable-knit sweater to keep me warm in the fall air, and white Keds. It wasn't what I would normally wear to an art gallery, but I wasn't ready to go back to skirts and heels quite yet. Since Heather and I set up our meeting for 10 am, an hour before the gallery opened, I wasn't worried about my appearance. It thrilled me to see Mr. Jorgensen's exhibit at last.

The door was locked when I arrived, so I knocked. Through the glass door, I saw Heather emerge from the back of the gallery like a goddess coming down from Mount Olympus. She was perfection, in her fitted red dress that flared to a ruffle around her knees and her four-inch matching red heels. I looked at her differently now that I knew she and Devon dated. Heather was class and elegance, and I wasn't. She was who he was attracted to in the past and that was the exact opposite of me.

She let me in and towered over me as we stood next to each other. We spent the next half hour looking at the exhibit. Talking about art with her made me feel a little less lacking. It was my thing and I could go toe to toe with anyone when it came to discussing art. She even seemed a little annoyed with me when I pointed out a lighting technique Mr. Jorgensen obviously used that she wasn't aware of.

We spent another half hour going through other pieces she had in her storeroom. She made some suggestions on which pieces might be used for our different exhibits. Overall, the visit made me optimistic about the success of our project. I thanked her for her time and her commitment to the project, and she walked me out. When we reached the door, she stopped before she unlocked it again.

"I'm so sorry to hear about your fall. That must have been absolutely terrible." Insincerity dripped from each word.

"Yes, it was. But I'm healing and I should be back to normal soon. Thank you for your concern."

I thought that would be the end of it, but she still didn't unlock the door.

"That was so kind of Devon to play nursemaid to you all week. He's such a selfless soul. Don't you just love his home?"

"Yes, his home was lovely."

"My favorite place there is the massive soaking tub in the master suite. We spent hours there together each weekend. Did he let you in there to take a swim in the tub?"

"Um. No. I was happy with the one in the guest room, though."

"We've talked repeatedly about getting back together and when I finally give in to him and agree to it, I want to redo the guest suite. I think it could use a little work."

Where was she going with this? Devon literally just asked me out a few hours ago. I couldn't imagine him being the kind of man who would toy with women, so Heather's words didn't add up. Was she trying to mark her territory? Was she trying to warn me away from him so she could make her move? I wanted to tell her about our kisses and our nights spent in each other's arms, but I also wanted to keep our working relationship friendly.

"Well, as a guest, I can say that I was completely comfortable there, so I wouldn't make any changes. But I do need to get going, Heather. I have a lot to do before our committee meeting later. Thank you again for showing me around."

She unlocked the door, but kept a hand on it, continuing to prevent me from walking out.

"I need to make sure we're on the same page here, Quinn. Devon is mine. You might have a little Nightingale Syndrome from having him take care of you, but he only did it because he felt responsible. Don't get your hopes up that you two are starting something. He has an enormous heart, in addition to his other enormous parts, but don't let that fool you into thinking you two are going to be something, because you're not. He belongs to me."

She was the worst. But what she didn't know was I've spent a lot of my life dealing with bullies. And bullies made me want to fight these days, not flee like she was hoping. I accepted our working relationship wouldn't be a friendly one, so I stopped pretending.

"Well, Heather, just to help you out so you don't sound so uneducated in the future, Nightingale Syndrome is actually where the nurse falls for the patient, not the other way around. So, that would be Devon falling for me, not me falling for him. And I'll make sure to go over your remodeling suggestions with him when we go out on our date tonight. See you at the meeting."

I stepped in front of her, opened the door myself, and walked out with my head held high. I hoped I was pulling off an air of confidence, because I was anxious jelly on the inside. Despite having bullies in my life when I was younger, I never stood up for myself. It felt kind of good.

I went straight to my office to try to get caught up on emails and phone calls. I was dreading the meeting today, but I knew I would get to see Devon there, so that made things better.

Luckily, the meeting went well. They kept the drama to a

minimum. Heather shot daggers at me through her stares, but I continued with the agenda, ignoring her attitude. The awkward part came at the end of the meeting when Preston asked me out for drinks again. Before I had the chance to answer, Devon stepped in, swung an arm across my shoulders, and informed Preston that I couldn't go out for drinks with him tonight because we had a date planned. He said it loud enough for Heather's head to whip around from her conversation with Millard. I didn't think she believed me earlier. She believed me now.

I told Devon I couldn't stay out too late, because the strain of my first full day back to work was taking a toll on me. We decided dinner would be enough. I told him I would meet him at the restaurant, so I could go straight home from there instead of having him drive me back to the Capitol to get my car. He offered to drive me home and pick me up in the morning to bring me back to my car, but I told him that wasn't necessary at all.

We met at a popular Italian place near my apartment. I wanted to tell him about my interactions with Heather that morning, but I didn't want to bring her into our date. So, we talked about everything else. For the first time since meeting him, he asked a couple of questions about my parents. I appreciated that he didn't ask those while I was staying with him, because I would have felt captive and obligated to answer him. Now, I felt like it would be okay to talk about them.

He didn't ask for any graphic details but wanted to know more about me and how I handled things. I told him the basics, the same information that was reported in the news during that time. Things like how I testified against my father and how I moved in with Aunt Betty across the street since I didn't have any other family. I told him how hard it was to live across the street and see where it happened every day.

The emotions came flooding back, so I asked if we could change the topic and he graciously agreed. The rest of the evening was wonderful. I was relaxed with him in a way I wasn't with many other people. When it was time to call it a night, I had a hard time leaving. My body was telling me I was still healing and needed some rest, but I wanted to stay up all night talking with him. We stepped outside the restaurant and he pulled me to him.

"Quinn, I'm intrigued by you. You've been in my thoughts all day long and it was torture not having you beside me last night. I shouldn't admit this, but I even spent last night in the guest room so I could feel closer to you. I don't know what to do about you." Then I felt his lips on mine, demanding a response.

My knees went weak as he kissed me. I wondered if I was building things up in my head that weren't real, but his kiss cleared all that up for me. All the emotions that swirled around inside me came through in my kiss. Everything made me think of him. I couldn't find the confidence to tell him that yet, so I showed it to him through our kiss.

When the kiss ended, I felt a loss. I needed his lips on mine. But it was time to go. He held out his arm to me, which I took, and he walked me to my car. I was floating. This man made me so happy.

But, as soon as we got to my car, the happiness was quickly replaced with cold and fear. Someone wrote BITCH on both sides of my car. My knees went weak for the second time in a few minutes, but for a different reason.

Devon saw my reaction and stepped between me and my car. He pulled me into his chest and wrapped me up. I was safe. I was going to be okay. I wasn't alone.

Once I got myself under control, I called Olivia. She was

working nights this week, so she was able to get Matthew out to us right away. We went through all the same questions we did when the flowers were delivered. Do you know who might have done this? Do you know of anyone with a grudge against you? But this time he asked if I had any difficult encounters with anyone since the last time we spoke.

Devon stepped in and said I was with him every day except today, so there wasn't anything new during any of those days. But he made sure to mention that Preston asked me out after our meeting and I shot him down.

"Was that the only difficult encounter since the last time we spoke, Quinn?" Matthew was making notes in his notebook as he asked. When I didn't say yes immediately, they both looked at me expectantly.

"Quinn, did anything else happen today?" Devon asked in a tone reminiscent of a third-grade teacher talking to a child.

"Well, there was one other thing today."

I gave them a quick summary of the conversation I had with Heather today. Devon was furious that she would treat me that way. I had to calm him down and let him know I handled her fine on my own, so he didn't need to swoop in and fix things.

"Okay, I'm going to go have a chat with both of them. I'll let you know what I find out. Quinn, I don't think you should be home alone tonight. Since Olivia is working nights this week, do you want to stay with Jillian and me?" Matthew asked me.

"She'll stay with me," Devon announced without hesitation. "You can find her at my place if you have any more questions." A small part of me was annoyed that he would make that declaration without speaking to me first, but there was also relief knowing I would be safe in his arms again tonight.

Devon made arrangements for my car to be picked up by

his car guy, then he drove me to my apartment so I could pack again. While I was packing, I could hear him talking to someone on his phone, but I couldn't make out the conversation.

"I'll talk to you more tomorrow. Thanks," I heard Devon ending his call when I walked out of my bedroom.

"Who was that?" I asked. Which I knew sounded nosy, but I wanted to know because I felt like I was the topic of discussion during his call.

"That was Sarah, the private detective I hired. I called and updated her about your car. And I also called my dad and let him know what was going on. He suggested, and I agree with him, that you should work from my house this week, until we find out who is doing this. My staff is amazing, so I trust them to run things while I work from home for another week, too."

All the excitement from the night was overwhelming me. I tried to keep my cool, but adding in everything that happened over the last week, I lost it. I started sobbing, right there in my living room, holding my suitcase in one hand and my purse in the other. I could only imagine how unstable I appeared, but it was all hitting me so hard.

Devon took the things from my hands and set them on the ground. Opening his arms for me, I threw myself into them.

"It's going to be okay, Quinn. We're going to get this all figured out. I promise," he said as he held me tight to his chest and kissed the top of my head.

When we got to Devon's house, he brought my suitcase upstairs and said he would run me a bath to help me relax. I went to the kitchen and made some tea to take with me upstairs.

Walking into the guest room, I didn't see my suitcase there. I thought of how sweet he was to unpack my bag for me again. I went to the dresser to find some clean clothes, but the drawers were empty.

Devon appeared at the door. "I hope I'm not being too presumptuous, or maybe too hopeful, but I put your clothes in my room. I would sleep much better knowing you were beside me."

"I would sleep better that way, too." I gave him a big smile as I walked out with him to the master suite where I heard the water running in the master bath. I froze.

"What's the matter, Quinn?" He looked at me, then things clicked into place for him.

"This is about Heather, isn't it?"

I nodded.

"She was telling tales, Quinn. The only time she could have been in my bathtub was when she was house-sitting for me, when I was gone. We were never in there together." I breathed a sigh of relief as he continued. "I wouldn't mind breaking it in with you, though." He gave me a mischievous wink.

"But not tonight. Tonight, I want you to go in there and relax. I'll get you unpacked and see you when you come out."

The one truthful thing Heather said to me was that the master bath was glorious. Devon put some bubble bath in the water and scattered candles around the room. I never wanted to leave. I could have spent the next few days in there, but I was looking forward to climbing in bed with Devon more than I wanted to stay in the bath, so I forced myself out of the water.

At the door, I took in the view of the master bedroom. Devon was lying on top of the fluffy white down comforter in a pair of hunter green boxers and tortoiseshell reading glasses, reading a book. He was breathtaking, like sexy professor breathtaking. Everything about him was perfection. His skin, still slightly tanned from the summer. Those tight abs that I wanted to touch so badly. His muscular thighs. Seriously, everything about him made me tingle. He closed his book and took off his reading glasses when he saw me come in.

He stood, walked to my side of the bed, pulled the covers back and held them while I got in. Then he climbed in on the other side to join me.

Something felt different from our other nights together. Maybe it was because this was his bed. His bed felt drastically more serious than the guest bed. Maybe it was the intimacy of the boxers rather than his normal pajama pants. Maybe it was because I wasn't a 'patient' here this time. I was nervous, but my excitement at the thought of sleeping in his arms again was so much greater. One night apart was too much.

He moved next to me and pulled me into his side, as if this was our normal routine we've been doing for a year.

"It was hard to sleep without you last night," he said in a gravelly, deep voice, then I felt his lips on my forehead. I melted.

"Same for me," I admitted.

I turned and put my head on his chest and slid my leg over his. The skin-to-skin contact set something off in my body. I gasped in air.

"Are you okay?" he asked.

"Yes, I just missed this," I said as I turned my face up to look at him while I spoke.

He leaned forward and kissed me. It didn't start soft this time, not like his other kisses. It was demanding. I used his chest to pull myself up closer to his mouth, and he growled.

I was so turned on by his growl that I whimpered into his mouth.

In a quick motion, he flipped me onto my back and was over me on his side. He never broke our kiss. The weight of his body on mine wasn't scary, like I would have expected it to be. It was sexy and enticing. I had no idea what I was doing, but everything he did made me want more. I ran my hands over his strong back and shoulders, and I could feel his hard muscles move under my fingers.

His lips left my mouth, leaving me devastated, until I felt him kissing his way down my neck.

"Quinn, you are so beautiful," he said between kisses. "I want to taste every inch of you."

"Please." My one word was all he needed.

His lips made a trail from my neck to my breasts, kissing the skin right above my tank top. He pulled the top down and to the side and I felt his tongue licking circles around my breast until his mouth closed over my nipple and sucked. I almost had an orgasm from that one act. I moved my hand up his back into his hair and pulled him closer. Even though I wasn't sure what I was doing, I knew I needed more of his mouth on my breast.

"God, Quinn, you taste so good."

His hand released my top and covered my breast again. I felt him moving his hand down lower, across my belly and down to the bottom of my tank top. He slid his hand under the hem of my top and it felt so good. As he moved his hand up and reached one of my scars, I panicked and sat straight up, pulling my shirt down and leaving him with a shocked look on his face.

"I'm so sorry," I said as I turned away from him, continuing to tug my shirt down, even though it couldn't go any further.

He moved in behind me and pulled me back so I was leaning against his chest.

"Was that a scar from the attack?" he asked after a minute of quiet.

I nodded, so embarrassed.

"How many are there, Quinn?" His voice was so gentle.

"Three," I whispered.

He pushed me forward and moved himself out from behind me as he laid me back down.

He looked me straight in the eye and ask me, "Do you trust me?"

Without hesitation, I nodded.

He moved further down the bed, so his head was near my belly, and slowly lifted the hem of my shirt. My scars were so ugly, so angry-looking. My level of self-consciousness over them was through the roof. I never wore anything where they could be seen, no bikinis or crop tops. I wanted them to be covered up, so nobody needed to see them. The only one that ever showed was the one on my arm. I learned over the years to accept the looks when people saw it, and I did my best to ignore them.

As the ones on my belly came into sight, one at a time, he didn't flinch. I took a deep breath when all three were showing and he could see them and all angry redness. He leaned forward and placed a gentle, lingering kiss on one scar. He did the same with the second one. And, finally, the third. Then he gently ran his fingers back and forth over all three. They stopped hurting long ago, but the emotional pain was still there.

"I wasn't lying when I said you were beautiful, Quinn. You are. Every part of you is beautiful. These scars, they made you who you are today, and I find that the woman you are today is absolutely magnificent."

His kisses on my abdomen moved lower. Soon, he was kissing right above the waistband of my shorts. He looked up at me as if to ask for permission. Not knowing what to say, I just nodded my head and he smiled.

14

DEVON

*S*he was nervous when she encouraged me to keep going. It felt like we were crossing over into unfamiliar territory for her, and I had to keep that in mind as I moved forward. It was more important for me that she enjoyed this than it was for me to have my own release. I moved up towards her and helped her take her top off. Her hair fell out of its messy bun when she pulled her top over her head and it spread across her naked skin. She looked angelic.

With my tongue flicking her pert nipple, I slid a hand under her shorts and into her panties. Her mound was covered in the softest down-like hair. Moving further down, I could feel how wet she was. I wanted her so much I felt physical pain. Restraint was killing me. My erection was pushing hard against the material of my boxers; trying desperately to join the party. But he needed to wait.

Licking and nipping at her nipple made her squirm beneath me. Then, I slid one finger between her folds and she practically launched herself off the bed.

Stopping everything, I put my hands up like a suspect

busted by the cops. I knew she was inexperienced, but I didn't know how much she'd actually done before. I knew I was going to be invasive, but I had to ask her a personal question and I hoped she trusted me enough to answer honestly. "Quinn, do you masturbate?"

Her cheeks turned red, a clear sign this was a topic she rarely discussed.

"It's okay, beautiful. It's important for us to talk openly about this. You said you're not very experienced, so I want to make this good for you, but I need your input. I need you to trust me."

"I touched myself a few times as a teenager, when I was just learning to explore my body, but after my injuries, I felt disgusted by the way my body looked, so I haven't tried since."

"There is nothing disgusting about your body. You are perfection." I kissed her again, then reached for her arm and kissed her scar there, so she would learn to believe me. "I need you to communicate with me. If I do something you like, let me know. If I do something you don't like, definitely let me know. Faster, slower, harder, softer, these are all things that are going to make this better, okay?"

I leaned her back again and kept eye contact with her as I glided my hand back over her body and underneath her panties again. I wanted the taste of her breast in my mouth again, but that would have to wait. It was more important that we focused on each other.

When I found her wet heat, I put my lips on hers as I slid a finger between her folds again. She moaned into my mouth and it was the sexiest thing I have ever experienced.

I started drawing slow circles on her clit with my finger, gradually increasing the pressure, and her hips bucked beneath my hand. I hadn't even moved my finger inside her yet and she was going off like a rocket. She wrapped both her arms around my neck and squeezed her legs tight together around my hand as her orgasm took over.

Neither of us moved for over a minute while she came back down from what I could only assume was her first orgasm.

"Devon...that...um...wow...that...was...amazing."

I laughed as she tried to make sentences happen through her panting, but then I saw the look on her face change.

"Oh, Quinn," I said as I kissed her lips, "I'm not laughing at you. I'm just loving the look on your face right now. Watching you experience an orgasm was the most erotic thing I have ever witnessed."

She relaxed in my arms. "I've never felt anything like that. My one time wasn't like this as all. If I had known it was supposed to feel like that, maybe I wouldn't have waited until now to try again."

The thought of her doing this with anyone else, of any other man touching her like I did, made me furious. An over-whelming feeling of possessiveness came over me. I was falling for this sweet, intelligent, beautiful woman. I wanted to be the only man that could make her feel like this.

I couldn't get enough of her. "I'm not done with you yet." Then I moved on top of her and slid her pajama shorts and panties down her body, kissing and licking as I went. I kissed the top of her thigh then right above her knee. From there I went down to her calf, kissing the smooth skin there, then I finally made it down to her ankle where I place another gentle kiss. There she was, completely naked and open in front of me. I had never seen a sight so glorious as her.

I kissed my way back up, this time separating her legs as I advanced. She quivered when I kissed her inner thighs, then she gasped when I reached her pussy and blew on it.

"Devon," she murmured, more to herself than to me.

Just hearing my name from her lips made my cock twitch against my boxers.

I put my tongue on her and let her adjust to the sensation, then I licked up to her clit. I think she stopped breathing. Her taste was better than a fine wine. One taste wasn't enough. I feasted on her, licking and sucking as she writhed beneath me. I had to hold her hips in place, or she was going to dislocate my nose with all the writhing she was doing under me. She was so wet, and I could tell she was on the edge. I only needed a little push to put her over. I took a long pass up her lips and nipped my teeth on her clit. That was it. She was gone. I kept my mouth on her while she rode through her second orgasm. It was as beautiful as her first.

After she came down from her second, more powerful orgasm, I got up and went to the master bath. With a warm washcloth in hand, I climbed into bed with her again. She looked a little embarrassed when I used it to clean her, but I assured her I only wanted to take care of her. After tossing the washcloth into the laundry basket, I went back to bed and pulled her to me again as I tugged the covers over us. By sheer willpower alone, my erection was slowly waning.

I could tell she wanted to say something to me, but I didn't push her until she was ready to say it.

"Um...Devon. What about you?"

"What do you mean, what about me?"

"Well, like you said, I don't have a lot of experience, but I'm pretty sure you didn't get much out of that."

She was so sweet. I had to hold in a laugh because I knew she would take it the wrong way.

"Oh, you have no idea how much I got out of that, my beautiful Quinn."

She looked perplexed.

"Getting you to orgasm twice was so erotic, I don't need my own. Hopefully, we will do more in the future, but if we did nothing more than this ever again, I would still die a lucky man."

She nuzzled her face into my chest, slid her arm across my abs, and crooked her leg over mine. Her naked body next to mine, with only my boxers as the barrier between us, made my erection reappear. I wanted her more than I wanted to breathe, but I knew we had done enough for her tonight. I enjoyed how things were unfolding slowly, but I was sure there would be a lot of cold showers in my future as we took our time.

I wrapped my arm around her warm body, kissing her forehead. After hearing her breathing become slow and even, I drifted off to sleep myself.

In the morning, I woke to her wrapped around my body, and in her sleep, her hand found its home on my cock. When I became aware, my body responded instantly. I didn't want to, but I knew I needed to get out of bed before Quinn woke. With as much stealth as I could come up with, I was able to sneak out without disturbing her. It was time for one of those cold showers.

Quinn was still sleeping when I came out. Wasabi had taken my place curled up next to her, so she was in good hands.

I spent my morning making some calls. I checked in with Officer Hadaway, who hadn't learned anything yet. Then I checked in with Sarah, who was in the same situation. I knew it had only been a few hours, but I wanted to know Quinn was safe. I wanted her to know that, too. Whatever this thing starting between us was, it couldn't be based on fear. I wanted her to look at me like a man she could have feelings for, not just a man she could run to in difficult times.

I wanted us to have a chance at a normal relationship, but nothing has been normal about anything since the moment we met. Things weren't going along the typical, boy meets girl, boy asks a girl on a date, boy kisses girl, girl falls in love with boy, they live happily ever after path. Maybe that would work in my favor, though. With Quinn's history, maybe normal wasn't what she needs. It's possible she wouldn't have let her guard down and let me in so quickly if we hadn't started this way. Maybe we could make our own steps and strike our own path.

With that in mind, I went upstairs to wake her up. Seeing her sleeping with Wasabi warmed me.

I crawled into bed next to her and held her tight, which caused her to stir and angered my cat.

"Good morning, beautiful. How did you sleep last night?" I asked as she stretched her arms above her head to get the kinks of sleep out of her system.

She turned to me and smiled, and my day was made.

"I slept like a baby, which is surprising to me with everything that's going on."

She snuggled up next to me and we stayed there for a while. When I couldn't keep my hands off her any longer, I cupped her cheek in my hand and leaned in for a kiss.

"What are you doing?" She freaked out and pushed herself to the other side of the bed from me.

"I was trying to kiss you good morning. I'm sorry if I upset you." This woman confounded me. She was trusting and relaxed in bed with me last night. Why would a morning kiss freak her out so much?

"But I have morning breath." Holding her hand up to her mouth, she looked embarrassed but sincerely concerned.

I had to laugh. Morning breath. That was her big concern. I got up on my hands and knees and crawled across the bed to her.

"I don't think there is anything about you that would ever make me not want to kiss you. So, can we try this again?" I asked, because I needed to feel those lips again. It had been too long.

I leaned in, and this time she didn't run away. This time, she met me in the middle of the distance between us and our lips connected. Even her morning breath was perfect, which I knew was crazy. I was starting to think this woman put a spell on me.

We both spent the day working from my home. She spent her day working on the layout for the first month's art show. I found myself distracted by her presence and kept wandering over to the kitchen table where she set up her makeshift desk. Each time I went out there, I saw Wasabi lying on the floor beside her. I think she was becoming as fond of her as I was.

I offered to take her out to dinner, but she preferred to stay in, which sounded fine to me. She wasn't anything like the usual women I dated. They wanted to go out all the time so they could be seen in public with me. Quinn seemed to want to spend time with me as a person, and I kind of liked that.

I made us some pasta while she made a salad to go on the side. I loved sharing my space with her. Working side by side doing completely domestic things. The thought that I could get used to having her with me every day was a little frightening because of how fast things were moving, but not as scary as I would have expected it to be.

Family was important to me and I've always known I wanted a family of my own, but I didn't have a long-term game plan on when I saw it happening. I didn't want it with Heather. That's why, in the two years we dated, I never once thought to propose to her. She wasn't who I saw my future with. But Quinn, who I'd only known for a couple of weeks, had worked her way into my future plans easily.

There was nothing better than waking up with her in my

arms and going to bed with her each night. I wondered if this was how love happened: unexpectedly. Did it sneak up on you when you weren't looking? Did you spend your time with the right person doing everyday things and then it just showed up? I wasn't saying I was in love with Quinn, because that would be a little premature, but I felt like I could see it happening with her and that was surprising. Trying not to put too much thought into an unknown future, I just enjoyed my time with her doing the most mundane things together.

She enjoyed watching reality TV. She blamed it on Olivia, saying she needed to keep current on the shows Olivia made her watch so they could talk about them, but I could tell she was totally into them. So, we spent the night watching a dating show based on an island. All the contestants were beautiful, half naked, and most often drunk. Quinn was absorbed.

Two of the contestants, Heath and Jessica, were clearly meant to be, but they didn't see it. I thought I could use them to get Quinn talking.

"Why isn't Jessica going after Heath? They seem to like each other a lot and they have so much in common," I asked.

"I guess Jessica isn't ready to let go of her past with Mitchell and let herself love again. She's been hurt before and that's a pretty gigantic risk."

"But it's clear they should be together, so can't she push past her fears for the chance at something wonderful?" I suggested.

"Maybe it's not that easy to let go. For some people, I think it might be impossible."

"Heath seems like a good guy. Maybe he could help her through if she let him in," I pushed.

"He could. But maybe he has to be patient with her. Maybe she has to go at a different pace than him to get there. And maybe he doesn't want to put in the time and effort to do that, so maybe that scares her. Maybe she's worried she's not worth the effort."

We weren't talking about Heath and Jessica anymore, but I continued as if we were.

"I don't doubt Heath would give her all the time in the world to work through her concerns as long as she let him in to help her."

I hoped my message was clear to her and didn't scare her away. I was willing to help her through the scars of her past. I wanted to let her take her time and grow to trust in me and let me into her world. She let me in a little last night when she let me see her scars, but I also knew her scars were only the tip of the iceberg.

"Are we still talking about the show, Devon?" Quinn asked tentatively.

"I don't think so," I said as I reached for her hand. "There is so much from your past that hurt you and changed you, but I want to get to know all of you. There isn't anything you could tell me about your past that would scare me away or change how I feel about you. I find you captivating, and smart, and creative, and kind, and so many more things I can't even name. And, and I'm so attracted to you that I can't think clearly when I'm around you. I know we're just getting to know each other, but I want to give us a try. I want you to let me be a part of your world. Do you think that's possible?"

I sat there, not breathing, while I watched her process everything I said. I dumped so much on her and I wouldn't be surprised if she got up and ran away. She looked at her hand in mine as she thought.

"Devon," she started, and I was sure she was going to break my heart.

"I have so much baggage in my past. After my parents, I knew I would never let someone in. I could never love someone like how my mother loved my father, or worse, like my father supposedly loved my mother. I didn't want to risk myself like that, so I didn't put myself out there. I didn't date, and I never dreamt of my future with someone else or planned out my happily ever after like other women have. I have been so focused on my artwork and getting my education that I didn't feel like I was missing out on anything. Even though Olivia continually told me I was missing out on so much, I didn't believe her."

Great. I'd already fucking blew it. She didn't even want to give me a chance. She wouldn't take the risk on me. I gently pulled my hand from hers, but she grabbed it back.

"But that was then," she said as she looked hopefully into my eyes. "I'm scared. I don't have a lot of positive relationships to reference. I don't know if I believe happy couples even exist, much less that it could be a possibility for me. But I think I would like to give it a chance."

So, that was what butterflies felt like. I didn't know guys got those. I wanted to say something so she couldn't have time to take the words back, but I didn't know what to say.

"But I don't know what I'm doing, Devon. I'm afraid of everything. It won't be easy with me, and I feel like you deserve more than the complications I come with. I don't know how relationships work because I've never been in one. I'm jealous of Heather and you're not even together. You don't need that. And, seriously, your face said it all last night when you found out I haven't even touched myself. The whole extent of my sexual experience is an awkward and uncomfortable three minute encounter. I take inexperienced to a whole new level. I'm a mess, and you should think twice about wanting to get involved with me.

I scooped her up and put her sideways on my lap so I could look directly into her beautiful, stormy eyes.

"That's for me to decide, and I've already decided I want you. The you that is made up of all your inexperience and insecurities. Because then I get the you that's so passionate about your work, so kind to others, so funny to talk to, and sexier than should be legally allowed. That's my decision, and I'm glad you're not going to take that away from me."

I kissed her hard. She wasn't as fragile as I thought, and I needed to stop treating her as if she was. Anyone that could openly speak about their concerns like she did was a strong person. I tightened my hands in her hair as I held her to me. She moaned into me as we kissed, which only made me want to devour her more. I couldn't get enough of her.

Annoyingly, there was a twinge in my chest that was trying to remind me I took a vow to go slowly with her. A vow I forgot the previous night, but I couldn't forget again. Her emotional stability was more important than my wants and I needed to be the man who would respect that, no matter how hard it was on me.

I stopped our kiss and pushed myself back, trying to ignore the shocked look on her face.

"I have some work to finish up. Why don't you head up to bed and I'll come up when I'm done? I'll be quiet, so I won't wake you when I come in."

I kissed her forehead as I stood, then reached for her hands to help her up and send her on her way.

"Okay," she said, more to the floor than to me.

I watched her walk up the stairs and forced myself not to follow her.

15

QUINN

*Y*ou should head to bed? I won't wake you up? What was that?

We were talking and connecting and kissing and it was all more than I ever could have imagined, and then he sent me to bed like a toddler. What did I do wrong?

I thought about last night. Oh, last night. In the tiniest of fantasies that I ever allowed myself to have, I couldn't have dreamt up anything that felt so life-altering and emotionally exhilarating than what we did in his bed.

I opened up to him, physically and emotionally. I let him in.

Then I was being sent to bed without dessert. Seriously?

Devon made me feel things that were crazy and new to me. Each time I saw him, I wanted to be closer to him, to feel him next to me. I wanted the closeness that I shunned away from with everyone else. I wanted his lips on mine again, and to feel his hands on my body, roaming and exploring again. I wanted. That feeling of desire was all so unfamiliar.

I spent some time swimming in his massive tub, brushed my teeth, and washed my face. I grabbed my normal shorts and a tank top to put on, because who did I have to impress? Then I crawled into bed and tried not to think about how hurt I was that Devon wasn't next to me.

Trying to distract myself from thoughts of Devon, I focused on trying to understand what was going on with my car and the roses. While I felt completely safe in Devon's home, I needed to find out who was doing this and put a stop to it. It was time to get back to my normal life. Flying under the radar was a life goal of mine for years, so I struggled to come up with who would be so angry with me they would feel the need to do these things to scare me.

Heather came to mind first. I didn't understand her relationship with Devon because that kind of connection was foreign to me. Although it only took a few weeks of being with him for me to feel possessive of his time, even though he wasn't mine. She made it clear to me I was standing in her way. Her entitlement concerned me, but I didn't know if she would do something malicious to get what she wanted.

I was ready to cross Preston off my list. He thought too much of himself. If a girl didn't respond to his advances, I felt he would just assume there was something wrong with her and move on to the next woman. I didn't see him retaliating. It didn't feel right to me that he would have done those things.

The only other person I knew of with any negative feelings towards me was my father, but he was in prison, and would be for the rest of his life, so I didn't have to put him on my list of suspects.

After another twenty minutes of going through all the people I knew, I ran out of ideas. I trusted that Matthew and the police would do their job and find out who was doing this so I could get back to my normal life.

But that freed my mind up to go back to thinking about Devon. Devon, who rejected me moments ago. His rejection hurt more than I expected and tears welled in my eyes. I curled up on my side and let the tears fall silently on my pillow.

The door to Devon's bedroom opened, and he tip-toed into his room. I tried my hardest to get the tears to stop and pretend to be sleeping.

In the darkness, I felt him lift the covers on his side and slide in. Then, he surprised me be moving over to my side and wrapping his body around mine from behind. His warmth was so reassuring and so frustrating at the same time.

His arm drew me in tighter to his chest and I could feel him put his hand near my face on my pillow. He sat straight up, leaned over to his nightstand, and turned the light on.

"Quinn, what's wrong?" he asked in a panicked voice as he rolled me over onto my back.

He looked at the pillow and the remnants of my tears.

"Your pillow is wet. Why are you crying? What happened?"

I sat up and looked him in the eyes, because I didn't want to be fearful around him like I was around others. I wanted to be strong and confident around him, even if I didn't feel it yet.

"Quinn, you're scaring me. What's going on?"

I just needed to be honest with him.

"Promise not to laugh or judge me."

"I would never do that to you."

I gathered my courage and blurted it out.

"I thought you were attracted to me. Well, I hoped at least. Then, you dismissed me downstairs, it felt...I don't know. Maybe I made it out to be more than it was, and that's on me. But when you went so cold and sent me away, it hurt."

He had a look of shock on his face that I needed to fix,

because I was making everything so awkward. I kept rambling, as if that would magically fix everything.

"I'm not expecting anything from you and I'm grateful for all you've done for me. I didn't mean to make last night into more than it actually was. Let's get some sleep and things will be normal in the morning. I promise."

Even though the conversation was extremely uncomfortable, I was so proud of myself for speaking honestly, if not a little defensively. I didn't hide from a difficult situation, which was a big deal for me.

He looked at me for a moment, then leaned forward and took me into his arms.

"The last thing I would ever want to do is hurt you. I didn't mean to make you feel rejected when I suggested you go to bed. That's the last thing I would want. I did that to protect you."

"I don't understand."

"Quinn, I want you so much more than you will ever understand. I walked away from you tonight because I was trying to respect you and take things slowly. I love kissing you so much that thoughts of carrying you up here and making love to you were all I could think about. But I don't want you to feel rushed. We need to take our time. I needed some distance from you for a little while to calm myself back down."

His words. Were they words that I could trust? I desperately wanted to trust them. I wanted it all to be true. But trusting was hard for me. Could I open myself up to the hurt that would most definitely come if he were playing with me?

I drew back from his embrace to look at him while I spoke, feeling the need to be bold and confident for once in my life. "Don't pull yourself away from me or slow yourself down. I feel things for you too, Devon. And I know I'm about as inexperienced as they come, so you'll just have to teach me, but I have always been an exceptional student."

His smile grew. "Well, I did consider being a teacher once upon a time."

Heat flooded through me.

"But I think we should take this slowly. It's important to me that what we have, or could have, isn't only physical."

My heart fell a little, and my expression didn't hide it well.

"Don't frown like that. You're killing me. I think we might have something special here, Quinn, and I don't want to mess this up."

I've always been a logical person. My father took away my opportunity to be carefree and wild. So, the logical part of me completely understood what he was saying and appreciated his willingness to take his time with me. But there was a new side of me coming out I didn't realize existed, and that part of me wanted me to tell him that slow wasn't what I wanted. That new side of me wanted more of what we had last night. She was shouting for it at the top of her lungs, drowning out the logical side of me.

"So, how slow are we talking?"

I leaned into him and gently kissed his lips.

"Oh, Quinn, you are killing me. I'm worried about my ability to stop myself with you. It was so hard, literally so hard, last night. I had to go take a cold shower and take care of my…situation. But I would continue to do that each night if it meant I got to taste you again."

The mental images he gave me made me wet, and I blushed. The thought of him in the shower taking care of himself gave me an idea.

"What if I helped you take care of your problem? I don't want to be greedy and take all the fun for myself. Show me how to…help your situation. Wouldn't that be an excellent compromise?" I smiled my biggest grin, as if I had just come up with a plan to cure cancer.

"Yes. That's the best idea I've heard in a long time." He said, then adjusted his sleep pants, drawing attention to the growing bulge there.

"Maybe you should show me now, since it looks like there's a teacher's aide available?" I said as I gazed at his pants.

His answer came as a kiss. Not a soft, getting-things-warmed-up kind of kiss, but rather an I-need-you-right-now-and-I-can't-stop-myself kind of kiss.

I needed to feel him. Guessing at how things worked, I ran my hand from his chest down his abs to the waistband of his sleep pants. I stopped and pulled away from his lips to look for any hesitation. There was only *GO* written on his face.

I slid my hand into his pants and found he wasn't wearing boxers. His skin felt soft as I worked my way down. Surrounded by short prickly hairs, he was rigid under my touch. My mind struggled to comprehend. He felt so soft but so hard at the same time. There was a lot to wrap my hand around. And he was so long. I gasped. There was no way Troy was that big. How would that ever fit inside me?

I was thankful at that moment that he slowed things down. I was about to have a panic attack trying to logic out how he and I would fit together, then I felt his hand on mine. He wrapped my fingers tighter around his girth and guided my hand back and forth over his length.

As if he could read my mind, he whispered into my ear, "Don't worry, you can trust me. I would never hurt you."

I took a breath and put my trust in this man.

Together, we moved my hand back and forth and back and forth and I forgot about everything else. His hand guided me to make swirling motions with my palm on the head of his cock. The sticky wetness at the tip smeared over every inch I touched and it was so tantalizing. My desire was growing and my fear subsiding. My only want was to please him.

I pulled my hand from his pants, which startled him. But I needed to see him, to watch what I was doing.

Grabbing both sides of his sleep pants in my hands. I lowered them as gently as I could, but I didn't quite clear the tip as I pulled. I couldn't contain the giggle that escaped when his cock bounced up and down.

"Oh, you think that's funny, huh?"

"I'm sorry. I do."

"Well, I'll remember that in the future."

He laid back on the bed and kicked his pants off completely. He was magnificent to look at. His muscles flowed from his shoulders, down to his abs that formed a V leading down to his powerful thighs. I wanted to run my hands over every inch of him.

Still unsure about what to do, I wrapped my fingers around him again and moved up and down. I was always an exceptional student, so I knew I could learn to please him, if only I could find the courage to ask.

"I'm…uh…kind of new at this. Tell me what to do. I want this to be good for you."

He wrapped his hand over mine and guided my rhythm. He deeply inhaled as our hands brushed over the tip and groaned a little when our hands reached the base. His eyes were closed and he tipped his head back as we continued, slowly increasing the pace. Watching him was doing something to me. I wanted so much more.

"Fuck, Quinn, I'm so close," he said after I removed his hand from mine and sped up my movements.

I was so emboldened by his reaction that I took a chance with something else new to me.

I slowed my hand and leaned forward over him. There was a growing need inside me to know how he tasted, so I reached my tongue out and licked the tip. Devon bucked his hips so hard I lost my balance and bounced back on the bed.

I looked and saw surprise on his face. But there was longing there too.

"Quinn."

My breathy name on his lips encouraged me. The look of lust in his eyes gave me confidence to continue.

With my hand in the middle of his chest, I pushed him back down on the pillows and wrapped my hand around his length. Slowly, I moved my hand back up and down. Leaning forward again, I licked his tip again and watched his reaction. It was so perfect.

After a few more licks, I put my lips around the head and sucked like it was a lollipop. He swung his arm to the side and hit the bed.

"That feels so amazing, Quinn. I'm going to come. I can't hold back any longer," he warned.

I continued to bob my head up and down. Because of his size, I couldn't take him deep into my throat, but Devon didn't seem to mind. I could feel him jerking in my mouth and then warm, salty fluid hit the back of my throat. Not knowing what to do, I kept going until it stopped and I could feel him going limp in my hand.

He pulled me up to his chest, which was heaving from being out of breath.

"Did I do okay?" I asked hesitantly.

"Oh, my god. Quinn, you nearly killed me. Yes, you did better than okay." He smiled down at me.

"With this being new for you, I have to ask, where exactly did you learn how to do that?" he asked.

"Liv is pretty detailed in her dating stories, and she is

always leaving magazines around the house and they can get pretty graphic. I might have read one or two of them."

"Well, thank goodness for Cosmo! Now, this is the one and only time that I will allow breaking the golden rule." He laughed and pulled me tight into his side.

"And what rule is that?" I asked.

"The rule where the lady always comes first, and preferably second and third too."

I blushed. It felt like such an intimate conversation to be joking about. I liked how he was still relaxed and fun. I thought sex was supposed to be so serious.

But his rule was apparently vital to him because he spent the next hour making me come three times. Once with his hand and twice more with his mouth. I was positive I wouldn't be able to move again for a week. Exhausted, I fell asleep in his arms, which had quickly become my favorite place to be.

DEVON

*T*he police didn't have any leads on who was harassing Quinn, so she continued to stay at my house. The days flew by and we fell into a comfortable routine. I made us breakfast each morning, and we discussed our plans for the day while we ate. We spent the days working from my house. She would pull something together for lunch and bring it to me in my office so we could both take a break with each other. After work, we ordered in dinner or cooked something together and spent the evening talking and laughing at stories. She never got too deep into her past, but I loved hearing the happy stories she had with her close group of friends from college.

She invited me to join her and her friends for her birthday celebration in a couple of weeks. Her actual birthday fell on Tuesday, but they couldn't all fit it in their schedules to celebrate that day, so it looked like Quinn would be free to spend her birthday with me.

Even though there weren't any more incidents like the roses or the car, neither of us brought up the topic of her moving back to her place. That gave us all the time in the world to get to know more about each other. I wasn't about to suggest we go back to seeing each other once a week for the project meetings.

Each night, we went to bed together and found new ways to please each other in almost every way imaginable. But, even though I wanted to be inside her more than anything else, we were taking that part slowly. And as frustrating as it was, not having sex with Quinn was quickly becoming one of my favorite things to do. I could explore her body for years and never get enough. And, with each night, she became bolder and more adventurous.

Saturday morning, I woke her by sucking on her nipple and bringing her to an orgasm with my fingers. When she came down, I reminded her we needed to go to Heather's studio to look at a piece she found for the January exhibit.

Heather called me Friday to let me know about a painting she found for the project and asked me to stop by her studio to check it out. Then she suggested that we get drinks afterwards. I made it crystal clear that I wasn't interested in drinks with her, and that Quinn would be joining me to check it out, since this was her project. Heather was annoyed by that but handled it better than I expected. I hoped that meant she had accepted that we weren't going to rekindle our old relationship.

After barely a month with Quinn, I realized how much had been missing when I was with Heather. Yes, Heather and I had sexual chemistry, but I didn't enjoy the rest of my time with her. We didn't laugh like Quinn and I did. We had little in common, so conversations were sparse and superficial. Quinn and I could stay up all night talking. Heather and I lacked a connection that I didn't believe existed out in the real world until I met Quinn.

Heather greeted us when we arrived at the studio, unlocking the door, since we were there before opening, and shaking hands with both of us. She held mine a little too long for my comfort.

"Quinn, you are absolutely going to love the piece I found. It's an Arthur Leary landscape of Dells Mill. I have it on loan from the owner through the exhibit." She preened as she spoke, looking for praise.

She brought us to the front window, where she had it on an easel. There, we found a picturesque painting of an old red mill next to a waterfall. It was a fall painting with the trees behind the water painted in the most vibrant reds, yellows, and oranges. His work was so believable that it felt like the water was truly moving over the edge of the falls. Quinn was breathless as she stared at it. I was breathless watching her.

"Devon, darling, would you mind terribly helping me move a crate while Quinn admires the painting?"

I did mind, because I didn't want to miss a moment of Quinn enjoying the artwork, but I nodded. I leaned into Quinn and told her I would be right back, then I placed a gentle kiss on her cheek and walked away.

"Well, that was cozy. Is there something going on between you two I should know about?" Heather asked as she led me to the loading dock.

"Heather, we aren't together anymore, so there isn't anything in my life you need to know about. But, yes, Quinn and I are together."

Wearing her skin-tight red pencil skirt, white silk top, and red stilettos, she stopped and turned to me with a tear in her eye.

"Why would you do that to me, Devon? You know we're meant to be together. I understand we're taking some time apart because I was inconsiderate, but you don't have to hurt me by dating little goody-two-shoes out there to show me what I had. I know now, and I won't take you for granted again. Can we please move past this little lesson you're trying to teach me and get back to where we were?"

Fuck. My temper raged inside me.

Was she honestly so self-absorbed to think I was seeing Quinn just to make sure she knew what a good thing she had? That was crazy. But, not as crazy as her thinking we were meant to be and somehow destined to get back together.

"Heather, you weren't inconsiderate. You were fucking my friend in my bed while you were supposed to be watching my cat. That's not inconsiderate. That is betrayal. And, honestly, I couldn't be more grateful that you did it. You and I didn't belong together. If you hadn't fucked Preston, I would never have been available to start something with Quinn, and that would have been a genuine tragedy. Because we have something great starting."

She went from teary-eyed to angry in a heartbeat.

"You aren't going to have something great with her. You're going to realize that you miss me and come crawling back to me because we belong together. Even your parents agree. So, I'm going to let you have this little dalliance so you can get it out of your system and we can be even for Preston. Then, when you realize your mistake, I'm going to take you back and we will never speak of this again. But the longer you take to come to your senses, the more begging I'm going to make you do when you're ready to come back. Is that understood?"

I didn't know what to say to get through to her that we were over. The fire in her eyes made me wondered if she could be the one responsible for the troubles Quinn had encountered. As I was about to make another attempt at correcting her misbeliefs, I heard a crash, followed by a scream and the gunning of an engine.

"Quinn" I screamed as I raced back to the front of the

studio.

Quinn stood, surrounded by glass from the shattered front window. All the color drained from her face.

Looking around her, I saw a brick laying on the ground, DIE QUINN painted on it in red.

"Don't move," I told Quinn, who was standing there in a state of shock. She wasn't crying, which I gave her credit for because that would have unnerved most people. She stood there, staring off. I knew I needed to get her out of here.

I walked over to her, the crunch of the glass under my shoes. When I reached her, she turned and looked at me. Confusion spread across her face, then she snapped out of it and the tears came. I picked her up in my arms and carried her away from all the broken glass. I put her down in the chair by the receptionist's desk and told her to wait there.

"Heather, call the police. Ask for Olivia Fletcher or Officer Matthew Hadaway. Tell them what happened." She looked truly frightened by what happened in her studio that I felt confident believing she wasn't the one fucking with Quinn.

I went back to Quinn and held her tightly while she cried. She kept asking, "Who hates me this much?" But I didn't have an answer for her.

She grew rigid in my arms and took a step back. Her tears stopped, and she looked like she was steeling herself for battle. She wiped her eyes and announced to me that she wouldn't be afraid anymore. It was time to find who behind all of this.

I made a call to Sarah, the private detective I hired, and she showed up at the studio.

Quinn did a great job recalling all the details she could for Sarah and Officer Hadaway. She didn't see the car for long, but the driver was a large man and he hung outside the driver's window of his black SUV when he threw the brick at her. She didn't catch the license plate, but she gave a pretty good description of the man driving.

Under instructions from Matthew, she called Olivia to fill her in on everything that had happened. When she was done, I suggested we call it a day and head back to my place instead of going to the farmers market like we had planned.

That seemed to shake her out of the daze she was in.

"No. I won't let this guy scare me away. I'm not going to change my life because some guy thinks scaring me is fun. Now, I would like to go to the farmers market like we planned and then go back to your place so you can teach me how to make soup. Can we do that?"

I loved her strength. She wasn't going to be pushed around. It was so hot, too. Although, everything she did was hot. How could I say no to her? I knew right then that there was nothing I would deny her. She held power over me and it didn't bother me at all.

So, we went to the farmers market and walked hand in hand through the aisles as we picked up fresh produce to make chicken noodle soup. I also picked up a bouquet of fall flowers and Quinn blushed when I gave them to her. It became my life's goal to do everything possible to put that smile on her face. I would do anything to see it over and over. She took my hand when she saw an artist that had paintings she wanted to check out.

They spent thirty minutes talking about the artwork and the artist was beaming at Quinn's praises. There was one painting of a wide-open field that spoke to Quinn, so she bought it. I tried to buy it for her, but she said art required sacrifice and she wanted to sacrifice for that painting.

I didn't believe her, but Quinn was right when she tried to explain how bad a cook she was. It surprised me that someone as accomplished as she was didn't even know how to chop a carrot. But, as she had pointed out to me in the past, she was a good student, and excelled when I showed her how. She was radiating happiness as the soup came together. Watching her take pride in her creation was everything.

We did the dishes in companionable silence. There was something on her mind, but I'd learned in our time together that she needed to tell me things in her own time.

When we were done, I asked her if she wanted to watch one of her reality shows. She turned to face me and shook her head.

"Would you like to work on our puzzle?"

She took a step towards me and shook her head again.

"Good book that you want to read?"

She took another step and shook her head one more time.

Quinn never started things in the bedroom. I didn't have to do more than kiss her and she was all in, but she never took the first step. With the coy smile on her face, I wondered if this was her making a move.

"Well, Quinn, what would you like to do?" I asked as I took a step forward, bridging the last of the distance between us.

She reached up and put her hands on each side of my waist and said words that knocked me out.

"Devon, I would like you to take me upstairs and make love to me. No more holding back."

That shocked me. We were definitely moving in that direction, but I thought she would need more time before she was ready.

Was this the trauma of the day messing with her? Would she regret this when the shock wore off? I wanted to throw caution to the wind and race her upstairs immediately, but I needed to know she was ready.

"Are you sure, Quinn? I know it's been a big day today. Does that have something to do with this?" I waited hopefully for her answer.

"Yes. It does."

My heart sank.

"It made me realize I'm alive and I don't have to be afraid to live. I'm not asking you to do this because I'm in shock or anything like that. All my mental faculties are in order, if that's what you're worried about. I'm asking you to do this because I feel something for you, Devon. Something overwhelming that I haven't felt before. I don't want to live my life in fear or shame anymore. I want to share this with you because I trust you."

She stared up at me, waiting for my answer.

Instead of words, I leaned down, took her face in my hands and put my lips on hers.

I've wanted this moment from the first time our lips touched. If I was honest with myself, I would probably admit I wanted this from the first time I held her in my arms, after she ran into me. There was something that felt so right about having her in my arms.

Leaning forward a little more, I wrapped an arm around her bottom and lifted her up. She instinctively wrapped her legs around my waist. Not breaking the kiss, I carried her up the stairs and to my bed.

Setting her down on the edge of the bed, I had to let her go. She started to take her top off, but I stopped her.

"No, let me do that." As thrilling it was to have her trust me enough to take her shirt off in front of me, when she was so embarrassed to do it only a short time ago, I wanted to be the one to undress her.

Moving her further up the bed, I lifted the hem of her shirt halfway up to her perfect breasts. I kissed each scar and all the warm skin around them. Lifting her shirt over her head, I worked my way up to her light pink lacy bra, pulling one cup down. The moment I put my mouth on her nipple, she arched her back pushing her breast closer to me.

"Devon, hurry."

"That's not going to happen, beautiful. You're going to get everything I want to give you to make this a night you'll never forget."

Unhooking her bra from behind, I slid it off her tiny frame as she laid back on the bed. She looked so delicate and fragile, but I knew that wasn't the case. She was strong.

"Quinn, you are so perfect," I said as I admired her laying before me.

Working her breast with my mouth, I slid my hand down her smooth stomach and into her panties. She was so wet already. Pulling my hand out, I brought her wetness to my mouth and licked it off, savoring the taste. Her gray eyes grew stormy as she watched. I couldn't stop myself from kissing her pale, plump lips again as I returned my hand to her heat.

"Devon." My name came off her lips like a whisper and made my cock twitch.

"Yes, Quinn? Tell me what you need."

"Devon, I need more. I need everything."

I was happy to oblige.

It didn't take long for her to reach her peak as I circled her clit while moving two fingers in and out of her slick opening. Feeling her soft thighs squeeze together as my fingers continued moving, she reached the edge of a powerful orgasm. Watching her fall over the edge and then come down was fascinating.

She laid naked in front of me, breathing hard, as I worked her pants and panties down her legs. With her shiny, soft, brown hair fanned out around her, she was angelic. I made quick work of undressing myself and reached over to my nightstand to grab a condom.

"Are you…clean?" she asked, hesitantly.

"I am. I tested after Heather cheated on me, and honestly,

I haven't been with anyone since. But that isn't the only reason for this," I said as I held up the condom.

"I'm on the pill," she blurted out quickly. "I have been for years because I have difficult periods. I, um, was, um, just thinking. Never mind. Never mind what I was thinking."

She trusted me enough to want to go without a condom. What did I do to deserve this beautiful woman? I didn't know how long I would last without one, though. It'd been a long time for me and my desire for her was raging. But the idea of feeling all of her was more than I could take.

"God, Quinn, it would make me so happy to have nothing between us our first time, but are you sure?"

"I'm sure, Devon. This is what I want. All of it. I want to feel all of you," she said as she nodded and bit her bottom lip.

I could tell she was nervous. Knowing this was only the second time she's done this, I worried that she wasn't ready.

"Stop looking at me like I don't know what I want. I'm ready. I want to do this. I want to do this with you tonight. You're not taking advantage of me. I'm literally begging you for this. This is what I want."

I believed her. She was ready, and I would be a fool to deny her anything.

I positioned myself between her legs and parted them slightly.

"I'm going to take this slowly, okay?"

Leaning forward, I kissed her lips as I entered her. Her warmth was sensational. I slid in further, letting her adjust to my size. She was so tight around me I knew I wouldn't last long. But I would make up for that with another round later.

Each inch made her moan, which was the sexiest sound I'd ever heard.

Moments later I was fully inside her and we stayed like that as I kissed her sweet lips. I could have died in that moment and felt like my life was complete.

Slowly I started moving in and out, then increased my pace. I wanted her to come from this more than I wanted anything for myself. Her moans let me know I was on the right track. I reached between us and rubbed circles on her clit, and she went off. Feeling her wrap around me like a vise, I couldn't hold on any longer. I came with her, holding her as she shook beneath me and around me. It was the best feeling.

Trying not to crush her, I rolled off to her side and onto my back, but kept her with me. I looked into her face, and she was exhausted. She could barely keep her eyes open. Even though I wanted another round, I knew I needed to give her some time. I helped clean her up and curled up back in bed with her. Her head rested on my shoulder, and the smell of her mint shampoo was comforting. She was lazily making slow patterns on my chest with her petite fingers. It was so relaxing and peaceful. What did I do to deserve this kind of happiness?

We laid there, slowly touching each other and discussing plans for her birthday party with her friends next week. Everything about that moment felt so natural, like we'd done that a hundred times before. It all felt so right.

Her trust in me was the greatest gift. I didn't want to take advantage of it, but I wanted to see if she felt ready to give me more of herself than just her body.

"Quinn, beautiful?" She looked up at me, almost drunk on exhaustion.

"Yes."

"You trusted me with your body. Will you trust me with more of you?"

"What do you mean?"

"Will you tell me what happened to you after your dad's trial?"

Her body stiffened next to mine, and she didn't speak for a long time. I was afraid I'd pushed her too far.

17

QUINN

I was floating on cloud nine. Physically and emotionally drained, in the best possible way. Why would he try to ruin something so perfect with questions of my past? Couldn't we stay in the moment and enjoy it? If I told him about what happened, his opinion of me would change. He would see there was no future for us. Would he question what we started? Would he change his mind about being with me when he found out I wasn't good enough to be with the CEO of Swift Corp? Someone would eventually recognize me and say something malicious out in public. He didn't deserve that. But it wasn't right to keep what people truly thought of me from him just so I could continue on in this fairytale world for a little longer.

His hand glided up and down my arm. Maybe if I didn't look at him, if I didn't see his face when I told him my story, maybe then I could get through it. So, I stayed tucked in his arm, maybe for the last time, enjoying the slow rhythmic rising and lowering of his chest as he breathed, and I went back to a time I wanted to forget.

"My grandparents all passed away, most before I was even

born. I didn't have any aunts or uncles. My mom was dead and my dad was in prison. I didn't have family left. Aunt Betty, my neighbor across the street, took me in after the police took my father into custody. She worked it out with the courts where she could be my guardian until I turned eighteen. Aunt Betty was my whole world while I was in the darkest part of my life. If it wasn't for her, I don't think I would be here right now."

His arm tightened around my body as I continued.

"I took the last few months of my freshman year off while I healed from my injuries and tried to recover from the trauma. Aunt Betty talked the school into letting me do my work from her house, so I didn't fall behind. Some of my friends visited me in the hospital, but it was completely awkward. They stopped coming around pretty quickly, and I don't blame them. It hurt that my best friend, Amy, stopped coming by, but I even forgave her. I wasn't the same person, and I didn't want to be around people. The trial was that summer. I was in counseling the whole time and when the trial was over, I was finally in a good enough mental place to start my life again. I was ready to reconnect with my friends and find my new normal."

I paused and took a breath, still not looking at Devon. I just needed to get through the rest and be done with it.

"My first day back at school was scary. I didn't know what to expect. Since I hadn't kept in touch with anyone, I didn't know what people thought about what happened. It quickly became clear to me that the small-town gossips didn't view me as a victim. Someone started a rumor that I was actually the one who killed my mom and that my dad took the fall for me because he was afraid of me. Since I wasn't there to stop it, that rumor grew for months. Kids whispered and pointed wherever I went. That continued for the first few weeks. I ate alone at lunch. None of my old friends would have anything to do with me. I spent a lot of time hiding in the bathroom. Teenagers can be vicious."

Remembering the past brought tears to my eyes, but I tried to keep them from falling.

"Homecoming week, when all the kids were playing pranks on each other, I came to school and there was a knife stabbed through my locker door. Aunt Betty tried to get the principal to do something about the bullying, but there was nothing he could do. Nobody was claiming credit for the prank. That was how he looked at it. A prank, not bullying. 'Kids will be kids,' is what he told her."

Devon tensed and squeezed me tighter, but he let me continue. I think he realized I wouldn't start again if I stopped.

"Each week, it was some new form of torment. One week it was 'Murderer' spray painted on my new locker. Another week it was posters made to look like a police mugshot with my face on them. The kids stopped whispering and were straight out shouting 'Killer Quinn' when I walked by and telling me I needed to be institutionalized for my deranged behaviors. Aunt Betty tried to work it out where I could switch school districts, but no other school would take me, so I had to stay there. 'Killer Quinn' became a thing, and I heard it daily. Parents were coming to school to talk to the principal about my disruption in the school. They said they didn't feel safe with their children in the same school as me. The rumors became fact in my school, so much so even the teachers and the principal started treating me with caution."

The first tear escaped and rolled down my cheek onto his chest. I wondered what he thought of me. I wondered if he questioned my part in my mother's murder or if I really was defective. By the end of my time at that school, I questioned it myself.

"The pranks and the bullying continued for weeks. They

progressively got worse. The last one was so bad that Aunt Betty finally pulled me out of school."

After I paused a little too long, Devon asked, "Tell me about it, Quinn. Let it all out."

"I got a note that was supposedly from my art teacher asking me to go to the art room during lunch. It was the only place in the school where I felt safe, so it was a relief to me to have someplace to go during lunch. When I walked in, the lights were off, so I turned them on. When I did, three of the students started a reenactment of the murder the way they thought it happened. The worst part was my former best friend, Amy, was pretending to be me. She had a prop knife from the theatre department and was pretending to stab a girl in the junior class. They even had fake blood and police sirens. The whole thing was surreal. When the kid playing my dad pretended to stab Amy in the stomach to stop her from stabbing the girl playing my mom, she set off fake blood pellets under her shirt. I ran as fast as I could to Aunt Betty's house and I never went back. But they recorded it and it was all over social media."

Reliving my most humiliating moments for him caused a pain in my chest. I couldn't stop the tears, but I needed to finish, so I continued on as the tears streamed down my face.

"Aunt Betty homeschooled me for the rest of high school. It was just the two of us. She let me lose myself in studying art as I healed. I spent the next three years doing more counseling. It helped me build the courage to go to college when I turned eighteen. I didn't want to, but Aunt Betty convinced me I would regret it if I let those kids have control over my choices. Not living my life would mean I let them win."

Devon sat up and brought me with him, pulling me onto his lap. His warmth and strength were soothing to my soul in that moment.

"My beautiful Quinn," he murmured into my hair as he

pressed me closer to his chest. "I hate that you went through all they put you through. I wish I could get my hands on each one of those kids. They are horrible people."

It was a relief to me that he didn't buy into the stories those kids told, but he didn't understand how it still tainted me and that could carry over to him someday. A strong fear grew inside me. I was being selfish. Being with me was so bad for him.

"Devon, it didn't end there. It still hasn't ended. You should do the smart thing and distance yourself from me before this affects you negatively."

"What are you talking about, Quinn?"

"People who know me as 'Killer Quinn' still cross my path all the time. They were at college with me. Someone even yelled 'Killer Quinn' when I crossed the platform to get my college diploma. It happened just a month ago at the grocery store. This thing hasn't ended. It won't end. If you stay with me, someone is going to recognize me and shout it out and it could happen anywhere. Then your character will be questioned just for being with someone like me. There is a reason I keep to myself and don't let many people into my life. It's to protect others. I need to protect you, too."

"There is no way I'm letting you run from me because you think you're protecting me. We have something. Don't you see that? I don't care what anyone says. I need you in my life. We need to see where this thing between us goes."

He spoke with such fire in his voice that I had no choice but to believe him. When he finished, he didn't give me the chance to argue with him. He pulled my face to him and kissed me like he was trying to kiss away anything bad that has ever happened to me. Like he was trying to heal me. But he wasn't listening to me.

"Tell me you don't feel the same as I do and I will walk away without hesitation."

I couldn't lie to him, so I didn't say anything.

"I didn't think you could." Then he pulled me closer to him again and his lips were on mine. His kisses made me believe we could conquer anything if we were together. But I knew I was fooling myself.

"Stop," I whispered.

He stopped immediately.

"You don't get it. You being romantically connected to me could ruin your reputation. It could come back to hurt your father. It could hurt your company. I can't let that happen. Gossip and rumors can get out of control. Lies get believed. Nobody cares about the truth, Devon. I won't do that to you."

I could see he was still ready to fight for this, so I told him the rest.

"Three years ago, Olivia was up for a promotion. She was the most qualified candidate for the position and it was clear she would get the job. I went into the office to meet her for lunch one day. When I was standing by her desk, a man walked by in handcuffs, being led by another officer. He started shouting about how he shouldn't be arrested if they weren't going to arrest 'Killer Quinn.' He kept going on and on about how I was a murderer walking free and it was a waste to arrest him for drugs when they had a murderer right in front of them. I was mortified, but Olivia stood up for me. She got in his face and shouted that he was full of shit and he needed to shut his fucking mouth. She went off on him, in typical Olivia fashion."

I hurt just remembering that day.

"After that, her boss called her into his office to talk about what happened. He said he was asking around about me and wanted to know what he could learn about my part in my mother's murder. He was considering it a possibility that I could have done it. Olivia refused to cooperate with him and she didn't get the promotion."

I put my hand on his cheek and turned his face towards me, so we were looking directly into each other's eyes.

"That is how powerful this lie can be. That's how much damage it can do to someone just for being friends with me. It would only be worse for someone I was dating. I need you to understand this."

"But you and I know the truth and that's all that matters. Fuck everyone else, Quinn. They aren't important."

He wasn't getting it. I needed to get him to understand.

"Think about what happens to your dad in the next election when his opponent grabs onto the story that the Golden Son of the Governor is dating a suspected murderer." I was practically shouting. I climbed out of bed and stood in his bedroom yelling at him.

"If we ever become public, there would be plenty of people willing to talk to the press about me. These aren't good people, Devon. They don't make choices based on right and wrong. They think it's okay to hurt someone as long as it isn't them getting hurt. Is that what you want?"

He gave me all his attention, but then, out of nowhere, he started laughing.

I crossed my arms in front of my chest and glared at him.

"Do you think this is funny, Devon?"

That just made him laugh harder.

I could see him trying to contain his laughter and when he finally got himself under control, he spoke.

"Quinn, beautiful Quinn, you are a spitfire. I have never enjoyed being yelled at as much as I'm enjoying you yelling at me right now, completely naked. I think this should be the only way I get reprimanded from now on." Then he broke into laughter again.

I looked down and realized that I was still naked from our lovemaking, and quickly grabbed the comforter off the bed and wrapped it around myself.

"Come on, Quinn?" He smirked. "Are you really going to hide yourself from me now? And, while we're talking about this, are you honestly going to be so cruel to use me for sex and then try to ditch me as soon as you got what you wanted? I never thought of you as a user." He was sitting upright on the bed, grinning at me and still laughing.

I knew he was teasing me, but that was what it looked like. I did just sleep with him and then try to push him away. What kind of horrible person was I? He should have been seriously mad at me, but he wasn't. He was taking everything in stride. The ever cool, ever calm and collected Devon that I had come to know and care for.

He stood up, and I felt lightning shoot through my chest when I saw him walking towards me in all his gorgeous nakedness. I wanted to forget everything we were talking about and run my hands over his tight muscles. I needed to protect him, but my resolve was slipping.

When I felt his hands on my arms, wrapping around to my back to pull me to him, my fear and anger melted away. As he held me tight to his muscular chest, I felt like maybe we could get through this. Maybe it could be okay. Maybe, over time, people would stop harassing me and Killer Quinn could be put to rest.

I leaned into him and let his strength comfort me.

"Quinn, you need to trust me. And I know trust is hard for you, but you need to let me in." He ran his hand over my hair to calm me. "I understand all the risks you're concerned about, but they aren't enough to make me walk away from you. I don't know what it is, but I think you and I have some-thing. If you run from it now, we'll never get to find out what this thing between us is, or could be."

"Devon, I don't know how to do this. This is all so new. I just don't want you to be hurt because of me. I'm okay alone."

He stepped back and tipped my face up to his. He stood

there, not saying anything for the longest time. Just looking at me.

"Do you feel something for me? Because I definitely feel something for you."

I couldn't lie to him. "I do."

"Is there a part of you that wants to see where we could go?"

Again, I didn't have it in me to lie to him. "There is."

"Then that's what we're going to do. We aren't going to worry about your past. We're going to focus on the future and nothing else."

He leaned down and kissed me. It started off soft and gentle, but it quickly grew urgent and demanding. I wrapped my arms around his neck as he lifted me into his arms and carried me back to bed. As soon as I felt his hand between my thighs, I forgot there could be anything in the world besides the two of us at that moment. Everything else dissolved away.

We spent the evening exploring each other's bodies and then I slept, exhausted, in his arms until morning.

18

DEVON

*T*uesday morning, I snuck out of bed to go make Quinn breakfast for her birthday. My family always did waffles in bed for each other on their birthday, and it felt natural to want to include Quinn in my traditions. I put the waffles on a tray with some bacon, orange juice, and a rose and carried it upstairs. She was right where I left her, laying naked in my bed with only a sheet to cover her. Even after spending hours making love to her last night, it wasn't enough. There was so much more about her I needed to explore. So much more I needed to learn. I wondered how long this feeling would go on.

I felt like a lifetime wouldn't be enough time to take in all of Quinn. I needed to know her thoughts and opinions on everything. With as much as I wanted to spend my time in bed with her, I wanted just as much to spend my time talking and laughing with her. She held a power over me that I couldn't explain but didn't want to lose.

With Quinn, I hated to be away from her for even a moment. When we weren't together, I was wondering what she was doing. When we were sitting together on the couch,

I had to touch her. I had to have some kind of connection between us. Holding her hand, resting my hand on her thigh, or wrapping my arm around her while she lay on my chest. There was something pulling me to her.

As I watched her sleep, I felt a stir. I knew I should wake her up gently and let her enjoy her birthday breakfast, but I was too greedy to let the opportunity pass. I set the tray on my dresser, stripped out of my pajama pants, and gently pulled the sheet off her silky skin. She was ethereal. There was nothing more beautiful than seeing her lay there, naked and relaxed.

Slowly, so not to disturb her quite yet, I slid between her thighs. She stirred, just a little, when I eased her leg, but then she settled back into sleep. A war waged inside me. I needed my mouth on her, but I couldn't stop staring at how beautiful she was when she slept.

Laying down between her legs, I blew a light breath over her perfect pussy. She didn't move. I slid one finger between her lips to part them and followed closely with my tongue. Her taste was better than the finest dining I'd ever experienced. I was obsessed with her. I slowly licked from her bottom up to her clit again, and she moaned quietly. Increasing my intensity woke her up as her hips started grinding against my face. When she was fully awake, she made a startled noise and looked down at me as realization settled in.

"Happy Birthday, Quinn." I smiled up at her.

She pulled my face back between her thighs and moaned as I continued to devour her. As she pressed harder into my mouth, I slipped a finger inside her. It didn't take long for her to be overcome by a powerful orgasm. I lapped up her juices as she came down from it.

I slid up next to her and pulled her to my chest.

"I made you breakfast for your birthday."

"It looks like you've already eaten," she joked, and then blushed when she realized what she said.

I loved how comfortable she was feeling with me and our burgeoning sex life to make a joke about it.

"I did. And it was the best birthday breakfast I've ever had. But now you get yours," I said as I got up and brought her the waffles.

"Devon, this is so wonderful. I've never had breakfast in bed before."

"Well, get used to it, because I kind of like starting my day with breakfast like this."

She blushed, and it was adorable.

We each had our own separate plans for the day. She planned on meeting up with Olivia and Jillian for lunch and I was taking Tate out to lunch. Tate was starting to retreat again and I couldn't let her slip backwards without a fight.

"How about you finish your breakfast and then I help you spend the rest of your birthday morning in bed?"

And that's exactly what we did until I forced us to get up and get ready to go to our separate lunch dates. I deserved an award for my restraint, but Quinn made me seem like a monster for putting a stop to our morning fun.

We walked to our cars to go our own ways. I directed her to my Land Rover and gave her the keys.

"No, Devon. My car is just fine."

"Yes, but someone has already messed with your car once. I'd rather them not see you driving around town. Especially since you refuse to take security with you."

She looked a little guilty about that one. We went round and round about security. She insisted that we'd gone long enough without something happening, so she was fine without it. I still worried about her safety.

"Would you please take my car. It would make me feel better."

I thought we were going to have to go a couple rounds on that one too, but she agreed.

I closed the car door for her, and she rolled down the window. "Ask Tate to join us on Saturday for my party."

"I thought that was something you did with your friends. Are you sure we won't be crashing the party?"

"Not at all. Jillian is bringing Matthew, and Olivia is bringing Trenton. It hasn't been just the five of us for a while."

I didn't like how her voice got rough when she mentioned Trenton. I was going to have to meet him and see what was going on there.

"Plus, I never bring anyone to my party, or theirs for that matter, so it's about time I do."

"Okay, I'll ask her and see if she's free. Say hi to Olivia for me."

She agreed and drove off.

I let Tate pick where we would meet for lunch, which meant we would be eating at Niko's, her favorite Greek place on State Street. She was obsessed with their gyros, so we always ended up there when she got to pick.

I got there first, so I placed our order, making sure to get Tate extra onions on hers, and found us a booth.

She looked exhausted when she walked in. I waved, and she came to the table and sat down. She appeared distracted and not fully with me, but when she saw her food, she snapped out of whatever funk she was in and smiled at me.

"Extra onions. You're the best." She smiled up at me.

"Of course." I smiled back at her and nodded towards her food. "Eat," I said, hoping to get her to relax.

After she had a couple bites and seemed to settle in, I brought up the party.

"So, what are you up to on Saturday?" I asked, knowing full well she didn't go out anymore.

"I have a hot date with a good book."

"How about you stand up your date and come with me to Quinn's birthday party?"

She hesitated, which I took as a better sign than her instant refusal.

"I don't know, Dev. I'm not so great with social situations these days."

"That's why I'm suggesting it. It's just going to be something small with a few of her friends at a bar they like to hang out at. I've met most of them and they're all great people. I think you'll like them. And I'll be there, so you'll know someone. This would be a good chance to try getting out into the world again."

And, knowing exactly how to get her, I added, "It was Quinn's idea. She specifically asked me to invite you."

I had her. I knew it.

"Fine. But I'm driving myself so I can leave when I've had enough."

"Deal. I'll text you the address and the time. Now, tell me what has you looking like you did when Mom told you that you couldn't get a hamster?"

She hesitated, looking down at her food as if she was considering not talking about whatever was on her mind, but I think the weight of whatever was bothering her was more than she could bear on her own.

"Preston stopped by the store this morning."

I saw red. My temper was immediately hot, and I wanted to strangle him. But looking at Tate's face brought me back to earth. My anger wasn't what she needed. She needed her brother to be there for her and listen.

"What did he want?"

"I don't know. He was all over the place. He started by telling me I needed to come back to him. But then he bounced over to questions about you and about Quinn. He wanted to know if you guys were dating and if I knew anything about Quinn." She looked so upset by this. "I didn't tell him anything. You know I'm not that kind of person. I would never do that to you, or to Quinn. She seems like a nice enough person. She shouldn't have to deal with Preston's shit."

I reached my hand across the table to hers. "Tate, I would never think that you were that kind of person. So, what happened?"

"I told him I didn't know much about Quinn and I haven't seen you in a while, so I was the wrong person to ask. Then he moved on to asking me when I was going to come back to him."

"Bastard." I couldn't keep it from slipping out.

"I told him I was never coming back to him and he should leave and stop coming by the store. He left but told me it was only a matter of time before I missed him so much that I would beg him to take me back. He said the longer I took, the harder it was going to be for him to forgive me."

Preston and Heather seemed to be cut from the same cloth. I was furious. What kind of man would treat a woman he supposedly cared for this way? I hated how I didn't see what he was doing to Tate before she told me. And what was with his questions about me and Quinn? That made me uncomfortable. I didn't want Preston around either one of them.

Quinn asked that we not have security at the house, but she didn't specify anything about when we left the house. So, to give me some peace of mind, I had someone watching out for her when she was out alone. I sent him a quick text to make sure she was okay. I got a reply almost immediately saying she was at the restaurant and not having any issues.

I knew she would be upset if she was aware I still had security watching out for her because she thinks nothing happening for three weeks is enough to let her guard down. But I didn't think we're done with this lunatic yet. Someone that upset doesn't give up. And if that someone is Preston, he's going to pay for it.

I was deep in thought when Tate kicked me under the table.

"What was that for?"

"That was for ignoring me for the last two minutes. I asked you how things were going with you and Quinn."

I hesitated because I didn't know how to answer that. Tate spent the last year dealing with depression. How could I tell her about how happy I was? But it didn't matter. She could read my mind.

"I want you to be happy, even if I'm not happy right now. So don't hold back on me or I'll tell Mom," she said with a laugh that eased my anxiety.

"Everything is going great. I'm so happy, Tate. She is such an amazing woman. She's so smart and funny when she lets her guard down. I know you guys are going to love each other. I worry about this guy that's threatening her, though."

"Do you love her?"

"Whoa. Do I love her? That's a big question."

She looked at me like she was going to sit there and wait me out for an answer. Some things never change.

"I don't know. I thought I might have loved Heather, but you know how that relationship turned out. And it took me years to even get to a place where I thought it might be possible with her. I've known Quinn for less than two months. Is it possible to love someone that quickly? I feel so much for her, but it's scary to risk that kind of pain again."

Tate kicked me under the table again.

"Seriously? Okay, what was that one for?"

"That was because you're being stupid. Listen to yourself. I feel so much for her, but I don't want to risk hurting again.

That's the dumbest thing I've heard come out of your mouth since that time you tried to convince me bears could tell the difference between boys and girls and that was why I couldn't go camping with you and your friends."

Remembering that brought a smile to my face. She was so frustrated that she couldn't be one of the guys.

"It's not that I'm protecting myself only. She has gone through more in her life than any one person should ever experience. You know Dad's going to run for president one day. I worry that being linked to me will have people digging up her past over and over again. Those are wounds that should be allowed to heal in private."

I had all the reasons in my head why I shouldn't let things go too far with Quinn, but my head wasn't always in charge.

"I feel things for Quinn that I can't deny. Her brilliance makes me want to encourage her to let her creativity go wild with this project. Her personality makes me want to spend all my time with her. She's so beautiful. I want to help her see it in herself. Her kind heart makes me want to protect her from ever hurting again. And she's so caring that I want to make her mine."

Saying the words surprised me. I felt foolish saying these things about a woman because I didn't move fast. I wasn't one to jump into relationships quickly and fall fast. But I did. Quinn brought that out in me. Then it hit me hard.

"Oh, man," I said as I rubbed my hands over my face. "I think I love her."

Tate grinned at me.

"That was the most fun I've had in a long time. Watching your face as you put all the pieces together was priceless. You haven't known her for long. What do you think you're going to do about your feelings?"

That was a great question. But I didn't have an answer for

her, so I ignored it and starting talking about Mom and her leukemia treatments.

Despite being grown adults, Tate and I both needed Mom to beat her cancer. She was the glue for our family. We all still needed her, Dad especially. He wouldn't be in the governor's office without her.

We agreed we would set up a lunch with her sometime soon. Then I looked at my watch and realized I needed to get going if I was going to fit in an extra stop to my day.

I walked Tate to her car and hugged her tightly, not taking her presence in my life for granted anymore. Kissing the top of her head, I told her I loved her and I would see her soon.

I needed to go take care of something.

It only took twenty minutes to cross town and get to where I was going.

I walked into the lobby of Henry Paper and went to the reception desk. It was time Preston Henry Sr. and I had a little chat. Name recognition got me in to see him without any issue.

Mr. Henry knew me from attending events for my dad and a couple of dinners Preston and Tate threw when they first started dating, but this was the first time we discussed anything other than typical party chatter. He came across as an honorable man the few times we interacted, but Preston knew how to put on a show too, so I wasn't sure if that was an inherited trait.

He brought me into his office and offered me a Scotch, which I took, even though it was only the middle of the day.

"Thanks for meeting with me, Mr. Henry."

"No problem, Devon. I've missed seeing you and your family at our parties since Preston and Tate decided to end things. I wish things would have worked out with them. I always thought Tate was a wonderful influence on Preston.

Helped him settle down a bit. But, we can't always get what we want. Now, what can I do for you?"

His comments made it clear to me that he had no idea what went on between his son and my sister. This was going to be a hard conversation to have. I hoped he would believe what I had to tell him.

Our talk lasted about a half an hour. There was a lot about Tate and Preston's relationship and breakup he didn't know about, and he appeared to be balancing between anger that his son treated Tate the way he did, and embarrassment that he didn't know any of it was going on.

Hearing your son did terrible things to a woman had to be hard to take, but Mr. Henry deserved credit for handling it the way he did. He listened intently, asked a few questions, and never tried to pass the blame from Preston to Tate. He earned my respect.

Back in the lobby, he gave me his assurance that Tate wouldn't have to worry about Preston anymore, and I believed him. Preston walked in as his dad was shaking my hand. He was clearly unhappy seeing us together.

"Devon, did we have a meeting today?" he said, trying to sound professional.

"No, today I was here to talk to your dad. We needed to work out a couple of issues together, which we did."

Mr. Henry's smile left his face when he turned to his son. "Yes, son, we had quite the enlightening conversation. Clear your afternoon because you and I are due for a long talk."

"Thank you again, Mr. Henry. I'll make sure to let my dad know how helpful you've been."

With that, I left the two Henrys to work things out between themselves.

19

QUINN

"*H*appy Birthday, Quinny!" Olivia shouted from the doorway of the restaurant as she and Jillian came in.

I stood up as Olivia ran to me like we hadn't seen each other in a year. Her hugs could cure cancer. Even though it had been less than two weeks since I last saw her, and despite talking on the phone daily, it felt like forever since I last hugged her.

She held me out at arm's length and looked me up and down. "You've lost weight."

Jillian pulled Olivia away and hugged me too.

"You're so dramatic, Liv. When did you become an Italian grandmother? She hasn't lost an ounce. Now sit down so we can all catch up."

Olivia stuck her tongue out at Jillian then laughed.

After we ordered, Jillian bounced in her seat like her pants were on fire.

"So, what's going on with you and the hot committee member?" Jillian did some weird thing with her face.

"Did you really just waggle your eyebrows at me?"

She did it again.

"Stop that. It's freaking me out."

So, of course, she did it again. Out of all my friends, Jillian was the silliest. I think it helped her release the stress that comes with being a pediatrician.

"If you give me all the juicy details, I'll stop," and she did it again.

"Fine. I'll tell you whatever you want to know. Just stop doing that. It's creepy."

We all laughed. It felt so good to be with them again.

"Well?"

"Wow, you're so impatient. I don't know exactly what you want to know. He's amazing. I like him…I like him a lot."

I could feel the blush warming my cheeks. I've never talked about my love life like this because I've never had one. I wondered if it would always feel this awkward. But these were my best friends. I knew I didn't have to hide anything from them.

"Okay, I'm excited every time I'm with him. Just sitting on the couch watching a show with him gives me butterflies. I want to be near him all the time. And, seriously, have you seen him? He's so sexy. And yes, we're sleeping together. And, not that I have anything to compare it to, but it's pretty fabulous. I don't even know how to explain the things that he makes me feel. But, wow, I didn't know that it would be like this. Is this normal?"

Jillian smiled and got a dreamy look in her eyes.

"Well I can only speak for myself, but even after three years that's exactly how I would describe how I feel about Matthew. Right down to the sexy part. That uniform gets me all worked up."

She and I laughed, but Olivia stayed quiet.

Living with Olivia for the last decade made us closer than

sisters. We started off sharing a dorm room and then moved into an apartment together. It's been weird not seeing her face regularly. Now that I was there with her in person, I could tell something was off.

Jillian gave me a knowing look that told me she saw it too. Knowing Olivia's history, I had a guess about what was causing her sadness.

"So, how are things with you and Trenton?"

Her expression let me know I hit the nail right on the head.

"It's over, guys. I couldn't take it anymore. You were both right about him being an ass-hat."

I was ecstatic that she was done with Trenton, but I was worried about what pushed her over the edge. For as long as I've known her, she's needed to be in a relationship to be happy. She found some sort of security from it. She wasn't usually the one to leave though, so something bad must have happened.

I took her hand in mine and gave it a light squeeze. Jillian took her other hand.

"Livy, what happened?"

She pulled her hands away from ours and took a deep, calming breath.

"So, you know how I've been saying I wanted to go see that new movie about the woman with amnesia who falls in love with the bad boy in town?"

"Of course, you've been talking about it for weeks. I'm so sorry I haven't been able to go with you."

"No worries, seriously. You've got a lot going on these days. I'm not pressuring you to do anything. That's not where I'm going with this."

She paused to take a sip of her soda.

"Well, I decided I would take the day off yesterday, since I've been working so many hours lately, and treat myself to a me-day. I started at the spa for a massage and a mani/pedi. Then, I decided I would go see the movie by myself and it was exactly what I needed. I was so relaxed and so happy when the movie ended, so I stuck around for the credits because I didn't want my day to end. While I was sitting there, I saw Trenton leaving the theater with his arm around Kimberly, a girl he works with at the gym."

Jillian slapped her hands on the table. "That bastard!"

"He didn't!" I yelled.

"Yes, he did."

"What did you do?" I asked, leaning so far over the table I was practically in the appetizers.

"Well, they didn't notice me, so I followed them out. I watched him walk her to her car and give her a two-minute kiss goodbye. So, when she drove off, I walked right up to him with a smile on my face. He was so surprised to see me there. He started looking around, trying to figure out if I saw what just happened and then said, 'Hey Babe', as if he didn't have his tongue down someone else's throat twenty seconds ago."

I couldn't speak, I was so angry, so Jillian spoke for both of us.

"He's such a fucking jackass."

"I was so mad. So I told him that anything he left at the apartment would be on the sidewalk for him in thirty minutes and he was never to speak to me again."

"What did he say?"

"He begged me to forgive him and give him a second chance. He said Kimberly meant nothing to him and he was only hanging around her because she was the boss's daughter and he wanted to stay solid with him. I got in my car and drove away. I gave him the thirty minutes I said I would, but he didn't go back to our place. So I threw all the stuff he left at the apartment on the sidewalk as soon as I got home, including his Xbox."

I hurt for my best friend.

"Oh, Livy, I'm so sorry. That is just the worst. He's the worst."

"I know, but I should have left him a while ago. I don't know why I didn't."

I wasn't going to kick her while she was down, so I stayed quiet. But I knew she didn't leave him because she's struggled with being alone for as long as I've known her.

"Maybe you should use this time to take a break from dating. Maybe don't dive right into another relationship right away and get to know you and all your awesomeness."

I was pretty sure I saw fear in her eyes.

"I don't know if I can do that. Quinny, I've had a boyfriend since I was sixteen. You know I believe Mr. Right is out there somewhere. How will I find him if I stop looking?"

I reached across the table and took her hand in mine. "Maybe if you stop looking and spend some time figuring out your self-worth, Mr. Right will have time to find you?"

I don't think she believed me, but I think she was finally at the point in her life where she knew something needed to change.

Jillian piped in to give her a shove in the right direction.

"Or maybe you've already met Mr. Right, but you've always been with Mr. Wrong, so you couldn't see it."

"Not this again. Jace and I are just friends and that's the way it has to stay. I can't imagine fucking things up so badly with him and losing our friendship forever. I wouldn't survive that. You guys know that. So it's never going to happen."

With that, she raised her hand and called for our check like the drama queen she was.

She looked defeated.

As amazing as Olivia was, she couldn't see it. Her mom did a lot of emotional damage to her growing up, and Olivia struggled to work through it all.

I would offer to move back home, but I knew she wouldn't let me do that. She's too selfless to put herself first.

We walked out of the restaurant to our cars and Olivia let out a howl when I walked up to the Land Rover.

"Nice upgrade there, Quinny!" Jillian joked.

"It's not an upgrade. Devon said he felt safer if I wasn't driving around in my car because the person that's been messing with me knows my car. It gave him some peace of mind, so I didn't argue with him about it."

Out of nowhere, Olivia burst into tears.

"Livy, what's wrong?"

"I...don't...know," she said in between gasps for air and sobbing. "I'm just...so...happy that...you found...someone wonderful...that cares enough...to drive your crappy car...so he can put you first." She wailed the last part.

In the whole time I've known her, I've only seen Olivia cry twice. Once when she dropped our couch while we were moving into our first off-campus apartment, breaking her pinky toe, and once when the White Stripes officially broke up. Her break-up must have hurt her more than she was letting on.

Jillian and I wrapped her up in a group hug and held her until her sobs subsided.

"Are you okay now?"

"I think so. Fuck, I'm sorry about that. I don't know where that came from. It must be all the shit with Trenton. Crying jag aside, I'm so happy for you and Devon. I feel like these are happy tears."

Squeezing her again, I told her that she would need time to get over this one and I asked her to be kind to herself.

"I'll be better in time for your party on Saturday." She wiped the tears from her cheeks.

"Oh, that's right. I almost forgot to tell you I asked Devon to invite his sister, Tate, to the party. She's had a rough couple of years and a low-key night out would be perfect for her. Do you mind?"

"Of course not. It's your party. She can take Trenton's place."

My heart was breaking for my best friend. I knew her relationship ending was ultimately the best thing for her, but I also knew what she was like after a breakup. She took them hard and took them personally. That was usually when she would start looking for the next guy. I couldn't help but hope this time would be different.

We said our goodbyes, and I got into the Land Rover to drive back home. Holding the steering wheel tight, I had to remind myself that I was driving back to Devon's place, not back home. Spending so much time there, it was starting to feel like home, and I needed to put a stop to that. I was getting too attached to his place, and to him. If I were completely honest with myself, I was even getting too attached to Wasabi too. She spent many hours curled up on my lap.

I didn't want to turn into Olivia and mourn the loss of a relationship. Watching her suffer each time was hard enough. I was afraid to go through that myself. I think it would break me. I needed to keep my heart guarded through this.

Walking into the house, I could smell something wonderful from the kitchen. I put my stuff down in the entry and wandered towards the heavenly smell. Devon stood in the kitchen, wearing a navy blue gingham apron and mixing fluffy white frosting. Three layers of cake sat on a cooling rack on the counter. Something simmered in a pot on the stove, which must have been what I smelled when I came in. His eyes landed on me and a brilliant smile crossed his face. His joy at seeing me was overwhelming.

He put the bowl and spatula down, strode over to me, then he picked me up and swung me around. I squealed in surprise.

He stopped spinning but didn't put me down. He held me up to his level and kissed me sweetly. Fearing falling, I wrapped my legs around his waist and kissed him back like this was how we always greeted each other.

We slowed the kissing, but he still didn't put me down. "Happy Birthday, Beautiful," he said as he walked me to the kitchen counter and set me down on it gently.

"I'm pretty sure you already wished me a happy birthday today." I turned red, remembering how he woke me earlier.

"I did, but it is your birthday for the whole day." He kissed his way up my neck. "So, I feel like celebrating you all day long is not out of the question. Don't you?"

I couldn't think clearly as he switched to the other side of my neck. So much for guarding my heart. I was so gone.

Trying to refocus, I asked, "What is that amazing smell in here?"

"You mean other than me?" he joked. "Well, I'm working on a bolognese sauce for tonight's dinner. And we'll have birthday cake for dessert. But that's not for hours and I can't wait that long to give you your birthday present. So, come with me."

He picked me up off the counter and set my feet on the floor, kissing the top of my head and taking my hand to lead me upstairs.

We reached the guest bedroom and stood in front of the closed door.

"If this is too forward, or if you don't like it, I won't be offended, so please be honest with me and tell me if I went too far. Can you do that for me?"

I was afraid to open the door. I wanted to love anything he would give me, but I also didn't want to tell him if something he did out of the goodness of his heart offended me. But I nodded in agreement and he leaned forward to open the door.

My breath caught when I saw what he had done, and tears flowed from my eyes.

"Oh, Quinn, I'm so sorry. I went too far. I'll take it all back and we can forget this ever happened. Okay?" He wrapped his arms around me from behind and murmured apologies into my hair.

I forced myself to stop crying and turned to him. "I'm sorry, Devon, I love it." To prove it to him, I turned back to the room and took his hand to bring him in with me.

An easel sat near the window of the guest bedroom. The bookshelves on either side of the window held enough painting supplies to keep me painting until I was old and gray. Canvases of all different sizes filled the other side of the room.

Feelings and memories washed over me. His gift brought me sadness. Painting would forever remind me of my mom and all I lost. Not only did I lose my mom, but I lost the coordination I once had to paint. But it also brought me so much happiness that he would even think to connect me with my passion again. That he listened to my stories and put it together how this was a part of my past that hadn't healed yet. So many feelings swirled around inside me that I couldn't stop the tears.

"Quinn, sweetheart, if you love it, why are you crying?"

Concern escaped from his lips. Where would I even start to explain my feelings? I calmed myself and led him to the guest bed, where we sat together on the edge.

"I was 15 when my father murdered my mom. That's the part people know. But my life sucked before that. My mom tried to make my birthdays special, but my father made it practically impossible for her when she did, so I didn't say anything to make her feel bad. After that, Aunt Betty would bake me a cake for my birthday and would sing to me, but that's all she could afford to do since she was suddenly raising a teenage girl." I wiped my eyes of the tears that fell, remembering how much my mom and Aunt Betty tried to give me a normal life.

"When I went to college and met Livy, Jillian, Sydney, and Jace, we were all pretty broke, so we celebrated each other, but we never gave gifts. We made it a priority to get together for the important times and give each other the gift of friendship."

I turned to look him in the eyes. "Devon, I can't remember the last time I was given an actual present. And for it to be the gift of painting. I've been so afraid to pick up a paintbrush again since my mom's death. For the longest time, it was the pain from my injury, but then it was the hurt from losing her."

Realizing I might be coming off as ungrateful, I added, "Please don't think that I don't love it, because I do. I'm just overwhelmed by all of this."

Not knowing what else to say about it, I stood up, stepped between his legs, and kissed him.

He kissed me back, but then broke the kiss and pushed me back so we were looking at each other.

"I'm sorry I brought up bad memories, but I hope once you try it, you'll reconnect with the wonderful memories of your mom, too."

I smiled up at him because the idea of wonderful memories was so appealing.

"It kills me that you don't know how to enjoy being given

a gift, but that is something you are going to have to get used to because I want to spoil you. I want to give you all the gifts, but I also want to give you all my time and attention. I want to give you all of me. And that's new for me. So you and I will travel through these new feelings together." He paused, looking at me. "Quinn, I'm falling in love with you."

20

QUINN

$\mathcal{N}$o words. There were just no words.

Sitting in Devon's kitchen, as the cheerful sunlight shone through the window like all was right with the world, I thought back over how awkward the last four days were.

After Devon told me he was falling in love with me, I panicked. Needing a reason to get away from the situation, I stepped out of his arms, told him I heard the washing machine buzz, and then left to switch laundry that buzzed before I even left for lunch.

We made polite conversation over dinner. He asked about my lunch with Olivia and I asked about his with Tate. That night, I fell asleep wrapped in his arms, like each night, but this time we felt so distant. He was right next to me, but we were in different worlds.

He was gone when I woke in the morning. That became our new normal. He would be gone to work during the day while I worked from his home. We would have a pleasant evening together, asking all the socially acceptable questions about each other's day, then we would go to bed, fall asleep, lather, rinse, repeat.

Drinking my coffee, I tortured myself over the last four days. I did that to him. I made an open and caring man push his feelings for me away because I was a monster who didn't deserve to be loved.

I wanted it so badly. To hear him tell me he loved me and to tell him it back with the same confidence. To feel like I was good enough to deserve his love. But I didn't.

Nobody should be subjected to my history. My past kept coming back to haunt me at the worst moments. I knew it would be better if I cut ties now and walk away. But I couldn't bring myself to do that, which showed how selfish I was. He deserved so much better than me. Maybe Heather was right, maybe they were meant for each other. She understood his life. She fit in his world.

My phone buzzed, and Olivia's name popped up.

Olivia: PARTY TONIGHT!!!

Me: I know. I'm looking forward to seeing everyone!

Olivia: Did you give Matthew the go ahead?

Matthew came to me a week ago and asked if it would be okay if he proposed to Jillian at my birthday party since all of her friends would be there and she would never expect it. He was so sweet to worry about taking the attention away from me on my day, but I told him that him bringing so much joy and love to Jillian would be the best birthday present he could give me.

Me: Of course I did. I'm SO excited! And I don't think Jillian knows anything about it!

Olivia: I don't think so either!

Me: Can you believe it? She's going to get married!

Olivia: She could say no.

Olivia: I couldn't even type that with a straight face!

Me: I'll see you there at 7.

Olivia: Devon and Tate are coming too, right?

Me: Yup. Devon is coming with me and Tate will meet us there. Say hi to her if she gets there before us. She's a little nervous about this whole party thing.

Olivia: You know me, the perfect hostess! I'll make her feel like she's part of the group!

Me: See you tonight!

Olivia: See you tonight!

Even when I was in my darkest moments, Olivia made me feel better without knowing it. Just texting with her and her enthusiasm for life helped me step out of my own head for a moment.

Now, being out of my head, I had to figure out how to deal with the whole Devon thing.

I had to show him I cared. Even though I wasn't ready to tell him I loved him yet, because that was way too scary for me, I felt things for him I couldn't explain. Feelings I didn't think I could feel. My heart has been caged in and locked up for years, mostly by my own choosing. I thought it was so well guarded nobody could reach it, but Devon was trying. And I realized I wasn't afraid of him succeeding. I wanted him to break through and reach me so I get rid of my walls completely. I wanted to take a risk and be vulnerable. But my heart wouldn't survive another loss like I felt for my childhood, for my mom, and even for my father.

Whenever I felt sadness for my father, guilt quickly followed it.

He was a terrible father, a worse husband, and a terrible human being. But he was my father. The only one I had in this life. My sadness was more about what should have been, rather than about missing who he actually was, because I didn't have good memories of him. I mourned the loss of family camping trips, having him teach me how to ride a bike or how to bowl, going to cut down a Christmas tree together, or even something simple like getting ice cream together, just the two of us. I still mourned for the dad I didn't have as a child.

Selfishly, I mourned for my lost high school years. But whenever I did, my guilt was immense. My mom lost her life, and I worried about losing some friends.

My father's actions changed me forever. During the two months I spent in the hospital after he murdered my mom, I felt lost. In the span of a couple of minutes, I essentially became an orphan. That was when I locked up my heart and hid it away. That pain was more than I could handle.

But Devon made me feel like it would be okay to take a risk and open myself up. And that was what I was going to do.

I smiled as I opened the walk-in closet in Devon's bedroom. In the beginning, he insisted I keep my clothes at his house, since I was going to be staying with him until we found the person harassing me. My clothes hung on the right and his on the left. It felt domestic. When I stepped in, I could smell him on everything. Seeing my things there with his clothes was encouraging. He was completely content to merge our lives together without hesitation. It didn't seem foreign to him, like it did to me.

I didn't buy sexy clothing because I never wanted to stand out. I flipped through hangers, looking for something specific and finally found it. The dress Olivia bought for me to wear to our college graduation party. It was the only thing I owned that would work for my birthday party. I didn't end up wearing it to the grad party because it put me so far outside my comfort zone that I had a panic attack when I tried it on back then.

Looking at it on the hanger, I noticed there was even less dress than I remembered. Olivia told me every woman needed to own a little black dress, and she knew I would never buy one for myself, so she bought one for me.

It was beautiful in its simplicity. The halter top tied at the base of my neck and the dress fell to the middle of my thighs. Turning the hanger around reminded me of what made me so nervous about the dress years ago. The back of the dress plunged so far down that one twist or turn in the wrong direction and people would know if I wore panties or not.

My anxiety grew, but I wanted to wear this. I wanted to look like a woman with confidence when I walked in on Devon's arm, even if it was only an act and not actual confidence, yet. It still felt like a step in the right direction. I was grateful Olivia stuck it in my suitcase.

Devon was going to pick me up in a couple of hours, so I went about getting ready, spending a little too long soaking in a bubble bath. Once I dragged myself away from the luxury, I dried and styled my hair. I went for an updo, because I was all in. I wouldn't hide myself behind my hair.

And I wasn't going to cover my scar with anything. Then I slipped into the black dress, making sure it was properly covering all the vital parts. Normally, I hid my arm with sweaters, jackets, or shawls. But I didn't want to do that tonight. I wanted to stop feeling shameful about my body and my past.

Devon texted that he was about five minutes away, so I took one last look in the mirror, grabbed my strappy black heels, and went downstairs to meet him.

Standing in the kitchen, putting the lunch dishes in the dishwasher, I felt panic growing. What was I doing? This wasn't who I was. I didn't dress sexy and try to impress people. Who was I kidding? I felt like a fool.

I put the last dish in the dishwasher and turned to walk upstairs to change when I heard the front door open. Ugh, I couldn't avoid him. I would have to go past him to get to the stairs to go change. This was the worst idea I've ever had.

I heard the door close behind him and his footsteps coming towards the kitchen. So, I just stood there, hands sweating; arms across my body like they would protect me from judgement.

"Hey, sorry, I was running late. I don't think I'm going to have time to shower before we go to your party. Jordan was talking my..." His words stopped when he reached the kitchen. I felt his gaze as it went down my body and back up.

His eyes rested on mine.

"Quinn," he whispered.

"Yes?"

He stepped closer to me and I automatically took one step back. I hated that I still had so much self doubt.

He reached a hand out to me, and I stepped forward and took it. He did the same with my other hand.

He spread my arms out so he could look at me, then let

one hand go and spun me around to see the back. I heard his breath catch. Then he spun me back around to face him.

"Quinn, there aren't words to describe how stunning you are."

I could feel my heart beating and was sure he could see it pounding through the thin fabric of the dress.

I reached my left arm over to cover the scar on my right arm, but he stopped me.

"Beautiful, you don't have to do that. You don't have to hide anything from me. I love you exactly as you are."

Despite my attempts to stop it, a tear fell from my eye.

He meant what he said. I knew it in my heart he did. I needed to stop second-guessing him, because he was a good man who wasn't going to hurt me. Somehow, I needed him to know I trusted him.

"Devon, you mean so much to me." I looked up into his crystal blue eyes as I gained the courage to tell him what he meant to me. A flicker of sadness crossed his face at my words. I couldn't tell him I loved him too, but I knew it was what he wanted to hear.

"I never thought I would feel something like this. That I would let myself care for someone like I care for you. I know I hurt you when I didn't say I love you back, but that doesn't mean you aren't someone amazing in my life. It's just that I don't know if I'm capable of loving someone. Loss hurts too much, so it's easier not to care. But I do care for you. I don't have words for what I feel for you, but whatever it is, it's strong, and I hope that means something to you. I hope that's enough for you right now."

He pulled me into his body and held me tightly. It was my favorite place to be.

"Of course that's enough for me. I will wait as long as you need me to wait," he whispered into my hair.

He took my face in his hands and kissed me. The kiss was

sweet, but also passionate and filled with all the words we both wanted to say to each other.

He ended the kiss but kept his hands on my face as he spoke to me. "I need to apologize for how I behaved over the last couple of days. Apologize for being an ass. I was upset that you walked away from me. Not that you didn't say it back to me. I don't have a problem with you taking your time with your feelings. I want you to get to where I am and I will give you all the time you need. And if you don't get there, that's okay. I have enough love for the both of us."

"How did I get to be so lucky?" I smiled.

"Oh, you're feeling lucky?" He smirked and looked at his watch.

"Well, we only have a couple minutes, but it's your party, so you can be late. Let's explore that feeling lucky thing." He slid his hands up the sides of my legs, pulling the hem of the dress with him as he went. Once it was up to my waist, he lifted me up onto the kitchen counter and I gasped when I felt the cold marble against my skin.

Grinning up at me, he pushed my knees apart and kissed his way up my inner thighs. At the apex, he kissed my wet panties, slowly slid them down my legs, then he walked away from me.

I heard a whimper, and it took a moment for me to realize it came from me.

I gazed appreciatively at his body as he walked around the kitchen island to open a drawer. His body was magnificent. Even with his dress shirt and slacks still on, I could see his muscles move under his clothing while he walked. I wanted to touch him, not skipping a single part.

From the drawer, he pulled out a dish towel and strode back to me.

"That dress is the sexiest thing I have ever seen. But, as sexy as it is, I know the marble is cold," he said as he kissed my neck. Putting the towel down behind me, he laid me down on the counter.

Looking up at the ceiling, I spread my legs for him and then felt his hot breath between my thighs. He hovered there, breathing rhythmically. It was torture. I wanted his mouth on me so badly. I needed it more than I needed to breathe.

Just when I thought I couldn't take it anymore, his lips were on mine as his tongue pierced me.

There was no teasing or easing into things. He was frantic. I felt like he was a starving man and I was his last meal. It took only moments, and I was screaming in ecstasy.

Before I even had the chance to come down from my orgasm, he was inside me. At a frenzied pace, I was out of my mind.

"Baby, I need this. I need you," he said as he thrusted. "Come for me, Quinn," and at that moment, we both fell over the edge together.

After catching my breath, I sat up and wrapped my arms around Devon. Feeling his body strong against mine was what I needed.

We stayed that way for minutes, then I remembered we had a party to be at.

"I must be a disaster. I need to go fix my hair so we can get out of here."

"Or, just an idea here, but we could always get more messy upstairs and be a little late," he said with a mischievous grin.

I slapped his tight abs to get him to back up.

"Did you forget that it's my party. I can't bail on it. But I do promise that we can pick up where we left off when we get home from the party.

After the awkwardness of the last few days, this felt right. Felt like we were back to our old selves again. That made going to the party much more enjoyable.

After more fooling around while we redressed, we finally made it to the party less than an hour late.

We met at my favorite bar, which was more upscale than our normal hangouts. The mahogany bar gleamed as it ran the length of the room. They kept the lighting at a dim, romantic level that encouraged intimacy. Its high-end atmosphere wasn't why it was my favorite, though. It wasn't loud, like other bars. People were having deep, involved conversations in small groups. It was intimate and perfect.

Even though most voices were low, it was impossible not to hear Olivia's laugh from across the room. All my friends were sitting at a large table at the far end of the room. Olivia was the center of attention, with Jace to her left, completely enthralled by whatever she was talking about, and Tate and Sydney to her right, enjoying the conversation. Jillian and Matthew were across from them, caught up in their own private conversation. There was so much love between them, I could feel it from across the room just by looking at them. For an orphan, my chosen family was pretty amazing.

Olivia squealed when she saw me and hugged me tight. "I never thought I would ever get to see you in this dress. You look fabulous!"

When Olivia finally let me go, my friends wished me a happy birthday. We all sat at a table together and the conversation flowed easily. Even though we weren't in college and seeing each other every day anymore, we were still the best of friends.

Matthew asked me to go to the bar with him to get the next round of drinks. I knew what he wanted to talk about. But he was stressing over nothing.

"Okay Quinn, I need to be one hundred percent positive that you're okay with me proposing to Jillian tonight. I know you are under so much stress with the guy that's harassing you and this is your night to relax and celebrate, so I'm completely okay with you telling me to do it another night." He looked so sincere.

This man was going to make Jillian so happy. He was so thoughtful and cared for her immensely. Nothing would stop me from encouraging him to propose to her.

"Matthew, I couldn't ask for a better birthday present than for you to propose to her tonight. Actually, since it's my birthday and my special day, I command you to propose to that woman right now." I stood as tall and regal as I could, as if I were a queen commanding her subject.

"As you wish, your majesty."

We carried the drinks back to the table, and I cuddled up next to Devon to watch the show.

Matthew stood and raised his glass as if to toast me.

"I would like to raise my glass to a fantastic woman tonight." Jillian's face lit up. One of her favorite things about Matthew was how he valued her friends as much as we valued him.

"She came into my life when I wasn't expecting it and changed my entire world. She brings me joy and happiness day after day and I couldn't imagine living a single moment without her ever again."

Jillian looked a little confused, assuming the toast was still about me.

"She is the smartest, most caring, beautiful woman I have ever met. And my life is complete because she is by my side." Jillian was finally catching on that she was who he was talking about.

"I would like you all to keep your glasses raised while I ask a quick question. Then I can finish this toast."

He set down his glass, dropped to his knee in front of Jillian, and pulled out a box from his pocket.

"Jillian Westwood, my love, my heart, would you do me

the honor of being my wife and walking through the rest of our lives together?"

We were all smiling, but Jillian was in shock and didn't speak as she stared at the stunning pear-cut diamond ring in the box he held out to her.

"Jilly, our arms are getting tired. Answer the man," Sydney prodded her.

"Yes! Of course! Yes!" she shouted.

He took the ring from the box, put it on her finger, and picked her up in a hug.

The table finished the toast; "To Matthew and Jillian."

"I'm engaged! Oh shit, I can't believe it. I'm engaged!" She was radiating happiness.

Devon squeezed his arm around my shoulder. I looked up at him and he was grinning as big as the rest of us. He was truly happy for them.

DEVON

*W*atching joy pour out of Quinn from Matthew and Jillian engagement was heartwarming. She loved these people openly and without reservation. It showed me she had love inside her to give to others and that gave me hope.

Later in the evening, Jace was updating our group on his plans to run for State Senator Spenser's seat. The political climate in Wisconsin had been in flux for the last decade, so running a campaign was hard to plan. You had to appeal to the unbending older generation who didn't want change, while also appealing to the younger generation, who wanted Wisconsin to move in a progressive direction. Luckily, my dad found balance, and both groups liked him, but it was hard for a new person to come in and do the same. I didn't envy Jace for the hard road he had ahead of him.

"Charlotte is on my case to find someone special. She said I need to appear family oriented," Jace said, exasperated.

"Who is this Charlotte chick?" Olivia spat out.

"Charlotte Adams, she is my new campaign manager. And she has strong opinions on what I'm doing wrong.

But, in her defense, she's been right about each flaw in my campaign she's found. Senator Spenser has been happily married for over 35 years and the public loves his wife. It shows he's willing to commit and stick with things that need work. It's going to be hard to beat him." He sighed.

According to Quinn, Jace's track record with women wasn't terrible. He wasn't one to bounce from one woman to the next, but he also called it quits before he was in too deep. There was always some reason for him to walk away. When we talked about him, she made it sound like Jace was hung up on Olivia, but she wouldn't let herself reciprocate the feelings.

"She wants me to find a serious girlfriend. One I could get engaged to before the election so people see I'm willing to settle down."

"You should fire her," Olivia shouted.

When we all turned to look at her, she tried to explain her outburst. "You shouldn't have someone working for you who wants to change you. She should see how perfect you are. I mean, how perfect for this position. You're perfect to be our next senator. I just think she doesn't get you, so she shouldn't be in charge of your campaign."

Seeing Olivia's reaction to the possibility of Jace finding someone to settle down with made me wonder if maybe Quinn's assessment of Olivia's feeling for Jace might be on point. It felt like more than your typical friendly feelings in her outburst.

"Well, I have a little time to think through things. I don't have to publicly announce that I'm in a relationship until the new year. Heck, Charlotte even offered to step in if I don't find someone by then. She said we could tell people we fell in love while working on the campaign and people would eat up the love story."

I'm pretty sure I heard Olivia mutter "bitch" under her breath.

"But I don't want to mislead people. I won't lie to them. That's not the politician I want to be. That's not why I want to get involved. I sincerely believe I can make a difference for Wisconsin."

Olivia's face relaxed with his admission until he continued.

"But I told her I would be interested in taking her out. She and I have similar beliefs and interests, so I didn't think it would hurt to try. If we are actually compatible, maybe I could kill two birds with one stone."

Olivia stood up suddenly. Looking a little shocked, she covered by picking up her glass and raising a toast.

"I would like everyone to raise their glass to our beautiful Quinny. She is the calm to my crazy and the heart of our group. She cares more than any other person I know and truly wants the best for each of you. For that, she deserves all the good in this world. Quinny, may this next year bring you nothing but happiness, and Devon, may you be worthy of our girl. Happy Birthday, Quinn. We love you."

Glasses clinked and her friends shouted, "To Quinn!"

Quinn stood and looked around at all the people who loved her.

"Thank you, guys. This has been the best birthday. I'm so blessed to have all of you in my life. Congratulations to Matthew and Jillian. You both deserve so much happiness and I'm so glad you found it with each other. Livy, Jace, and Sydney. My world is immensely better because of you. Tate, it was wonderful having you join us tonight. I look forward to getting to know you better. And, Devon, I don't have words to explain how I feel celebrating with you here. I didn't look for you, but you found me, and I'm so grateful for that." A little tear dropped from her eye. "So, I raise my glass to all of you. And with that, I need to get some sleep. We will see you all later."

Quinn's friends stood to leave, but it looked like Jace and Olivia were going to stay for one more drink. I was confident Jace was about to get an earful from Olivia, and based on the look on her face, I didn't envy him.

I helped Quinn with her coat and she took my arm as we walked to my car. Pride filled me walking down the street with this woman on my arm. It's been a roller coaster ride since the day we met, but I wouldn't change any of it. I stood taller with her beside me, like I could be the man she thought I was.

Driving home, I reached for her and held her hand as we drove in peaceful silence. Glancing over at her, she was stunning, smiling softly as she watched the road pass by the window. With all the chaos in her past, she had a calm about her that carried over to me. This was the perfect night.

My calm ended when we were close to my house. There were lights, sirens, and smoke.

"Oh my God, Devon, your house is on fire!" Quinn screamed next to me as we pulled up to the fire trucks in the street.

I turned to Quinn and asked her to stay in the car to be safe, but I knew that wasn't going to work. She jumped out of the car and ran with me to a firefighter by one of the trucks.

"I'm sorry, sir, you're going to need to stay back. This is an active fire, and we need to keep this area safe." The large firefighter in full gear held up his arms and looked like he meant business.

"This is my house," I yelled over the sounds of the fire.

The firefighter looked at the fire ravaging my house, then back at me. The look on his face told me everything I needed to know. My house was destroyed.

"My cat! Wasabi is in the house!" I shouted. I knew I could replace all the things in my house, but not Wasabi. She needed to be okay.

"Don't worry, sir. She was meowing by the window when we got here. She's safe in a pet carrier. I'll have someone get her for you. But you are going to need to stay back while we work. I'll let the police know you're here. They're going to have questions for you."

Relief washed through me, knowing Wasabi was okay. We've been through so much together. I wasn't prepared to lose her.

The fireman ushered us over to the side of the driveway. It was surreal standing there watching my house burn to the ground. My front door, the door I walked through every day for years, was charred black instead of the bright red I was used to seeing. The fall colored plants my mom put in planters on my porch were burnt and dead. There wasn't anything joyful about looking at my house anymore.

I wrapped Quinn tight in my arms. She was okay. Wasabi was okay. Everything else was replaceable.

A police officer walked up to us carrying a pet carrier. I could hear Wasabi making her dissatisfaction known from inside. She was going to need a lot of attention to get over this one.

Quinn reached for the carrier before I had a chance, and as soon as Wasabi saw her, she stopped howling. They had bonded during Quinn's stay and both seemed relieved to see the other.

"Mr. and Mrs. Swift, I'm Officer Stevens. I'm sorry you guys are going through this tonight."

Quinn was about to jump in and correct him, but I liked the sound of Mr. and Mrs. Swift, so I spoke first, interrupting her. "Thank you, we appreciate that."

I knew the answer to my next question, but I had to ask it, anyway.

"Officer Stevens, do you know how the fire started?"

I held Quinn tighter. As if my strength would pass through me to her.

"Well, it's only preliminary thoughts right now. We won't know for sure until it's completely out and we can get in there to investigate, but at first look, it appears to be arson."

Quinn flinched, and I held her tighter.

"Your neighbor reported hearing a loud explosion, but I won't know anything solid until I can get in there and look around closely. I noticed a car in the driveway. Are you sure nobody was home?"

"That was my car," Quinn said, her voice quiet and shaky. "Devon drove us to the party."

"Are you guys often out at night?"

"No. Actually, we're usually at home in the evenings spending time together. Her birthday was a few days ago, so we went out with some friends to celebrate. But since she has someone harassing her, we usually stick close to home," I explained.

I could feel when it all clicked for Quinn. She tensed in my arms. She wiggled out of my hold and turned to both of us with panic in her eyes.

"They tried to kill me. They saw my car was here, and they set a fire expecting I would be home. Someone burned down your house because of me. If we were here, they could have killed you."

I wanted to tell her she was wrong. I wanted to tell her it was an accident, and it had nothing to do with her, but I couldn't lie to her. Despite that, I needed her to understand this wasn't her fault. I took her hands in mine and lowered myself until I could look her in the eyes.

"Baby, the person who did this has a sickness. It isn't

anything you caused. We're going to find them and put an end to this, but this isn't your fault. Tell me you understand that and you believe me."

She kept slowly shaking her head back and forth in disbelief. She wasn't ready to accept the truth. She was taking the weight of this on herself and was going to carry it with her.

"Quinn, we are both okay and it's just a house. Houses can be rebuilt. This isn't your fault."

"Ma'am, you should listen to your husband. When people do things like this, it is on them, not on the victim."

"He's not my husband," she shouted. "He's just the poor man who got stuck with me and all the craziness that follows me wherever I go! He's the man whose house burned to the ground because he has a kind heart and he cared about the wrong person!"

"Stop it," I yelled.

I threw up my hands in frustration. Why wouldn't she understand that I wasn't with her out of pity. How the hell could she not know by now how mad I was about her.

The officer was considerate enough to step away.

"You aren't a burden I took on, and you aren't a charity case I couldn't walk away from. You are the love of my life. And it is killing me that someone is trying to hurt you and I can't keep you safe. I'm not staying here because I feel obligated to. I'm staying here because I would die if someone hurt you. My life wouldn't mean anything if you weren't in it. With or without this lunatic, I love you. You are my world and that isn't because I have some white knight complex. It's because I fell in love with the woman you are. God, Quinn, I wish you could see yourself the way I see you."

She stood there, clearly stunned. Maybe I went too far. I shouldn't have yelled at her right now, not after the shock of the night's events. That was a dick move.

But then she set Wasabi's carrier down and threw herself into my arms and held me tight as she cried.

Wrapping my arms around her helped me relax. It felt right when she was against my body. Like the rest of the world would disappear.

I whispered calming words to her as it sank in that I was in love with her. That I was with her because of who she was, not because of the situation she found herself in. I could feel the anxiety and doubt leave her body as she let it all out. Finally, we could start moving forward together.

My parents showed up. The Fire Chief called my dad when he found out it was my house. My mom insisted on taking Quinn to their house, saying it was after midnight and Quinn didn't need to be here to watch this. I was in complete agreement with her. My dad stuck around with me while I answered questions and watched my house burn.

Eventually, Matthew showed up.

"Seriously, man, you didn't need to do this to get my attention. If you wanted to spend more time with me tonight, you could have stayed at the bar."

That was the first laugh I had since we pulled up to the house a few hours ago. I was definitely starting to like Quinn's friends.

I recognized the starstruck look in his eyes when he saw my dad standing next to me so I took I introduced them. Then Matthew switched into officer mode.

"They told me what happened and what they suspect. I know we won't have anything definitive for a couple days, but we're going to go forward with the assumption it's the guy after Quinn, since that's what all signs are pointing to."

I nodded.

"Is she safe?" he asked.

"She went home with my wife," my dad answered. "They'll stay with us at the Maple Bluff mansion for now.

Our place is already well-guarded, but I'll get some extra security to help." Being level-headed in a crisis was part of his job and he did it well.

"That sounds good. Devon, you should probably head over there now. Go be with Quinn. There isn't anything you can do here tonight. I'll get all the information I can and I'll meet up with you guys tomorrow." And, almost as an afterthought to himself, he added, "We're going to get this guy."

Dad and I both thanked Matthew and left in my car. I watched my destroyed house in the rear-view mirror as we drove away. The fire department had the fire under control and almost completely out by the time we left. I knew it was only a thing, but I had so many happy memories there, most from the last month with Quinn. My heart hurt for the loss, but I would make new memories somewhere else with Quinn. My world would be okay as long as she was safe by my side.

When we got to my parent's house, my mom was still awake. She came over to me and gave me a big mom hug. The kind filled with love and feels like home.

"How's Quinn?" I asked.

"That girl of yours is pretty strong, Devon. I could tell this was getting to her, but she didn't complain or break down. I don't know if I could be that strong. But when it all hits her, it's going to hit her hard, and she's going to need you."

I nodded in agreement. She was carrying so much and not allowing herself time to let the emotions go through her.

"I set her up in the guest bedroom at the end of the hall upstairs. When I checked in on her a while ago, she was out like a light. She needs some sleep. I can set you up in another guest room if you want."

I didn't think she was trying to be modest or old-fashioned by offering me a different bedroom. She was trying to make sure Quinn wasn't disturbed, which was exactly the caring mom she was. But I couldn't be away from Quinn, not after everything that went on.

"Thanks, Mom, but I think I'm going to stay with Quinn tonight. I'll be quiet as I go in there."

I could see the look of disappointment on her face.

"I need to be near her tonight, Mom. We need each other. I'll be as quiet as possible. I promise."

"Okay, but you let her sleep. That sweet girl has been through a lot and she needs her rest."

I kissed my mom on her forehead and wished them both a good night.

A weight lifted from my shoulders as I walked up the stairs, only moments away from holding her in my arms again. I wasn't sure when it happened, but I needed her with me to feel like myself. When she wasn't with me, I worried about her and I could breathe easier when she was near. I was so wrapped up in her.

I opened the door to the guest room quietly and saw her asleep. She looked so tiny on the king-size bed.

Walking around the bed, I undressed and gently lifted the covers, sliding over until I felt her body next to mine. She stirred a little as I pressed my body up to hers, but then her breathing settled back into its slow, rhythmic pace as she slept. This was where I needed to be.

22

QUINN

I felt warmth surrounding me when I woke up. Some from the sun shining through the windows, but mostly from Devon's body wrapped up next to mine.

It took me a moment to remember where I was, because this wasn't Devon's bed or his room. It didn't take long for the events of last night to come back to me, though.

Slowly sliding out of Devon's arms so as not to wake him, I got out of bed.

Standing in his parents' guest room, I realized the only thing I had with me was the black dress I was wearing last night. When I took it off the night before, it smelled of smoke. I could still smell it in my hair. That wasn't exactly how I wanted to go downstairs to greet his parents this morning.

I went into the en-suite bathroom to see if I could clean up a little and saw that his mom had already taken care of all my concerns. She left towels on the counter, along with a basket of different soaps and hair products, toothbrushes and toothpaste, and a pair of sweatpants, t-shirt, and sweatshirt for each of us. She was an angel.

I ran a bath, staying in longer than I should because it felt so good to let my worries soak away. Suzanna was nice enough to leave a hair dryer on the counter with all the other items she thoughtfully left, but I decided against drying my hair. I didn't want to wake Devon.

With damp hair and stocking feet, I snuck out of the guest room and found my way downstairs to the kitchen. Suzanna was already up and prepping for breakfast. Out of nowhere, a wave of sadness washed over me.

This is what it would feel like if my mom lived. I hadn't walked into a kitchen to find a mom making breakfast for so long. I didn't have a mom to take care of me when things went bad. To come running to when something happened and I needed a shoulder to cry on. To leave clothes out for me when I was unexpectedly staying at her home. To think about me and my needs. To show me love and kindness. My dad stole that from me and I hated him for it.

Right there, in the middle of the Governor's kitchen, I broke down. The tears came so uncontrollably fast and I sobbed as I crumbled to the floor.

Suzanna rushed over to me. She sat down on the floor next to me and wrapped her arms tightly around me. Her comfort made the sobs come even harder because I hadn't felt any kind of maternal caring in years.

Even though she wasn't my mom, I couldn't help but take comfort in Devon's mom, and it was the most wonderful feeling. Aunt Betty was kind, but she wasn't a demonstrative woman. I was barely a teenager the last time I felt this kind of maternal care.

I heard someone running down the stairs.

"What's going on? Quinn, are you hurt?"

Suzanna and I both turned to see Devon looking down at us on the floor.

"Quinn is fine. Sometimes we women just need a good

cry. Devon, sweetie, why don't you go take a shower? We're going to make breakfast," Suzanna said so matter-of-factly, like someone breaking down on her kitchen floor was the most normal thing in the world.

Devon looked at me. I could see the pain in his eyes and I ached knowing I was the cause.

"Your mom is right. I'm okay, Devon. Go take a shower."

He looked at his mom and back at me and accepted that he wasn't invited to this meltdown. I knew it must have been hard for him to let his mom take care of me. He was the kind of man who liked to solve all the problems. But he had enough love and trust in his mom to leave me in her care. As he left, he told us both that he loved us.

It was a strange feeling to hear him tell me he loved me so openly in front of his mom. Like he wasn't ashamed or embarrassed of me.

Suzanna looked at me until I lifted my eyes to meet hers.

"If we don't cry, we break. You're carrying a load that is too great. You need to let someone else help you carry it."

I gulped back a few more sobs, so I didn't start crying again.

"Share the load with me."

She spoke with such kindness that I couldn't help but talk to her.

"Do you know about my past?" I asked with a little shame in my voice.

"I do. And I know you did nothing to cause what happened to you and your family."

People have told me that in the past, but it was never something I could trust in and believe.

"Now, what brought this on this morning?" She asked warmly.

"Walking in here and seeing you cooking breakfast for your family," I whispered.

She leaned in and hugged me again.

"And you remembered all you lost when your father took your mother from you, didn't you?"

I whimpered and nodded as tears fell again. I couldn't speak.

"Oh, my sweet Quinn, you didn't deserve this. And I'm positive your mom would have done anything she could to be the one here to make you breakfast."

She released me and wiped the tears off my cheeks.

"Let me tell you something about moms. We're a unique group. Almost a secret society of sorts. We take care of each other. And, when we lose a member too early, the rest of us step in and finish the job. That's how the world keeps turning. I need you to let me step in for her. I don't want to replace her, and couldn't even if I wanted to, but I can be here when you need a mom to lean on. Even if things don't work out between you and Devon, I will be here for you. You are not alone. Will you let me do that?"

And, like I hadn't cried enough, the tears and sobbing started all over again at the thought of having a mom that wanted to care about me.

She didn't hurry me and make me feel bad about all the tears. She let me cry until I was done. It felt cathartic to let it all go.

When I was all out of tears and my breathing regulated, she helped me off the floor and gave me a hug.

"Now, let's start breakfast and you can share more of your burden with me. Have you ever made Dutch Babies for breakfast? They're Devon's favorite type of pancakes."

I shook my head. I still felt like I would burst back into tears if I spoke.

She pulled out ingredients and explained to me how to make these big fluffy pancakes that Devon liked so much. We worked side by side and I eventually got my emotions fully under control well enough where I thought could speak without bursting back into tears.

"I'm in love with your son."

I don't know where it came from, but I needed to say it and I needed her to hear it.

"I thought that might be the case. Have you told him yet?"

"No."

"May I ask why?"

"Honestly, I'm not sure. I've been so afraid of him loving me that I didn't take time to think about me loving him. You have to know I don't want to hurt him. But I also don't want to be hurt when he realizes I'm not good for him. You know some of my story. My past is going to cause problems for him. And now that I love him, I know it's going to hurt that much more when he realizes I'm right about this and leaves me."

Putting words to my fears and speaking them out loud was scary. But it was also freeing. I couldn't see a happily ever after for us because I was 'Killer Quinn.' I was tainted, and he was perfect. I didn't want to love him because I knew it would hurt so much more when he wasn't in my life if I loved him. But it was too late. I was madly in love with Devon Swift.

"What if he doesn't leave you?" she asked, while she continued to slice strawberries. "What if he stays with you and you guys have a beautiful life together?"

"I don't know if a beautiful life is in my future. I don't know what one looks like."

She set down her knife and turned to me, waiting until I turned to face her.

"Do you think Devon deserves a beautiful life?"

I nodded.

"And can you imagine what his beautiful life could look like?"

I nodded again.

"So, is it you don't know what one looks like, or is it you don't feel like you deserve a beautiful life?"

For what felt like the millionth time that morning, tears flowed down my cheeks again because she was absolutely right. I didn't feel like I deserved to have the same sort of life I wished for everyone else to have, because my mom didn't get one.

"Seriously, why is she still crying?" I heard Devon say from the doorway, looking freshly showered.

"Devon, relax," his mom scolded him. "She's just getting some stuff out that has been weighing her down for a while. Go get your dad and let him know that breakfast is going to be ready soon."

Being dismissed again, he sulked away against his will.

"Sweetheart, everyone deserves a beautiful life filled with joy and happiness. Some people don't get that, and it breaks my heart your mom didn't get that, but you still deserve nothing but the best. So, you need to get it out of your head that you're not good enough or that you don't deserve everything life has to offer you. You are a good person who is putting wonderful things out into this universe, and you have suffered enough. I can't think of anyone better for my son than someone as caring and wonderful as you."

Before I could stop myself, I blurted out, "Even Heather?"

"Especially Heather. She is too selfish and self-centered to be part of this family. But you are the exact opposite."

She gave me another hug and a kiss on the cheek and that was that. We went back to making breakfast.

Tate showed up as we finished cooking. Sitting at the table with the whole Swift family was an adventure. There was banter and memories and support of one another. It surprised me that it didn't make me sad for all I missed out on. Honestly, I found it comforting.

"So, I'm assuming Quinn is going back to her apartment, so where are you going to stay, big brother?" Tate asked as she and Devon fought over the last piece of bacon.

That caught me off guard. I hadn't even thought about where we were going to live. I mean, of course I would go back to my apartment. But I was so used to sleeping with Devon by my side each night that the idea of living in different places was painful.

"You could always stay with me?" Tate offered.

"Or you could stay with me at my apartment," I suggested, looking down at my plate so I didn't show how hopeful I was.

"Well, that would be tight living with Olivia there, too. Wouldn't it?" Tate asked.

I knew she wasn't saying this to be difficult, but I needed his little sister to butt out.

"Actually, I think I'm going to have to find a place to rent for at least a few months. Seeing how bad it looked last night, I think my house is going to take a long time to rebuild."

My heart sank. He didn't want to live with me. I kept my focus on my pancake so he wouldn't see the hurt in my eyes.

"I didn't exactly want to have this conversation at the breakfast table with my family watching, but Quinn, I don't want to be without you. And this isn't because someone is trying to hurt you and I feel like I need to protect you. I'm so in love with you and the idea of not sharing a home with you is unimaginable to me. Will you come with me to find a place of our own to rent until my house is repaired?"

I looked up and couldn't contain my smile.

"I would like that very much."

"If you don't think Olivia would mind, we could stay at your place until we find something?"

"No, I don't think she would mind at all. I'll call her after breakfast."

"Well, now that all of that's settled, let's finish breakfast," Suzanna said.

Right then, the doorbell rang. It was Matthew.

"Why don't you guys go into the living room to chat? Your father and Tate will help me clean up from breakfast." Suzanna said to Devon.

Devon and I sat on the loveseat across from Matthew. He was dressed in his uniform, so it was clear it was a professional visit.

"Matthew. I'm so sorry for all of this interrupting your engagement night. Was Jillian upset?" I asked.

"No. Of course not. She was worried about you and annoyed with me when I told her she couldn't come with me when I got the call. But she was better when I got home and told her you were okay. Don't worry about her. She's pretty resilient."

I knew he was right. Jillian could handle anything with Matthew by her side.

Devon thanked him for coming and asked what they had learned since last night.

He looked from Devon to me and seemed a little hesitant to answer him.

"Well, the fire inspector was able to check things out this morning and she found that someone put a homemade explosive device on top of the refrigerator in the kitchen. It was set to go off on a timer and was definitely made by an amateur. "

He gave us a moment to let that sink in before continuing.

"Unfortunately, the fire was going for a while before the fire department was called. I'm sorry, Devon, but your house is a total loss. You're gonna need to start from scratch and rebuild."

When I heard that, my stomach clenched over all that

he lost because of me. Devon stopped Matthew to remind me that it wasn't my fault and I shouldn't worry, because that was what insurance was for. He knew what I was thinking.

Once I nodded understanding, Devon got the conversation back on track.

"Do you guys have any idea who did this yet?"

"Nothing concrete yet. We're following a lead, but I don't want to get into with you guys yet until I know if it's going to take us anywhere. I promise to keep you guys in the loop as we find solid info though."

I trusted Matthew, so I didn't push for any more information. It gave me hope that there could be an end to this someday.

We walked him to the door and he gave me a big hug before leaving.

Devon put his arms around me. "Jillian is lucky to have him. He's a good man. I'm really looking forward to getting to know him better when all of this is done."

I had to work hard to contain my excitement. Not only did he like my friends, but he was thinking in terms of a future together after all this craziness ended. I wanted to stop him right there in the hallway and tell him I loved him, but I needed it to be special. It would be the first time I ever told a man I loved him. I wasn't exactly sure how to go about saying it, but I wanted to make it memorable.

Devon's mom and dad were in the kitchen when we got there. It was still a little surreal to be in the kitchen with my boss. But I needed to get over it.

"So, what are your plans for the day?" Martin asked me.

"Well, Mr. Swift, I think I need to head to work to get backups of things that were lost in the fire. Luckily, I back up my computer to the cloud. Otherwise, I wouldn't have anything ready for tomorrow's committee meeting."

He and Devon both had furrowed brows. It was easy to see the family resemblance between the two of them.

"First, it's Martin, not Mr. Swift," he said sternly.

"Sorry, Martin."

"And second, I don't know that going to work tomorrow is the best idea. You guys have been through something pretty traumatic. I think you both should take some time off to get your feet back under you."

"I agree with you, Dad." Devon jumped in.

I looked at both of them like they were aliens. I had a job to do and there wasn't anything either of them could say that would stop me from putting on the best art show ever.

We all spent the next twenty minutes arguing the pros and cons of me holding the committee meeting tomorrow. Luckily, Suzanna took my side, so I didn't feel like it was me against all the Swifts. The guys had a valid point that it wasn't the safest thing for me to be out and about while this person with a vendetta against me was still out there, but I had a solid point with the fact that I couldn't put my life on hold forever because of this lunatic.

We eventually agree that Devon and I would stay with his parents for a couple more nights and we would hold the committee meeting at his parents' house. Suzanna was giddy when I mentioned how I would love it if she joined us and how I felt her thoughts and opinions would be a welcomed addition to the committee.

With our living situation finally decided, Devon and I went to my apartment to pick up some of my things. He tried to tell me he was going to replace my entire wardrobe, but I insisted that the things I still had at the apartment would be completely fine. He sulked a little and I couldn't help but find him adorable.

Then, we went shopping for clothes for him since he lost all his possessions in the fire. I could see when moments of sadness hit him a few times while we were shopping. There was a tie that was similar to his favorite tie, but not quite an exact match, and I could see him cringe a little, but he tucked that emotion away and carried on. He lost everything. I wanted to fix this for him, but I didn't know how.

23

DEVON

$\mathcal{W}$aking up with Quinn in my arms at my parents' house was weird. Even when I was younger and living at home, I never had a girl sleep over under my parent's roof. It would have been impossible to sneak one in when I was a teenager, with all the security we had. And I never wanted to bring a woman I was dating over for anything major at my parent's house. Part of me felt confident my parents wouldn't barge in, but another part of me worried they would and I would get an earful. I guess you never stop feeling like a kid around your parents.

Feeling her rhythmic breathing next to me soothed my anxiety as much as possible. She was safe, and that was what mattered. Knowing she was safe was one thing, but keeping her that way was another. My level of frustration over not being able to protect her was over the top. I needed this guy to be caught so we could start, what I hoped to be, a long life together. But right now, I was looking over my shoulder at every turn. I had the best security in the state working for me and Matthew was putting all of his time into finding this guy, but Quinn was still scared and I couldn't take that away from her.

Quinn sighed as she woke up. I leaned in and kissed the tip of her nose.

"Good morning, beautiful."

She smiled up at me as her hand grazed over my chest. That was all it took. One touch from her was enough to get me going.

I slid my hand up the length of her side and she quivered. Normally, I was a patient lover, but with her, I had no control, even in my parent's house with them right downstairs.

I rolled over her and kissed her neck, then worked my way down until I had one of her perfect nipples between my teeth. She gasped as I gave it a little nip and her hips pressed up towards me.

"Little impatient this morning?"

"Devon, don't play with me. I need this."

She reached between my legs and guided me to her. She was already wet and ready.

So, it was going to be like this. I liked it when she took what she wanted.

Not to give her all the power, I pushed in at a torturously slow pace while she moaned at my speed.

"Devon, now. Stop playing with me," she demanded.

She had grown confident in what she wanted and felt comfortable enough with me to ask for it without embarrassment or hesitation.

I picked up the pace a little, but clearly not as fast as she wanted it. Her nails were digging into my shoulders, trying to get me moving faster. I wasn't sure how long I was going to last because the feel of her wet heat enveloping me with each movement was rapidly pushing me to the brink.

To balance the scales, I slid my hand between us and

rubbed her clit with my thumb and she cried out, but quickly covered her mouth, realizing where we were.

I didn't stop teasing her clit, though, so she grabbed a pillow and screamed into it. She came undone, her whole body shaking beneath me, and I followed right after.

A quickie in the morning with her was something I could get used to, but what I wanted was to take my time savoring each part of her body, somewhere my parents were not. Finding a place of our own to rent moved up higher on my to-do list.

I pushed her hair away from her face and saw her flushed cheeks.

"What time is it?" she asked with a yawn.

"It's almost eight."

"Oh," she said as she sat up. "We need to get moving. We have a lot to do today."

My hand found its way up her inner thigh and my smile let her know what things I wanted on our agenda for the day.

"Other than that. We have to get ready for the committee meeting and we have to go to the costume shop to pick out our costumes for the Halloween party."

She was so excited about going to this party, which seemed odd to me, since she was a rather introverted person.

"What is it about this party that has you all worked up?"

She looked a little embarrassed, which I didn't like at all.

Trying to bring a little fun to the conversation, I pushed her back onto the pillow and climbed on top of her, taking a wrist in each hand and holding them over her head. I was ready to go again, looking at her pert breasts aimed up at me.

"Tell me, or I'm going to tickle you."

She hesitated, so I let go of one hand and started tickling her side. She screamed. I didn't realize how ticklish she was. That knowledge was going to come in handy in the future.

"Stop. Stop. I'll tell you, just stop!"

I eased up on the tickling, but I stayed on top of her.

She wouldn't look me in the eye, but when she looked down, she was staring at my hard cock, so she finally looked back up at my face. I smiled at her and she blushed. It was adorable.

"I'm not a big party person, but Olivia throws this Halloween party each year, and each time I go I end up being a little envious of the people who show up in couples costumes. There is something wonderful about two people who care enough about each other to look silly together. It might be dumb, but I'm a little excited to go with you as a couple. I never thought that was something I would do."

I've never been one to dress up for Halloween before, but to see that light in her eyes, I would wear a costume every day of the week.

"That's not dumb at all. We need to find the best couples costume ever. I think it needs to be something that says something about us, though." I was fully invested in making this happened for her.

"Thank you for doing this, Devon."

I kissed her soft lips, which led to us being even later at starting our day than we already were.

While looking through the costumes at the shop and not finding the winning costumes, we came up with our own idea for a couple's costume that they didn't carry there. But we could pull each of the costumes together with our own things or things we could easily find, since all my stuff burned to the ground the night before. So, we went that route.

Then, against my protestation, we went to Quinn's office at the Capitol to pick up some papers for the committee meeting. I gave an extra glance to each person we passed, wondering if they were the one that wanted to hurt Quinn.

Even with two of the bodyguards I hired with us, I still worried for her safety.

We got in and out without any issues, though, and Quinn had the paperwork she needed.

Quinn was using work to avoid dealing with the emotions that came with our situation. If that was what she needed, I was going to do everything I could to help her and I would be there for her when she was ready to let her feelings take over.

Even with myself and my dad telling her we could postpone the project, Quinn wouldn't listen. She insisted she was going to meet her deadline and pull together the best art show possible because that's what the people deserved.

She was so unselfish. After the childhood she lived through, to continue to put others first was unthinkable to me. She took pride in her work, but not in a look-at-me kind of way. She did what she did to make lives better.

Sitting at the dining room table, we worked through the meeting details. Despite the events of the last few weeks, Quinn had us on track to have the first collection ready by the planned New Year's Day opening, so the agenda was focused on February's collection. I felt anxious about February, because that collection heavily depended on Heather following through on her connection to her photographer friend, Andrew Jorgensen. I worried Heather would find a way to ruin things for Quinn, and I wouldn't let that happen.

My mom, ever the hostess, was baking treats for the meeting and asked Quinn to join her. As I did some of my own work from Dad's study, I could hear laughter coming from the kitchen. I was so in love with Quinn. How did I get so lucky?

It was strange, having the meeting at my parents' house,

with my mom greeting people at the door, but everyone seemed okay with it, so I got over it.

"Mrs. Swift, it is so wonderful to see you again. It has been way too long." Heather gave my mom a big, enveloping hug, that my mom was too polite to refuse.

Being the Governor's wife put my mom in many situations where she had to handle people she disliked, and she always did it with grace. I could see that grace coming out as Heather hugged her.

My mom gave Heather many opportunities to show her that she was a person worthy of her son, but it never turned out. Heather always showed her superficial, self-centered personality. Then, she would pout to me that my mom never gave her a chance. I should have taken that as a sign, but I didn't, and I paid for it with heartbreak. But all of that washed away from my mind the moment I met Quinn.

"Yes, Heather, it has been a long time." My mom agreed with the one thing she could, without saying she missed her or that it was too long. Always the diplomat.

Preston was the next to show up. From his stiff, reserved demeanor, it was clear his dad had a serious talk with him. If I were to guess, it involved his inheritance disappearing if he continued on the way he was with Tate or Quinn. Though it surprised me that he even showed for the meeting, I was hopeful that he was finally going to stop causing trouble. And his connections to the art world would still come in handy.

My mom and Millard reconnected like old friends. She worked with him to choose the decor for my dad's office when he was first elected, but she wasn't involved in much after that because Millard was great at his job.

The meeting was productive. Instead of putting a block between Quinn and Andrew Jorgensen, Heather played it up. She rambled on about how much time she and Andrew spent together and how, because of her, he would be completely willing to do whatever she asked of him for the project.

I knew she was trying to make me jealous. She tried that when we dated, too. We would be at a party and she would flirt with all the guys, trying to make herself appear desirable, but it didn't work then and it wouldn't work now. I realized I was over her long before we even broke up. So her stories of time spent with Andrew didn't bother me at all. I needed the meeting to be over so I could spend time with Quinn.

But Heather wasn't about to let things end so easily. I could tell my lack of interest in her exploits with another man bothered her. So, she moved on to another tactic to attempt to hurt me.

"Sorry, I have gone on and on about Andrew. I get so excited to talk about someone so passionate about his work." She looked at me.

"But we do have one thing that could put a kink in our plans for using his work for February."

Quinn, who ignored most of Heather's peacocking, perked up to attention at the possibility of something not going as planned.

"What would that kink be, Heather?" Quinn asked.

"You," Heather said spitefully.

"Me? I haven't even met him yet." Quinn spoke quietly. She was pulling into her shell again.

I wasn't going to let that happen. I wouldn't stand by while Heather played with Quinn. "Heather, Andrew doesn't even know Quinn yet, so what kind of game are you playing?"

Upset that I stood up for Quinn, Heather turned to me and said with venom in her voice, in front of all the committee members and my mom, "Well, he hasn't met her yet, and he doesn't want to. He's concerned about being associated with 'Killer Quinn' and I don't blame him." She made air quotes as she said the vicious nickname.

I saw all the color drain from Quinn's face. This was what she told me about. Her biggest fear of us being together was that her past would come back to hurt me. I didn't want her to use this to run from me. My blood was boiling to know that Heather would sink so low to use this to hurt Quinn.

"What are you talking about, Heather?" Preston asked; the first words he spoke during the meeting.

Heather sat up straighter, as if she was about to address the nation.

"Well, our dear, sweet Quinn is under suspicion for killing her mom when she was a teenager and blaming it on her dad. It's also believed that she even let her dad go to prison for her." Heather glared at Quinn, then turned again to tell her lies to the rest of the committee, focusing on my mom.

"From what Andrew and I have heard, nobody from her hometown believes that her dad was the murderer. I guess he was a model citizen and a doting husband and father. But the police looked the other way and let her dad take the blame because Quinn was sleeping with most of the officers. She was known to get around back then and played multiple men against each other. I see some things haven't changed."

She turned to Quinn and asked, "You like playing men against each other, don't you, Quinn? It's what you've been doing with Devon and Preston for the last couple of months, isn't it? That's why I believe everything I've been told. I told Andrew as much, too. He is protective of his reputation and doesn't like the idea of having his name associated with a murderer. I asked him if you stepped down, and I took over the project, would he consider carrying forward with the project, and he agreed. So for the good of the project you care so much about, I think you should do just that, Quinn. You need to step down."

Quinn's face showed all the emotions that she went through. I wanted to hold her and help her through this. She didn't defend herself when the kids at her school started these terrible rumors, and with the recent turmoil, I didn't think she was going to now either.

I opened my mouth to defend her, but I didn't have time to speak before Quinn spoke for herself.

"Well, Heather, then we are going to have to move on without him. I'm sorry to hear Mr. Jorgensen won't get the recognition that being part of this project would bring him. I'll email him personally to let him know he is off the hook. If anyone has suggestions for a new theme for February, let me know. We're going to need to get moving on it as soon as possible. Maybe we can move things for March up a month. And, Heather, since you're so uncomfortable with me, please let me know if you have any suggestions for your replacement on the committee."

Heather was dumbfounded. That wasn't what she expected at all. To be honest, it wasn't what I expected either.

"So, you're going to stay associated with this project, tainting it with your sordid past?" Heather spat at her.

I watched as my meek little kitten decided to roar.

"Heather, I have been dealing with small-minded mean girls like you since I was 15 years old. I watched my father murder my mother. I sat through a trial, where I had to tell the world every detail about that night; where I had to tell the world how my father almost murdered me too, his only child. Then, because things weren't bad enough in my life, I went on to be bullied at school, which isn't even a strong enough word to describe the torture they put me through."

She stood up, leaning forward with her hands on the table.

"I let people take from me. I let them take my confidence, my courage, my belief in myself, my happiness. I did that because I didn't think I deserved any of those things. Those people made me feel dirty and tainted and I let it happen. I almost walked away from an amazing man because of how other people's lies made me feel. I won't let that happen again. I know what happened. And I know you do too, but you are the cold-hearted type of person who likes to make people feel small because it makes you feel better about yourself. Well, I'm not letting you do that to me. I'm a good person who deserves good things in her life. I'm not walking away from my dream job, or my dream man, because you are a shitty human being filled with hate."

The room was silent.

Quinn stood up tall, looked around the room, then dismissed Heather with a calm, "Heather, I think it's time for you to leave now. The committee will be better without you."

Heather stood and turned to me with a pleading look on her face.

"I'm with her," I said as I walked over to Quinn and put my arm around her shoulder.

Heather looked to my mom for help, which was a poor choice. Did she honestly not know how my mom detested her? How could someone be so completely oblivious to reality?

"Heather, please leave my home now and never come back," my mother said, as she also came to stand by Quinn.

Heather gathered up her paperwork, then turned to Quinn. "You don't even realize the enemy you made in me tonight. I will shut every single door you try to open. Your project will fail. And Devon will bore of you soon enough," she yelled, red-faced.

"Bye Heather," Quinn said as she squeezed my side.

We finished the meeting with my mom jumping in to save

the day. She mentioned she also knew Andrew Jorgensen and said that she was going to talk to him tomorrow to clear things up. I didn't want to doubt her abilities, but I was concerned with how many lies Heather told him. But if anyone could talk him into still working with us, it would be my mom.

When the last person left, my mom excused herself and I was finally alone with Quinn.

She looked down at her feet, like she did the day we met, and I wouldn't let her crawl back into her shell.

I tilted her face up to meet mine. "You were amazing tonight. I have never been as proud of anyone as I was of you standing up for yourself. I hope you believe every word you said, because you do deserve happiness and everything wonderful that this life can offer you. And you deserve me. It's me that doesn't deserve you."

I couldn't wait any longer, so I leaned down and kissed her hard.

24

QUINN

*T*he next couple of weeks flew by. I felt so much more confident in myself after I confronted Heather. It was like all the self-doubt and feelings of unworthiness I held on to for so long disappeared. It took over a decade, but it was finally settling in that I deserved to be loved. I should have accepted it long before now because Olivia, Jace, Jillian and Sydney spent years showing me how important I was to them, but it didn't sink in. I think I needed to find my own value, and hearing all the lies that came out of Heather's mouth made them sound so ridiculous. It made me want to stand up for myself for once. And it felt good.

I went along with Devon as he looked for a place to rent while his house was being rebuilt. They needed to start from the ground up, so he wanted it to be a place where he would be comfortable living in for up to a year. He insisted I go with and give input because he wanted me to live with him.

Olivia and I spent an entire night, and many bottles of wine, discussing me moving in with Devon. Despite my newfound confidence, I still struggled with bringing my issues into his world. Each reason I gave her to justify not moving in with him, she countered with me being afraid. Which was true. But I was also sad at the thought of living without her for the first time since our freshman year of college. She was my best friend. But she insisted we would still see each other all the time. She also said it was time for her to start working on herself and having the place to herself would force her to do that. That worried me, because in my eyes she was perfect, exactly as she was.

She wasn't her usual self since she broke things off with Trenton. It wasn't her normal break-up where she was ready to get right back out there and dive into another relationship. Something was different with this break-up, but she wasn't ready to talk to me about it yet. I would give her time, but not too much.

So, I took the leap and Devon and I moved into an adorable cottage, not far from his parent's house. It was tiny compared to his house, but he agreed to it when I fell in love with it. It only had one bedroom and the rest of the house was a large open space, so even though it was small, it didn't feel that way.

I didn't have much, and Devon had nothing but his cat left, so moving in took little work at all. Suzanna showed up on the first day with boxes full of gifts for every room in the house, insisting they were essential for us to have. It was nice to be cared for like that. With her help, we had the boxes unpacked by the end of the first weekend and the cottage felt like we had lived there for years.

We had a few more successful committee meetings since the Heather incident. Suzanna joined the committee to fill Heather's spot, since she had so many good ideas. She met with Andrew Jorgensen the day after Heather made all her threats and found out Mr. Jorgensen knew nothing about 'Killer Quinn' and was still planning to work with us. When he found out about the lies Heather was spreading, he pulled his exhibit from The Palette Studio and encouraged two of his colleagues to do the same. I wish I could have seen Heather's face when she found out.

Suzanna quickly became a confidant. She was so easy to talk to that I frequently forgot that I'd only known her for a short time. I wanted to do something for one of the month of the project dedicated to the eleven recognized tribes in Wisconsin. Suzanna sat with me for a couple hours as we tossed ideas back and forth on how to make that work. Then she added her idea of focusing one month on the students of Wisconsin and we spent another hour discussing and debating ways to make that one work as well.

It was just as easy for me to love Devon's family as it was to love him.

It took a lot of convincing for Devon and his dad to let me work from my office, but we were only two months away from the launch and I had so much to do that it was just easier to do it from the Capitol, so they finally gave in. But I had to let one of Devon's bodyguards go with me any time I went somewhere. I agreed. Devon and his family went out of their way for me, so any sense of security I could give them would be worth it.

Looking down at my watch, I was glad I brought my costume with me to work because I was going to have to change there and meet Devon at my old apartment for the Halloween party.

Looking in the mirror, I couldn't help but smile. I had a knee length jean skirt on over dark brown tights, a paisley long-sleeve button-down shirt with a buttoned sweater vest over it, a bulky purse worn across my chest, large tortoiseshell glasses, a bobby pin holding back some of my hair, and chunky, orthopedic brown loafers. I nailed it.

Devon and I decided we wanted to go as Dr. Sheldon Cooper and his girlfriend, Dr. Amy Farrah Fowler, from the Big Bang Theory. We enjoyed watching the show together, so it felt like an us kind of thing to do. I couldn't wait to see him as Sheldon.

He was probably going to worry soon, so I sent him a quick text.

> Me: Sorry - I'm running late. I changed here. I'll meet you at Olivia's. Can't wait to see you, Sheldon!

> Devon: Thanks for the update, Amy. I'll see you soon. And I think there might be coitus in your future.

I laughed out loud at his attempt to text me the way Sheldon would.

> Me: Oh, Sheldon! *Blush*

> Devon: Don't forget to bring Bobby with you.

> Me: Well, talking about the bodyguard sure is a buzz kill. :(

> Devon: Sorry, but I need my Amy safe and sound.

> Me: Okay Sheldon - I'll see you there.

Walking out of my office, Bobby flanked me immediately. He was a nice guy. We'd gotten to know each other pretty well over the last few weeks. He was in his late forties and happily divorced, as he liked to put it. Jaded by love, but happy with life. He was my favorite of all the different bodyguards because he would joke around with me. All the others took our conversations so seriously.

On our way out of the building, I ran into Devon's dad.

"Wow, you look great, Quinn, or should I say Amy?"

"Thank you. Have you seen Devon's costume yet? He's been keeping it from me, so I'll be surprised, but the wait is killing me."

"No. I haven't yet. But make sure you guys take a lot of pictures, so I have something to hold over his head if he ever gives me trouble about coming to my campaign rallies." He laughed.

"Oh, I definitely will. I was going to anyway because I think tonight is going to be a night to remember." I smirked.

"Really? Why is that?"

I was dying to tell someone. Devon's dad would be perfect.

"Because I'm in love with your son and I'm ready to tell him. Tonight's party feels like the right time to let him know."

I've known for weeks, but I wasn't sure how to tell him. Each time he told me he loved me, I wanted to say it back, but I didn't want the first time I told him to be a reaction to him telling me. It needed to be special.

I watched the smile cross his face and turn into a full, toothy grin.

"Quinn, that is the best news I've heard all day." He hugged me and told me I better get going because I didn't want to miss the perfect evening ahead of me.

I kissed his cheek and followed Bobby to the SUV. He insisted on driving, which was making me crazy, but I wasn't going to let it bother me. Not when I had important things to do.

Bobby was acting weird, so I asked, "What's up, Bobby?"

He looked a little guilty.

"Well, Ms. Hill, I didn't mean to eavesdrop, but I couldn't help but overhear you tell the governor you were going to tell Mr. Swift that you're in love with him."

My heart sank. Was he going to tell me I shouldn't do it? That I wasn't good enough for Devon? Or maybe that he was seeing someone else?

"Okay."

"Well, I just wanted to let you know that I'm rooting for you two."

Wow, that wasn't what I expected, knowing Bobby's rough history with love. Even with my newfound confidence, I guess I still naturally went to doubting myself.

"Thank you, Bobby. That's real sweet."

"I think you're good for him. I've worked for Mr. Swift for a lot of years now and I don't think I've ever seen him as happy as he is when he's with you. That Ms. Winston lady made him miserable, so I'm glad he's found someone like you."

Tears started falling from my eyes and I couldn't stop them.

"Oh no, Ms. Hill. I'm so sorry. I didn't mean to say anything to upset you." He was looking like he was going to pull the SUV over, but I stopped him.

"It's okay, Bobby. I'm fine. It's just your words were so sweet. I'm honestly okay."

We drove in silence for a while. I sat there with a smile on my face, watching the buildings turn into suburbs as we left the busiest part of the city. It was dark and the streetlights zipped by one at a time.

The vehicle jerked, and I looked to Bobby.

"What was that?"

Then it happened again.

Someone ran into the back of us.

"Hold on, Ms. Hill. We need to get out of here. Maybe you should call the police."

Bobby spoke to me in such a calming voice, as if we were out for a stroll in the park. Like two friends having a lovely chat, while in reality, I was about to have a breakdown.

He sped up, and I dialed Devon.

"Hey Ms. Fowler, are you ready to take me up on my offer for coitus?" Devon answered.

The car behind us crashed into us again and I screamed.

"Quinn, what's going on?" I could hear Devon shouting through the phone, even though my hand holding the phone bounced away from my ear with the crash.

"Devon, someone keeps rear-ending us."

I heard him yell to Olivia to call Matthew.

"Sweetie, where are you?"

I gave him the details and heard him pass them on to Olivia, who was most definitely passing them on to Matthew.

Crash

That time, the force was greater than before and I was thankful for the seatbelt, otherwise I would have gone through the windshield.

"Baby, I'm coming. Stay with me," Devon yelled.

He stayed on the phone with me for the next few minutes, while Bobby tried to evade the car that was hitting us. But we were on a two lane road in the country, so there wasn't anywhere to go.

Then I heard a gunshot, and I heard Devon shout through the phone.

I heard sirens right before I felt another hit. Bobby was doing his best to keep the SUV on the road, but it felt like it was pulling to the side. They must have shot the tire.

The police lights and sirens brought me back to the night

my mom was murdered, but I was trying so hard to stay in the present moment.

I was looking over at Bobby when I heard another gunshot. Instantly, Bobby's head went limp and tilted to the side. The SUV followed as his hands went off the wheel. He was hit, but I couldn't tell if he was still alive or not. I screamed as we crashed into the ditch.

I jerked forward and dropped the phone, but I could still hear Devon yelling for me. The airbag hit me so hard in the face that it dazed me for a moment. I immediately felt a headache coming on. There was a smokey smell, but I didn't see fire. I knew I needed to get us out in case there was a fire, but someone was out there trying to hurt me.

I shook Bobby, trying to wake him up, but I could see they hit him in the head. Blood was streaming down the side of his face. He was laughing a few minutes ago and now he was dead. I screamed.

"Quinn. Baby. Answer me." I heard Devon from the cell phone, but I was so out of sorts that I couldn't locate where the sound was coming from. His voice sounded muffled, so the phone must have slid under the seat.

I couldn't stay there. I needed to get out. But I didn't want to leave Bobby behind.

I needed to see what was going on around me and find a way to get away from the guy that was rear-ending us. I should run. If only my head would stop hurting. If only I could think straight.

I opened the door and the man driving the car behind us was coming at me with a gun raised up. I didn't recognize him. He was short, but his weight made him look intimidating. It looked like most of his weight was muscle, so I knew he could do some harm if he tried. How could someone I'd never met want to hurt me? I wanted to ask him if he had the wrong person because he was a complete stranger to me, but I didn't have time.

I heard a familiar voice. It was calm and steady. It made me feel safe.

"Quinn, get down."

Pop. Pop. Pop.

I screamed as three gunshots went off and I fell to the ground.

25

DEVON

*G*unshots.

Those were gunshots.

I couldn't drive fast enough. The sirens ahead let me know I was getting close. I needed to get there and to hold her in my arms. I couldn't lose her.

"Quinn. Quinn, are you okay? Baby, talk to me." I kept yelling into the phone, but I didn't get an answer. Why wouldn't she answer? Was she hurt? Was it something worse?

Olivia was next to me, telling me over and over that everything was going to be okay. That Quinn was going to be okay.

Traffic was slowing down and backing up, but I hadn't gotten to where she was yet.

I honked my horn, knowing full well it wouldn't do anything, but I felt so helpless.

I pulled over to the side of the road and ran.

Moment after moment with Quinn flashed through my head. From the first time we met when she ran into me in the hallway, to sitting with her and working on puzzles together as we talked about our days, to making love to her, to hearing her share her past with me, to looking for a place together. It all played through my mind like a movie.

She was a part of my life now, and I needed her to be okay. I finally felt whole, and it was all because of her.

Out of breath, I reached the police tape. I knew whatever happened was over because they were already taping off the area, but I was too far back to see anything. Searching, I couldn't see Quinn.

When I thought nobody was looking, I lifted the police tape to sneak under but an officer stopped me.

I argued with him, telling him my girlfriend was there, but he didn't care. He kept telling me I had to wait on the other side of the tape. I tried multiple times to push past, but he wasn't budging.

"Sir, I'm going to have to detain you if you can't wait on the other side of the line."

"Daniel, let him through," I heard Olivia say from behind me. She was out of breath from running to catch up.

"Olivia, do you know him? What's going on?" he asked, at least willing to hear her out. Thank goodness she worked for the police and knew these guys.

"He's with me. My best friend was in the car that was hit. We need to find out what happened."

He looked indecisive for a moment, then quietly said to Olivia, "I heard that the people in that vehicle didn't make it." He pointed to Bobby's SUV.

I roared in pain. My world crashed down around me.

Olivia spoke with the officer for another moment, but I couldn't make out what they were saying because of the ringing in my ears.

"Devon, he's going to let us through." I felt a hand on my arm as Olivia guided me under the police tape.

As we walked around the police cars that were blocking most of the scene, I saw two bodies on the ground, both with a white sheet over them. When I looked at the car, I saw Bobby there, clearly dead. There were officers wandering around as if this was usual and happened daily, while the love of my life lay under a white sheet on the ground.

How was this happening? Why didn't I go with her to work? Why didn't I make her work from home? What was wrong with me that I couldn't protect her? My chest was tightened and my breath came faster and out of control.

"Devon, you need to calm down. Let's get you over to the paramedics to get you looked at. I think you're hyperventilating."

She guided me past the bodies under the blankets. I wanted to lift it to see if it was my Quinn, but Olivia was on a mission to get me to the ambulance.

I turned around and ran to the body on the ground, still breathing too quickly, and lifted the sheet.

It wasn't her. It was a man I'd never seen before. Was this him? Was this the man who wanted Quinn dead? I lost all control. I dropped to the ground and pounded on the dead man's chest and screamed as if screaming could turn back time and make her come back. Moments later, I could feel Olivia pulling me away from him, knowing I shouldn't lift the second sheet and see Quinn that way. As I stood there, she wrapped her arms around me and I sobbed into her hair. How was I supposed to go on?

When the sobs turned back into quick breaths, she told me she still wanted me to get checked out by the paramedics and guided me back towards the ambulance.

When we walked around the ambulance's opened doors, I froze. Quinn was there on a stretcher, alive.

I wasn't sure if my mind was playing tricks on me, but our eyes locked and I knew it was her. I could feel the air flowing back into my lungs, rushing in as if I were drowning but finally surfaced.

Somehow, my feet figured out how to move and I slowly walked towards her, hoping I wasn't imagining her there.

"Baby?" I whispered my question to her. So much was in that one word.

"I'm okay," she whispered back. She looked exhausted.

I looked her over, top to bottom, and back up again. She had a brace on her lower leg and scratches on the side of her face, but other than that, she looked like she was whole.

"Devon, Bobby is dead." She looked down at her hands on her lap. As if I was going to blame her for that.

I sat on the side of the gurney and held her tight as she cried.

"It will be okay."

"It won't. He wasn't the only one that died." She whimpered between sobs.

"I know, sweetheart. I saw the guy when I got here, but I didn't recognize him. And I'm not going to feel bad about someone dying when they were trying to kill you," I said, but then it hit me. There was Bobby in the car and two white sheets covering people. She wasn't talking about the man that was trying to kill her.

My chest tightened. I was sure that I knew what she was going to say, but I had to ask her, "Sweetheart, who else died?"

Her sobbing grew harder.

When she calmed down enough to speak, she put words to what I feared.

"It's Matthew. Matthew's dead."

Olivia burst into tears alongside Quinn. I had never seen Olivia cry. She always put on a tough exterior. Seeing her this way made her seem a bit more human. But my heart broke for all of them, knowing that soon Jillian was going to be feeling the same pain I was in just moments ago. Only her pain wouldn't have a happy ending.

That was when the anger hit. Why did this happen? I needed some answers.

Seeing how tightly Quinn and Olivia were holding each other, I knew they needed some time together to mourn Matthew's loss, so I went to find someone in charge.

After being passed around between different officers, I finally got to speak to the officer in charge. They didn't know much yet. What he did know was the man rammed Quinn's car and then shot the tire. Bobby kept the car on the road, so the man shot him through the back window, causing him to drive off the road. Quinn got out of the car and so did the man. That was also when Matthew got there. He yelled for Quinn to get down, which she did. The shot the man took went past her and hit Matthew, but not before he got off two shots of his own. The bullet missed Matthew's vest and hit him in the neck. He died quickly. Both of Matthew's shots hit the man who was trying to kill Quinn. The one to the head was likely the one that killed him. He didn't have details about who the man was yet, but he said he took all my information and said he would find me at the hospital or at home when he knew more.

I went back to the ambulance, and they had Quinn loaded up and ready to go. Olivia wiped her tears as she came up to me.

"Go to the hospital with Quinn, she needs you. I'll follow in your car."

"Thank you. I'll see you there."

I gave Olivia my keys and hopped in the ambulance with Quinn, vowing to never leave her side again.

My vow ended quickly. When we arrived at the hospital, they took her away from me so they could x-ray her ankle. I sat in the exam room, alone, for the first time since I thought I lost her. Having a moment of quiet was all it took for me to break down. The stress and fear of the night hit me hard.

There was so much loss tonight, but I was given more time with Quinn and I wouldn't waste that gift.

Minutes passed, and I calmed myself down and sat there waiting for Quinn. I should have called my parents or texted Olivia to see where she was at, but I didn't have it in me to do those things. It was overwhelming to know I lost her and then I got her back. I had to sit there and let all the emotions run through me.

"Devon?"

I looked up to see who said my name. It was Jillian. Looking at her calm demeanor, she didn't know about Matthew yet.

Where was Olivia? Jillian should hear this from someone she's closer to. Not me. We've only hung out together a few times.

"Devon, what are you doing here? And what are you wearing?"

I looked down, having completely forgotten I was still dressed as Dr. Sheldon Cooper for the Halloween Party. The khaki pants and Green Lantern t-shirt over a long-sleeved orange t-shirt weren't my normal attire. So much had happened since I put those clothes on.

"Oh, god, I look ridiculous, don't I? Quinn and I were going to Olivia's party as Sheldon and Amy from the Big Bang Theory."

"That's so perfect for you guys."

Her face lit up. I didn't want to take that joy away from her.

"We were going to go to Liv's party, but Matthew and I both got stuck working tonight."

Her expression changed to one of concern, as if she just remembered where we were.

"Devon, what are you doing here? Where's Quinn?"

Looking around for Olivia, hoping she was near, I realized I had to be the one to tell Jillian what happened. Fuck.

"The man who's been harassing Quinn tried to kill her tonight." I didn't want to add more stress to her night, so I quickly added, "She's okay. She hurt her ankle as she went to the ground. They're taking x-rays now to make sure it wasn't a fracture and a CT to make sure her head was okay because she hit it when she went down. But they think she's going to be okay."

She let out the breath she was holding and sat in the chair next to me.

"Thank goodness. Did they get the guy that's been messing with her?"

"Yes, he's dead."

"Oh, that's so good that this is finally over for her!" I heard another deep release of breath from her. Happy to know Quinn's nightmare was over.

"Matthew's on duty tonight. Did you see him? Is he still at the scene?"

"Yes, I saw him." I didn't expand. I wanted her to feel like her world wasn't crashing down around her for a moment longer. Maybe I was still hoping Olivia would find us and break the news to her. I didn't know her well enough to be the person to tell her that all of her dreams and her happily ever after were gone.

She pulled her phone out of her scrubs and looked to see if she missed a call or a text. "I'm surprised he hasn't called me to let me know Quinn was coming in or that it was all over. He must be caught up in paperwork."

Clearly looking at me to explain why her boyfriend hadn't called her yet, she turned to me.

I turned my whole body towards her and took her hands in mine.

"Jillian, he was shot. He didn't make it."

I watched her go through every emotion I went through when I thought it was Quinn.

When I saw it fully sink in, I pulled her into my arms and held her while she cried. She lost her love so my love could live. There wasn't any way I could fix that for her.

That was when the tech wheeled Quinn back into the room. It didn't take long for her to understand what was happening. She pulled Jillian onto the gurney with her, and they cried together.

I gave them some privacy and went to find coffee.

They kept Quinn overnight to make sure there weren't after effects from hitting her head.

She was resting the next morning when the officers I spoke to the night before found me. I snuck out of Quinn's room. I didn't want her to have to hear anything that could cause her alarm while she was recovering. He filled me in on the details they found, and I knew I had another round of bad news to deliver. But I wouldn't do it until I knew Quinn was feeling better. I wasn't sure how much more she could take.

We went home that afternoon, and she slept until the next morning. I was making breakfast for her when she came out of the bedroom in the Green Lantern t-shirt I was wearing on Halloween. It looked so much better on her.

"Hey beautiful," I said, making her blush.

She held her hand up to the scratches on the side of her face from when she fell. I walked over and took her hand in mine.

"A couple of scratches won't change how gorgeous you are."

Leaning down, I kissed her gently. She wrapped her arms around me and pulled me in for a deeper kiss. I didn't want to rush things while she was still recovering, so I let her lead the kiss. Her murmuring let me know she was okay.

"Is that bacon I smell?" she asked as her stomach growled.

"It is. I'm guessing the last time you ate was lunch yesterday, so I took a shot at you being hungry this morning."

I watched her eat. There was food in front of me, but I couldn't tear myself away from looking at her to find my fork. I almost lost her, so every moment felt like a gift. I wanted to keep her safe in our cottage forever.

"You have to stop staring at me. You're stressing me out," she teased.

"I would say I'm sorry, but I'm not."

"Devon, I know the police talked to you at the hospital yesterday."

I nodded, even though I wasn't ready to get into the details with her yet. But she wouldn't let me push it off much longer.

She put down her fork and reached across the table to put her hand on mine. "I need you to tell me, Devon."

"What if you're not ready to hear it?"

"What if I am?"

I led her over to the couch and sat down next to her. I wanted her to be comfortable. She looked at me with her stormy grey eyes and I wanted to shield her from the bad in the world. But I knew I couldn't. She was the type of person who needed to understand things. And she proved time and time again that she was much stronger than people gave her credit for. To survive what she went through over the last decade, and not become a jaded person, showed her strength.

"He went by the name Gutter."

I could see her trying to find some connection to a man by that name, but she wouldn't find it.

"I don't know anyone named Gutter. So why was he trying to hurt me? Who sent him?"

It was time to rip off the band-aid.

"Quinn, he was sent by your dad."

I watched as she went from surprise to shock to anger, then to sadness. I thought she was going to break down, and I was ready to be there for her, but she didn't. She straightened up, took a deep, steadying breath, and asked me for all the details.

"According to the officer, Gutter shared a cell with your dad for years. He was in for murder, but had a shorter sentence because the evidence against him was tainted, so they could only get second degree murder charges to stick. Apparently, your dad helped him out when he got to prison, kept him safe, so Gutter felt like he owed him."

She sat with her hands folded in her lap while she listened. Her face was expressionless, which concerned me.

"Your dad told him you were the reason he was in prison. A prison guard heard him telling Gutter that you were actually the one the murdered your mom and you begged him to take the blame. And, because he was such a loving father, he agreed. He said you weren't going to take the stand at the trial, so he had a better chance of not being convicted, but then you changed your mind at the last minute. Gutter believed him when he said you turned on him. It didn't matter to him that all the evidence clearly showed it was your dad and not you. He believed you were the reason your dad was in prison."

She continued to sit there, unmoving, and I worried the news was too much for her. But she needed to have all the information.

"Gutter was released this summer and started following you to pay back your dad for watching over him in prison. He was in constant communication with your dad over the last few months. Your dad kept tabs on you the whole time he was in prison, so he knew where you were and that you took on the project for my dad. He gave all the information to Gutter, and he used it to harass you. Your dad didn't want him to hurt you right away. He wanted to torture you, to make you feel unsafe and on edge for as long as he could before he killed you."

Quinn burst into laughter. She was almost hysterical.

"Baby, what is so funny?"

She caught her breath and spoke between laughter.

"My dad, the man who couldn't even tell me my artwork was pretty or that he loved me, took a murderer under his wing. He couldn't be a father to me, but he could be a father to someone named Gutter. It's just hilarious."

Then the tears came.

"What was so wrong with me that he couldn't love me?"

"It wasn't you. Baby, it was never you. It was always something wrong inside him."

I watched as my words sank in.

She dried her eyes and stood up. She had a look of determination on her face.

"You're right. He is the one with the problem. I'm done letting him make me feel bad about myself. He has taken too much from me to let him continue affecting my life," she declared.

"My mom didn't deserve what happened to her, and I'm letting him win each time I hold myself back from finding happiness. I can't let him keep winning. I won't let him have that control over my life anymore."

She pulled me up from the couch so I was standing in front of her.

"Devon, I'm not going to be afraid anymore. I need you to know something."

She took a deep breath and looked me in the eye.

"I love you. And it's not some crazy confession because I'm under stress. I was planning on telling you yesterday. You can ask your dad. So I need you to know that it's real."

Her words were the most beautiful words I'd ever heard. She was mine.

She was about to continue on, trying to justify loving me, but I didn't want her to. I knew it was true.

I pulled her into my arms and kissed the woman that loved me.

26

QUINN

TWO MONTHS LATER

I woke up to sunlight shining in our bedroom window. I sat up and stretched. The room was a mess. I saw the beautiful lavender sequined gown I wore to the New Year's Eve party last night lay on the floor, not too far away from Devon's tuxedo jacket and tie. The rest of our clothes from the night before were spread across the room.

Devon and I attended the Governor's New Year's Eve Gala at his parent's home. His dad invited all of my friends, since they were also Devon's friends now too. Olivia, Jace and Sydney were able to make it.

When I asked Sydney if Jillian was going to show up, she told us she took another extra shift at the hospital. That was how she was coping with Matthew's death. She worked. That was all that she did. She took any extra shift offered to her.

I worried Jillian was using work to avoid dealing with Matthew's death, but I couldn't judge her for it. I would want to do anything I could to avoid thinking about Devon if I lost him. But she was also shutting her friends out of her life. Even Sydney would go a whole week without seeing her. We were all worried about her. Eventually, the pain of loss was going to catch up to her, and she was going to crash. My only hope was for her to let us be there for her when that happened. Sydney made her apologies and left early to go to the hospital and check in on Jillian.

Olivia was not herself at the party, either. She didn't want to talk to me about what was bothering her, no matter how much I pressed her. She was quiet for most of the night and left long before the clock struck midnight. Jace left right after Olivia. My heart hurt for my friends. I felt guilty over my happiness, like I didn't deserve it when my friends were hurting.

Devon and I spent the rest of the night mingling with his parents, their friends, and Tate. She was doing much better since Preston finally stopped coming around and bothering her. I think she was on the path to healing, and that took a tremendous weight off Devon's shoulders.

We stayed at the party until the countdown. At the stroke of midnight, Devon kissed me so passionately I forgot people surrounded us. Then, he leaned into me and whispered suggestions I couldn't turn down. It surprised me we waited until the bedroom for all our clothes to come off when we got home.

Devon was sleeping so peacefully that I hated to wake him. But it was the opening of the Art for the People project at the Capitol and there was much to be done.

I looked at the clock and decided we had a bit of time to spare.

Lifting the cover, I slid my hand down his chest. He didn't take long to come to attention as I stroked him under the covers. He moaned, but kept his eyes closed.

I rolled on top of him and sat up with my hands on his

chest. As I slid my wetness over his length, he opened his eyes.

"Good morning." His husky morning voice always did something to me.

"Good morning."

Without warning, he grabbed my hips, lifted me up, then pulled me down on his length. Not wanting him to have all the control, I took his hands from my waist, crossed them over his chest and held them there while I set the pace.

The pace I chose was definitely slower than what he wanted. It felt good to be in control, and I didn't speed up. It was my turn to drive.

It didn't take long for him to move his hips to change how fast I was going, but I slid off his cock.

"Hey, what's that for?" he asked, shocked.

"You don't always have to be in control. Sometimes you have to let me be in charge."

He smiled. He was always pointing out to me how proud he was that I was taking charge of my life. I didn't think he was proud that I was doing it here in bed, but he lifted his arms above his head and let me lead, which I did, all the way to both our orgasms.

Lying next to him in his arms, he told me he loved me. I heard it many times each day, but my heart still fluttered each time he said it.

Walking into the living room, I noticed a long tube with a red bow tied around it on the coffee table.

"Devon, what's this on the coffee table?" I yelled, assuming he was still in bed.

"It's a present."

I jumped, because he said that standing right behind me.

Turning to him, I asked, "For who?"

Standing there without a shirt on, I was almost too

distracted to hear him tell me that the present was for me. How was this man mine?

"You're gawking, sweetheart." He chuckled and my attention went up to his face again.

I blushed, knowing that he caught me.

"Sorry."

"No apologizes needed. I'm pretty happy that I make you gawk."

He led me over to the couch and we sat down. Picking up the tube, he turned to me.

"I wanted you to be the first one to see these." He popped the cap off one end of the tube and slid out a bunch of papers.

"The architect dropped them off yesterday. They're the blueprints for the house. The foundation was salvageable, so it will have the same footprint as the old house, but he changed the original layout. I wanted to get your thoughts."

He rolled out the blueprints on the coffee table in front of us and pointed out what each room was. It was going to be beautiful.

The first floor was open, with one room flowing into another.

"I wanted to make sure that if someone was in the kitchen, they wouldn't be separated from whatever people were doing in the living room. It's important for a family to stay connected."

His family comment caught me off guard, but he moved right on.

"You can see each side of the house has French doors leading to the backyard, so if someone is in the house, they can keep an eye on anyone playing back there. It's not so blocked off this time."

Kids. He was building this house expecting there would be kids playing in the backyard.

Before I could say anything, he flipped the page to show me the second floor. There were so many rooms, clearly preparing for a big family. The master bedroom and en-suite bathroom were huge. There was another set of French doors that led out to a deck overlooking the yard.

Looking over the other rooms, I noticed a set of stairs. Was he going to have a third floor?

"Where do these lead?" I pointed at the stairs.

He smirked. Then he flipped to the next blueprint, and I gasped.

The entire third floor was a wide open space with the staircase coming up in the middle and windows on all four sides. It had to take up at least half the footprint of the house. Like on the first two pages of blueprints, the room was labeled. It was called the art studio.

I wiped away the tear that fell from my eye and looked over to see Devon, down on one knee between the couch and the coffee table, holding out a ring to me.

Taking my hand, he said, "I know in my heart you and I are meant to be together forever. I know this is moving fast, but it is right and you are all I need. I built this house for us. For you and me to live together and start a family there, when we're ready. There's just one more thing needed to make this house perfect. Quinn, will you make me the happiest man on earth and be my wife?"

He looked at me, so hopeful. It was overwhelming to think about how much my life changed since I met him. He gave me the courage to be who I want to be. To stand up for myself and take control of my future. When I thought about it, I couldn't imagine that future without him in it.

"Yes! Yes! Yes!"

I flung myself into his arms and we rolled onto the floor as I kissed him. He rolled on top of me.

"I have never been this happy," I said as I pulled him down to kiss me again.

He broke the kiss and pushed himself back up. "Don't you want the ring?"

I forgot all about the ring. I rolled us over so I was on top of him and looked at his hand to find the ring. He laughed as he took my hand in his and slid the most brilliant princess cut diamond solitaire on my finger. I held my hand out to admire it.

"You did good, Mr. Swift. Real good."

He rolled us back over so he was on top again and he looked down at me with love in his eyes.

"Thank you, soon-to-be Mrs. Swift." And his lips met mine.

EPILOGUE

QUINN

*W*e arrived at the Capitol for the opening of the Art for the People gallery. Walking into the rotunda with Devon at my side, I couldn't help but think back to four months ago when I walked through those same doors to start my new job.

I still had the same sense of awe and wonder when I looked around. I hoped I would never lose that feeling.

Our trip to Door County was very fruitful. Mrs. Elmsworth was a delight and shared so many stories and paintings with us. We ended up spending the entire weekend there, learning everything we could about Arthur Leary.

Mr. Leary's artwork was on display throughout the rotunda and people were milling around, looking at it, discussing it, and enjoying it. That was what this project was about. Making the artwork assessable to all. And I think we accomplished what we set out to do.

I saw a mom with her young daughter, admiring "A Winter's Walk." I could see myself and my mom in them. Remembering her taking me to an art museum when I was about that little girl's age brought a smile to my face, rather than tears. I took that as a sign I was ready to move on and let the past go. Now that I could see a happy future for myself, I could envision someday walking hand in hand with my own child at the museum.

Looking around, I saw Olivia and Jace in a heated conversation. We walked over to them, and I heard Olivia. She was pretty worked up.

"You can't do this. She will ruin your life!"

"Hey, Quinn and Devon are here," Jace said in a cheerful voice, as if he wasn't just getting yelled at by Olivia.

"Hi guys," I said, a little hesitantly.

Devon must have heard what was going on as well. He stepped in and offered to show Jace the Governor's office. He knew Jace would jump at that offer, even though he's been there before, but it would get him out of his current predicament.

I waited until they were far enough away, then turned to Olivia for answers.

"Livy, what was that?"

She was still worked up and failed at keeping her voice down.

"He told me last night that he is going to marry Charlotte because she thinks it's the best thing for his political career." She looked at me. When I didn't start speaking fast enough, she yelled, "He's going to marry her!"

I gave her a moment and was about to try speaking again, she blurted out, "And I slept with Trenton last night."

That was a lot of new information. I wasn't sure which one to start with, but I felt like both of those things were actually connected.

"Tell me what happened last night. Start with Jace."

"Jace and I were talking at the party about his campaign and about how Charlotte was pushing him to settle down because that was what the voters wanted. Apparently, We the

People will only vote for someone in a stable relationship," she said in a mocking tone. She didn't think fondly of Charlotte. But neither did I.

"I told him he needed to hold off on making any major decisions. He wanted to talk more about it, but I told him that Trenton reached out to me and asked to meet him last night. So, I had to leave. I told him we could talk things through today and come up with a better plan than getting into a relationship to get votes, but he lost it. He said he didn't need to wait for me to think about things for him to make up his mind because he already decided to take Charlotte up on her offer to get married. I mean, who does that?"

Someone who loved a person who was leaving to meet up with her ex-boyfriend. I thought it but didn't say it to her.

"So, I left and met up with Trenton. He begged me to give him another chance, and I was so upset about Jace that I ended up sleeping with him. I freaked out this morning when I woke up next to him. I told him it was a mistake and we wouldn't be getting back together. He wasn't thrilled with that."

Trying to get through to either Olivia or Jace was absolutely pointless. They refused to see what was right in front of their faces. They were perfect for each other, but neither would admit it. Now Jace was going to marry someone else and Olivia was going to take some destructive life path because of it.

"Livy, I don't think yelling at Jace in the middle of the rotunda is the best way to get him to change his mind."

She agreed.

We set up a lunch date for next week. Maybe if I could get Jace to come, we could talk this out and find a better solution for both of them.

We found Devon and Jace in the governor's office. Devon's expression was trying to tell me something, so I assumed Jace let Devon in on his marriage plans as an explanation of why Olivia was yelling at him.

But I was wrong. Devon was trying to let me know he already told Jace our good news.

"Quinn, I can't believe you're getting married! Congratulations!" He scooped me up in a hug and swung me around.

"What? You're getting what?" Olivia turned and yelled at me. "Why didn't you tell me?"

She reached out for my hand and yelled again when she saw the ring.

"Oh my God, I'm so happy for you guys!"

Olivia insisted I tell her everything, so I retold the story of how he proposed. It felt so good to be happy, but that was something I wanted my friends to have, too. After popping some champagne and toasting to our engagement, Olivia could tell I needed a little time alone with my fiancé, so she made an excuse for her and Jace to leave.

I led him down to my office and shut the door.

He started telling me what Jace was planning to do with Charlotte, but I stopped him from speaking by kissing him.

"We can deal with all their issues tomorrow. Today, I want to enjoy being the future Mrs. Swift."

He kissed me and said, "Well, let's enjoy that all over your desk, future Mrs. Swift."

And we did, twice. Neither of us saw much of the opening day of the project, but there wasn't a word of complaint from either of us.

The End

ACKNOWLEDGMENTS

This is my first book and I thank you, the reader, for taking a chance on a new author. I truly hope you enjoyed reading Quinn and Devon's story as much as I enjoyed telling it. But this book wouldn't be in your hands to read if it weren't for some amazing people who deserve to be acknowledged.

First, my wonderful husband, for his love and patience as this story came together.

My family and friends for their love, support, and even for the nagging about when it was coming out. Big thanks to Kiley and Tracy for beta reading and giving me wonderful notes.

And, finally, to the "Lovely Ladies" for giving me the encouragement that I needed when I doubted myself as a writer. Your support means more to me than I could ever put into words!

Watch for Book 2 of the Capitol Romance series to see if Jace and Olivia find their way to each other!